finding
heather

ALSO BY ALISON RAGSDALE

TUESDAY'S SOCKS
THE FATHER-DAUGHTER CLUB

finding heather

ALISON RAGSDALE

Published by Lake Union Publishing, Seattle

www.apub.com

Amazon, the Amazon logo, and Lake Union Publishing are trademarks of Amazon.com, Inc., or its affiliates.

ISBN-13: 9781503939899
ISBN-10: 1503939898

Cover design by Laura Klynstra

Printed in the United States of America

For Tom.
He is not gone, as long as he is remembered by all
of us who loved him.

CHAPTER 1

The baggage carousel churned around, snaking inside its metal riverbanks. One solitary bag circulated. Dark green and medium size, the case had red overstitching and an old-fashioned leather tag, the kind that her parents had always buckled to their luggage when traveling. Long plastic tentacles pattered on the surface of the conveyor belt where the bags emerged. Heather Forester stared, anticipating that some company for the solitary piece of luggage would slide through. Nothing came.

As she watched the bag circle, she wondered why it hadn't been claimed. Had the owner missed it in the earlier chaos of multiple flights arriving? Had it been put on the wrong carousel? Had the person it belonged to taken ill on the flight and been whisked away in an ambulance, leaving the suitcase to revolve endlessly? Heather smiled and shook her head at her tendency toward melodrama.

It was the graveyard shift at Washington's Dulles airport, and, as usual, her husband's flight was the last in from Denver. She had, at one time, considered asking Brett to get a cab home when he was arriving this late but had thought better of it when he had told her how much he loved seeing her there as he walked through the doors onto the concourse. After all the years that he had been flying, she was the only wife among the group she knew who still showed up in the middle of the night to pick up her pilot husband.

Her neck was pinching, so Heather switched her bag over to the opposite shoulder. She instantly felt a knot of tension release at the base of her skull.

A handful of people wandered around the overly cold arrivals area. Some sat in the row of hard metal chairs with their backs to the luggage carousel, and others paced, checking their phones and yawning. She noted that they all looked as tired and disheveled as she supposed she did herself.

The lone suitcase shuddered as it passed her again. The tag was dragging on the conveyor belt, hopping with the tectonic movement of the plastic plates beneath it. Heather checked her watch and then glanced at the information board. She calculated that it had been fifteen minutes since Brett's flight had landed. With crew privileges and a fast-track pass, which came with the uniform, he should be walking toward her any minute.

Yawning, she focused on the glass doors at the back of the arrivals area. A few more minutes passed, and then, as she continued to stare ahead, icy cold ran up her back. Something was wrong with this picture—with this entire situation.

As had happened to her numerous times over the past few months, stark realization dawned. Brett was not going to walk through those doors. He wasn't going to tip his captain's hat at her and smile his rumpled smile. He wouldn't drop his pilot's case onto the hard, polished floor and sweep her up against his chest, breathing in the scent of her hair and squeezing her waist. No—because Brett was gone.

She'd had momentary lapses of memory since he died—still laying a place for him at the table or calling his cell to see when he'd be home—but this was the first time she had risen with her internal alarm and, in a fog of sleep, driven to the airport to meet him.

As she ran a hand through her lank hair, the scene before her blurred. What the hell was she doing here? Had anyone been watching her? Could she get out of here without people seeing that she had both arrived and was now leaving alone?

Heather swallowed and slung her bag back over the opposite shoulder. The car park ticket burned a hole in her pocket as she reached in to grab it. She had to get home. She had to get out of here.

Walking back to her car, she tipped her chin down and pulled her collar up against the biting wind. As her booted feet moved soundlessly over the tarmac, she frowned, trying to remember where she had parked the Volvo. Aisle sweet sixteen, or was it lucky-for-some thirteen? She couldn't remember the mnemonic that she had hummed to herself as she'd locked the door and turned toward the terminal less than twenty minutes before.

Pressing the button on the key fob in her hand, Heather looked around for an identifying blink of light, straining to hear the friendly beep of response. An orange flash caught her eye, and she turned to her left. Sweet sixteen it was.

After hauling herself into the driver's seat, she slammed the door, filled her lungs, and screamed at the windscreen—months of pent-up pain escaping into the silence of the car. Throwing her purse onto the passenger seat, she wiped a hand over her face and then pressed her fingertips viciously into her eye sockets.

Opening her eyes again, she noticed a small group standing behind a car farther down the row. As the family moved around the vehicle, Heather's pain slowly turned to anger.

A middle-aged couple hugged at the side of the car, and a younger woman spoke to them over her shoulder as she put a baby into a car seat. The woman's clean-cut partner loaded two suitcases into the trunk and then, smiling, gallantly opened the rear door for the older couple. So much ease in their togetherness, so much shared joy in their obvious reunion. Heather couldn't stand it. She squeezed her eyes closed to shut them out.

As she waited for her heart to slow down, she remembered a passage that she'd read recently in a self-help book about mourning. It had said that it was common to be disgusted by the way life goes on all around you and that other people seem to cloud your vision, becoming an unwelcome distraction, which can make solitude seem like the only survivable state.

The idea of solitude was comforting as she pictured her and Brett's bedroom: the bright windows draped with pale cream curtains, the mossy-green bedcover, and the carved Balinese headboard they'd bought on their honeymoon. She hadn't slept in there since he had died. She could not be in that bed alone—not yet.

As she kept her eyes tightly closed, Heather was reminded of the solitary suitcase heading away from her on the carousel. As she saw the lonely item in her mind's eye, she decided that the person it belonged to did not feel bad about its loss. Unburdened by the case, and all the connotations of its contents, they would move on—as she must now, too. This moment was as low as she could ever allow herself to go. All that was left was up.

Sliding the key into the ignition, Heather glanced at herself in the rearview mirror. She was a mess. Nothing new there, but as she stared at her reflection, what was new was the tiny light of determination in her eye.

CHAPTER 2

Heather let herself back into the house, careful to tiptoe along the hallway to avoid waking her sister-in-law, Chrissy, who was asleep in the
guest bedroom. As she gently pushed her children's door open, she saw
Max and Megan, her seven-year-old twins, lying in their bunk bed.

Megan's strawberry-blonde hair formed a pale pink halo around her
full cheeks, and her eyelids fluttered as she dreamed. Heather pulled the
quilt up over her daughter's tiny chest and laid her palm flat on top of
the covers. She could just feel the light beats of the heart that was so
intrinsically linked to her own. A gossamer thread of motherhood was
tugged with her daughter's every breath. The thread was stretched with
each cry and vibrated almost audibly when the child laughed. Then,
that was the only sound in the world.

Max was, as usual, curled up under his quilt. Being fourteen minutes older, he had claimed the right to the top bunk, and as one Spider-
Man–clad leg hung over the edge of the mattress, his small foot with its
high arch and perfect toes pointed toward the floor.

Heather lifted his leg and covered him up. As she was about to turn
toward the door, Max sniffed and ground his fists into his eyes.

"Mom?"

"Yes, honey?" She tiptoed back to the bed with her index finger against her lips. "Don't wake Megs." She smiled at her tousled son as he looked at her coat and frowned.

"Where'd you go?" The little boy pushed himself up on one elbow. His voice was thick with sleep, and he watched her face as she tucked the duvet tightly back around his legs.

"Just went for a drive. I wasn't sleepy." Heather patted the pillow, and Max lay back down. She ran a hand over his tight curls, a darker shade than Megan's. He was the yin to her daughter's yang, the shadow to Megan's light. As she stroked her son's head, Heather wondered if that was why he drove her so crazy at times. Max was her own reflection, and Megan was Brett's.

"Can you read to me?" He yawned.

"No, sweetheart. It's too late. You need to go to sleep." She held his small hand in hers. "I love you, Maximus." The nickname Brett had given their son sounded tinny in the quiet room.

The little boy gave a sleepy smile, kissed her fingers, and then contracted into a ball as she patted his back.

"See you in the morning." She pressed her lips to the side of his face and padded out of the room.

The house was dull. The lights were dim and the decor uninviting. The muted earth tones that she and Brett had chosen together had seemed chic. Now, the rooms felt cold and impersonal, and as she crossed the empty living room, Heather longed for some color.

She flipped on the light in the kitchen. The granite glistened where she had cleaned it that day. As she opened the fridge, searching for the open bottle of sauvignon, Heather felt the usual surge of guilt at drinking alone—something she hadn't done since working as cabin crew.

It had been eight years since Heather had stopped working for the airline, and now, as she sloshed wine into an oversize glass, she remembered the chance crew rotation that had caused her to meet Brett.

She had been assigned to the crew on a Newark-to-Edinburgh flight when Brett had taken over at the last minute, a substitute for the intended pilot, who had been taken ill. The first thing that had attracted her to him was how he made her laugh. Within a few moments of meeting, he was yanking up his trouser legs to show her the one blue sock and one black he had pulled on that morning in his rush to leave his Manhattan apartment.

There had been something so disarming about Brett's self-effacing humor that Heather had wanted to defend him from himself. He had teased her about her Scottish accent and her red hair, and when he smiled, his warm eyes and the way his two front teeth overlapped slightly had made her blush. His broad frame and thick sand-colored hair had reminded her of her brother, Murdoch.

During the flight she had volunteered to take food up to the flight deck. Brett had been animated, talking to her over his shoulder and asking her about Scotland as she watched the instrument panel in front of him flicker. The copilot had been a quiet man from Nantucket, and Brett, with his Brooklyn twang, had won her over by the time they landed in Edinburgh.

They were both unable to sleep that night so had texted each other and then met in the bar for drinks in their hotel on Princes Street. The rest, for Heather, had been history.

Reminded of her brother, she glanced at the clock. It was early morning on the Isle of Skye, so he would be out on the croft, caring for his sheep in the predawn darkness. As she pictured him in his mud-spattered overalls and ubiquitous boots, his breath spiraling smokily into the pink-gray morning, a surge of homesickness caught her by surprise. She could almost smell the gorse and the dew-covered grass of Scotland.

Draining her glass, Heather decided to call her mother. By this time, Elspeth MacDonald would be up, preparing breakfast for the guests at the Forge Bed and Breakfast in the village of Portree. Murdoch often dropped by the B&B for breakfast after the first part of his long day was done. If she called now, she might catch them both.

As she dialed, Heather pictured her mother already showered and dressed, laying tables and brushing up any hints of dust or crumbs before the dining room filled up with guests. The old house overlooking the harbor in Portree had originally been a forge, and as a child Heather had loved to help her mother sweep the flagstone floors on the main level and clean and prepare the bedrooms upstairs. In her teen years, having reached her adult height of five foot three, she would duck under the low beams on the top floor and vacuum the heavy canopies that hung around the four-poster bed in the largest room. Each bedroom had a fireplace, a porcelain sink hidden behind a large wooden screen, a series of thick woven rugs across the scrubbed wooden floorboards, and a wide, paned-glass window overlooking the garden at the back of the property.

Elspeth had been running the business alone since her husband, Matthew, had died two years earlier. Heather had taken the twins back to see her mother only once since her father's passing, and the memory of the Forge without him was chokingly sad.

Waiting for her mother to answer the phone, she glanced around the room. This place was choking her now, too, for the want of Brett. A wave of empathy toward her stalwart mother threatened to close her throat before she had even spoken the first word to Elspeth.

Heather heard the familiar click, and then Elspeth's voice trickled like melted butter over her raw skin.

"Darling, is that you?"

"Hi, Mum. How's it going? Is this a bad time?" Heather sank heavily onto a stool at the breakfast bar and shrugged her coat from her shoulders until it lay bunched around her hips.

"Fine, fine. How're you, love?" Elspeth sounded concerned. "It's awfully late there, isn't it? Why are you no' asleep?"

Heather felt her eyes prickle. Sympathy, or concern in any shape or form, was still so hard to accept gracefully. Along with those sentiments came the sting of recognition that this was real, and that slap of reality preceded the inevitable taste of tears.

"I went to Dulles." Heather's voice cracked, and she winced. "I went to pick him up." She turned the phone away from her face and sniffed, pulled a paper towel from the roll, and wiped her nose. "I'm losing it, Mum."

"Oh, darling. I'm sorry. Did the kids know?"

Afraid her voice would betray her again, Heather shook her head in the empty room. She swallowed over a walnut.

"No. Chrissy is spending the night again. She's trying a case in DC tomorrow. I snuck out while they were sleeping." Heather waited for her mother to say something, her eyes scanning the room behind her in case one of the twins had wandered in and overheard her. Satisfied that they weren't within earshot, she went on. "I just can't seem to get past it." She sniffed.

"Well, it's not been that long, Heather. It's a huge adjustment for you and the children. You can't expect to just brush yourself off and move on, love. You lost your husband."

Heather could hear the sad smile in her mother's voice. She knew that Elspeth would be winding a tight twist of hair around her index finger as she spoke. It was something she did when she was pensive or anxious, and Heather had recently noticed Megan doing the same thing when she watched TV. It had made her smile and then crave her mother's presence.

"I know. I just thought I'd be coping better by now. It's been almost six months."

Heather closed her eyes as tears slipped over her cheekbones. She could see the outline of her reflection in the refrigerator, hunched over the breakfast bar, her shoulders rolling forward under the weight of her life.

Straightening her back, she pulled herself up. She badly needed to get her hair cut. The lush red tendrils Brett had loved to touch, which usually just grazed her collarbones, now lay lank and uncared for down her back. Her green eyes looked deeper set these days, the weight loss having changed the balance of her face. Her cheeks were sunken and her collarbones, clearly visible beneath her skin, looked like scaffolding around a crumbling building.

Elspeth's voice was soft as she carefully talked her daughter down from yet another cliff edge. Heather let the familiar tones wash over her, sucking them up like a sponge, letting their comfort seep in through her pores.

"I just feel like I want to bring the kids home, Mum." The words out, Heather instantly felt lighter. The plug in her throat loosened, and the idea that she'd had in the airport car park began to take on weight. "What do we have here now, anyway?"

Elspeth was quiet as Heather let the question hang in the room.

"Well, come home for a wee break, then. It'd be wonderful to see you. The place is quietening down now the winter's coming, so there's plenty of room." Her mother sounded pleased but hesitant.

"No. I don't mean that. I mean come home to stay." Heather felt a tiny buzz of excitement, the first tickle of optimism that she had experienced since Brett's shocking aneurysm had ripped her life apart.

She heard her mother catch her breath.

"Oh, God. Heather, are you sure? It's a lot of change in a short time. I mean, I'd love it. Murdoch would be over the moon. But are you sure?"

Heather swiveled around on the stool and took in the room behind her. The pale colors chilled her, making her stomach flip.

"I'm not sure of much at the moment, but I know I can't stay here if I want to stay sane." There. She had said what she'd been thinking for weeks. Suddenly, her surroundings felt less muted. The idea of leaving the place where she and Brett had spent most of their married life was less terrifying than the prospect of more time shuffling around inside this shrine to the past that was crushing her with its emptiness.

"What does Chrissy say? She'd miss the kids so much."

"Well, Phil's started at college, and she's moving to Atlanta in a few weeks. Frank's been transferred to their law offices down there. They're excited about it." Heather nodded to herself. "She's been fantastic these past few months. She's spent more time here than at her own place. But they're leaving Virginia. It'll just be me and the twins here, and I'm not sure I can stand that." A sob escaped with her last word, and Heather listened for her mother's comfort once again.

"Now listen to me, Heather MacDonald. Sorry, Forester. You need to get a grip. Those children need you to be strong and make good decisions."

Heather bit down on her quivering lip.

"Are you there?" Her mother's voice was firm. "If you decide to come home, lock, stock, and barrel, you know we'll welcome you with open arms. But it has to be for the right reasons. Come to come home, by all means. But don't come to run away."

Heather let the words settle as she dabbed her face with the damp paper towel that was now screwed into a ball in her fist. She heard what her mother was saying, and while it stung to be called out this way, Elspeth's advice was, as ever, sound.

CHAPTER 3

In the past, Chrissy had occasionally stayed overnight with Heather and Brett when she had an early court case the next day. Her own home, out in the tranquil hills of Virginia wine country, while beautiful, was a long commute from DC. Since Brett's death, she had been staying two or three times a week, and Heather, rather than resist the support as she might have in the past, gladly accepted it, appreciating Chrissy's company.

She loved Chrissy like a sister, and her increased presence over the past few months had helped Heather through some of her toughest moments. On the days when she felt as if someone had tinkered with gravity, when she couldn't lift her head from the pillow, let alone care for the twins, Chrissy had taken the reins. Her sister-in-law had taken care of the twins, fielded offers of help from friends and neighbors, and protected Heather from the sympathy that Chrissy knew she couldn't yet bear to receive.

When Heather told Chrissy that she felt bad about her neglecting her own home, Chrissy had deflected.

"Now that Phil's at college and Frank's in Atlanta during the week, I'm lonely out in the country."

Heather understood that not only was Chrissy sensing that Heather needed her around, but that spending more time with her and the children had obviously helped Chrissy cope with her own crushing grief at losing her little brother.

The previous evening, Chrissy and she had drunk hot chocolate together and watched a slapstick movie until just after ten, when Chrissy had fallen asleep on the sofa. Heather had nudged her off to bed before slipping into the twins' room and settling into the armchair near the window. She'd only been there a couple of hours before getting up and driving to the airport.

Now, as Heather passed behind Chrissy at the kitchen table, she laid her hand across the capable shoulders that had held her up so frequently.

"Morning." She squeezed Chrissy's arm then leaned over to kiss Megan, who was nose-diving into her cereal bowl. "Honey, can you sit up straight, please?" She smoothed the cloud of curls and winked as her daughter raised her head and met her eyes.

"Uh-huh." Megan spooned more flakes into her mouth.

"Where's Max?" Heather looked over at the empty bowl sitting at his place.

"He was here a moment ago." Chrissy spun around and scanned the room. Her long dark hair was twisted into an elegant roll at the back of her neck, and small diamond studs glinted in her earlobes.

Heather had always admired Chrissy's togetherness. This morning, her pale blue silk shirt was immaculate, a knee-length black skirt and classy black heels sang out *professional woman*, and Heather, suddenly self-conscious, yanked at her pajama bottoms and then smoothed her unbrushed hair with her palm.

"He's outside." Megan spoke through a mouthful of cereal.

"Mouth is full, missy." Heather scowled at her giggling daughter as she walked toward the french doors. She pushed the door open and stepped out onto the cold slate patio.

October mornings were chilly in Virginia, and Heather loved the subtle dampness of them. The fall here reminded her of autumn on the Isle of Skye. She inhaled the musty scent of the leaves beginning to rot. The wet soil around the plants and shrubs was tangy and pungent, mixing with the morning smells of coffee and car fumes as neighbors headed off to start their days.

She wrapped her arms around herself and looked across the backyard for Max's familiar form. Over by the fence, under the willow tree, she spotted a dark leg. Max had taken to slipping outside to sit under the long boughs when he was working through something. He would take his book and read under the green canopy for hours, sometimes falling asleep, until someone came and found him. Heather had noticed him disappearing out there more frequently over the past few weeks, and his increased tendency to remove himself from the family was troubling her.

"Max. Maximus. Can you come in, please, honey?" She caught sight of her breath and shivered. "Max?"

"Coming. What's the time, anyway?" Max dipped under the trailing willow tendrils and emerged onto the lawn. He had a book in his hand, and his sweater had ridden up his back.

"Were you lying on the wet grass?" Heather caught the irritation in her tone. "Max, seriously?"

The boy padded across the grass, leaving dark impressions in its spongy green surface.

"It's not that wet." He looked up at his mother and rolled his eyes as she turned him around and began brushing the beads of dampness from his back.

"You're soaked." She held him by the shoulders and looked into his eyes. The intensity of the green irises, an identical shade to her own, still occasionally took her by surprise. Unlike hers, Max's were flecked with tiny dots of gold that could catch the light in a startling way.

"What am I going to do with you?" She shook her head and smiled at her son.

Max shrugged and thrust his free hand deep into his trouser pocket. "Love me and let me be."

The saying had been one of Brett's. He had responded that way whenever Heather would tease him about his bad habits. She knew it was Brett's gentle way of saying "back off," and hearing the words from her son made her catch her breath. Max hadn't said it to hurt her, but the impact of the statement was like a jab to her sternum. She was instantly angry.

"Get inside and change your sweater. Hurry up. The bus will be here soon." She held his shoulders and turned him toward the patio door. "Fast, mister—move." She shoved him gently forward.

As his curly head disappeared into the kitchen, Heather felt her stomach dip. Had she been too hard on him? What was it about Max that brought that out in her? He was a child and had no bad intent. She needed to get a handle on the way she reacted to him, before it became a deep-set dynamic between them.

Stepping into the kitchen, Heather watched as Chrissy helped Megan on with her coat and then Max with his clean sweater. Heather lifted the two packed lunches from the counter and handed one to each child as they passed her.

"'Bye, Mommy." Megan stood on tiptoe to receive Heather's kiss.

"'Bye, sweetheart." Heather cupped the pink cheeks in her palms and smiled into her daughter's blue eyes, Brett's eyes.

Max slung his Spider-Man backpack over his shoulder and headed for the door.

"Hey. Where's my hug?" She reached out and grabbed the pack's strap.

"Sorry." Max looked up at her and bit his lip. "Love you, Mom."

Heather wrapped her arms around him and hugged him close.

"I love you back, Maximus." Her voice caught and she coughed to disguise the emotion that was threatening to take over. "See you guys later."

She followed them out onto the front porch and watched as they trotted down the driveway toward the school bus. The yellow double doors concertinaed open, consumed her children, and then closed behind their curly heads. She waved to no one and turned back into the house.

Chrissy had filled her mug with hot coffee, and a slice of toast lay on a plate with the marmalade next to it.

"I've got to run. You OK?" Chrissy had her jacket on and a black leather laptop case in her hand. Her dark eyes assessed Heather's face as Heather slid onto a stool at the island.

"Fine. Thanks, Chris. You're a star." Heather lifted the mug and took a sip.

"I'm coming back here tonight, OK?" Chrissy's heels clicked across the wood floor toward the entryway. "Maybe we can have a glass of wine and watch another movie?" She lifted a pile of manila folders from the hall table and checked her reflection in the mirror, tucking an imaginary strand of hair behind her ear.

Heather swallowed the hot coffee and nodded.

"That'll be great. I'll get the kids to bed early so we can have a chat, too."

Chrissy stopped her progress toward the door and turned.

"A chat? Is this a we-have-to-talk kind of chat, or just a chat chat?" She widened her eyes and pulled her mouth into a comical grimace. "Have I been bad?"

"No, nothing like that. I've just been thinking about what to do next. We can talk tonight. Go—you'll be late." Heather flicked her hand toward her sister-in-law, dismissing her. "Go. Seriously."

Chrissy nodded, shifted the pile of files up in her arms, and pulled her car keys from her pocket.

"OK. Sounds good. Get a decent bottle of wine tonight. Not that vinegar you bought the other day." She rolled her eyes and walked out the door.

"Ha—funny girl," Heather called after her as the door clicked shut in the frame.

She was alone. The day stretched out in front of her, and she had no idea how she'd get through it until the twins got back from school. She would start with a shower, then go into town for a haircut. It was a start, at least.

CHAPTER 4

Elspeth MacDonald stretched a clean sheet over the mattress and tucked it tightly under the edge. Her mother had spent years working as a nurse for the National Health Service and had taught Elspeth how to do hospital corners when she was nine years old. Elspeth had never forgotten it and had, in turn, taught Heather the same technique when she had turned nine.

As she snapped the cotton blanket up into the air, high above the bed, she caught the scent of fabric softener. The satisfying floral smell wafted around her as she centered the blanket across the mattress and then smoothed it over the sides.

Only three of the six rooms were occupied this weekend, and Elspeth was glad of it. She was beginning to feel the strain of coping with the Forge Bed and Breakfast alone, although she would never admit that to her son. She did well for her sixty-eight years, but some days her arthritis got the better of her, and she didn't have the reserves of energy that she used to. However, if Murdoch knew that she was struggling, he would push her to sell, and that was more than Elspeth could bear to think of. This house was where she and her husband, Matthew, had raised their two children and spent all their married life and where

Matthew had taken his last breath. No. The only way she was leaving this place was in her coffin.

Matthew had been born on Skye. His father had been a third-generation farmer, but Matthew had broken the mold by leaving at eighteen to go to university in Aberdeen. Four years later, he had returned to the island with a business degree and a fiancée from Perth.

Despite his dreams of travel and seeing more of the world than his island had to offer, Matthew loved Skye with a passion. The Hebridean island, with its peninsula fingers radiating from the mountainous fist of the Cuillins, had rocky slopes and dramatic scenery that he had never tired of. Elspeth, too, had fallen for the place soon after arriving, and it had quickly become as much a part of her as it was of the man she loved.

Elspeth gathered the linen she had removed and cast an eye around the room. It was spotless and ready for the next occupant. She nodded, satisfied with the results of her labor.

As she headed for the staircase, she recalled how Heather had liked to help her prepare the rooms. It had surprised her that the young girl was interested in the mundane tasks of cleaning and dusting, making beds, and carrying laundry, but she had seemed to enjoy it, and Elspeth had been grateful for the help. While Matthew was passable in the kitchen and was a welcoming host and a meticulous bookkeeper, his contribution to the business had not stretched to the housekeeping.

Thinking about her daughter, Elspeth frowned. Heather's call the previous morning had put her on edge. She knew that her child was suffering, and, in Elspeth's opinion, that was purgatory for any parent worth their salt. Over the past few weeks, rather than feeling that Heather was regaining her strength, Elspeth felt that she sounded increasingly distracted. She was more apt to dissolve into tears, as she had done in the initial days after Brett's death, and she seemed to need more emotional support than she had a month or two earlier. The notion that her fiercely independent daughter was still so fragile was unsettling.

As their conversation replayed in Elspeth's mind, frustration at not being able to take her daughter's pain away ate at her. She knew better than most the time-stopping impact, the utter devastation, of being widowed, but for it to happen to Heather while she was still in her thirties—and with two young children—was an embittering twist.

Elspeth walked down the stairs and deposited the linen in the canvas-lined trolley she kept for the purpose. She pushed it toward the pantry where the washing machine and dryer were housed. The October sun was shining weakly through the thick glass of the paneled windows, casting white bars across the furniture in the living room.

She shivered, and for the first time since the previous winter, she thought about lighting the fireplace that dominated the long room. Murdoch had stacked a massive woodpile against the outside of the kitchen wall and had instructed her exactly where to pull from first to get the driest wood.

She smiled to herself at the thought of her son. He had turned out to be a bear of a man, like his father. Six foot four and build like an outhouse, as her own father used to say, Murdoch had a heart of putty and the kindest green eyes she had ever seen. His thick sandy-colored hair sprang up mutinously from his head, like a symbol of his inner rebel. When he laughed, she swore that his best friend, Fraser Duncan, who lived on the next croft two miles away, could hear him.

Murdoch had been rocked by his brother-in-law's death. He had stayed on in Virginia for a week after the funeral, not wanting to leave Heather. If it hadn't been for the sheep and the croft to manage back on Skye, Elspeth knew that he would have stayed even longer. She also knew that Heather had eventually shooed Murdoch off, telling him that he needed to get home.

Elspeth's children talked to each other at least twice a week, and that knowledge gave her tremendous comfort. She was thankful for the closeness between them and grateful that they were kind to each other.

She was luckier than some of her contemporaries whose families were fractured by old arguments and petty misunderstandings.

The linen trolley bumped across the kitchen floor as Elspeth headed for the pantry. The kitchen was warm now as the Aga sent a steady wave of heat throughout the ground level of the house, and the smell of baking bread made her hungry. She had put the loaves in before going upstairs, and her timing, which she had down to a fine art, was perfect.

Having filled the washing machine, Elspeth pulled on her oven gloves and took the loaves out. The golden tops crackled as she turned them out onto a cooling rack. By force of habit, she pushed them to the back of the stove top so Charlie, her errant Labrador named for the bonnie prince, would not be able to reach them with his twitching nose.

Just as she was pouring boiling water into the teapot, the back door flew open behind her and Murdoch stood in his filthy boots, grinning.

"Morning, Mother. Any tea in the pot?"

"Take those boots off and I'll think about it." She tutted at her son and pulled another mug from the cupboard. His habit of dropping in for breakfast was a bright spot in her day, and no matter how early the hour or how dirty he was, she looked forward to it.

Murdoch stepped into the kitchen in his socks and closed the door.

"It's gettin' cold out there." He gently pushed his mother out of the way and held his big red hands over the Aga. "Got any eggs on the go?" He winked at her, towering over her head. She leaned against his giant frame, pushed him back, and laughed as she made her way to the fridge.

"Fried or boiled?"

"The usual, please." Murdoch padded over to the long wooden table and pulled out a chair. The newspaper was folded neatly at his father's place, and the sight of it made him pause. Elspeth loved that about him. Despite his cheery nature and his tendency to jolly folk along, she knew how much Murdoch had loved his father and how precious Matthew's memory was to him.

"Can I have a look?" He pointed at the paper, asking permission of his mother, who nodded. "So what's happening in the world?" He scanned the headlines.

Elspeth carried the container of eggs to the stove and laid them next to the freshly baked bread.

"I meant to tell you Heather called yesterday." She cracked two eggs into a hot cast-iron skillet and reached for the spatula.

"Oh, aye? How is she?" Murdoch closed the paper and focused on his mother.

"Not good." Elspeth stared down at the pan, the utensil suspended in midair.

"What's going on?" Murdoch stood up and walked back over to her side.

"She's miserable. Says she wants to come home—for good." Elspeth bit down on her treacherous tongue. She had not wanted to blurt it out that way or to get Murdoch's hopes up before she knew if Heather was serious.

"What? When?" Murdoch reached over and took the spatula from his mother's hand. "Let me." He stepped in front of her and nudged the edges of the egg whites away from the bottom of the pan while Elspeth poured the tea.

"I don't know for sure. She may change her mind, but there was something in the way she said it. I think she meant it." Elspeth cut two slices of bread and popped them into the toaster.

"Well, you know what I think." Murdoch lifted the skillet and slid the eggs onto a plate. "She should be with her family, and so should those bairns."

Elspeth sat down at the table and ran a hand over the time-softened wood. Matthew had made the table for her as a gift when they had bought the Forge, and not a day went by that she did not sit at it and think of him. Matthew would have agreed with Murdoch about Heather coming back to the island, she was certain of that.

"It's not our place to tell her what to do. The children are Americans, Murdo. They've no idea what it would be like to live here. Can you imagine the wee souls?" Elspeth shook her head. "I mean, I'd love to have them all here, but such a lot of change in a short period of time— it's too much." She sipped her tea.

Murdoch grabbed the toast from the toaster, sat down opposite her, and cut into his eggs.

"But if she is talking about it, Mum, don't you go discouraging her." Murdoch waved his fork at her. "Skye's her home." He bit off a huge chunk of toast.

"I know that, young man," Elspeth snapped.

Murdoch flushed and muttered into the food in his mouth.

"Sorry. I just think . . ."

"I know what you think, but we need to remember that she's still grieving. It might not be the time for making such momentous decisions." She looked over at her son and smiled. She could never stay angry with him for long. "Besides, she'd be taking the children away from their home, their school, their friends, from Chrissy and everything that's familiar to them. It just goes on and on, son."

They sat in silence as he finished his breakfast, and then Murdoch stood up and put the plate into the sink. Elspeth looked at his broad back and remembered her husband standing in that exact spot on many a morning as he washed the breakfast dishes. The image brought a lump to her throat.

Perhaps Murdoch was right. Brett had no family in Virginia other than his sister's, and they were moving to Atlanta. Heather would soon be marooned there with two children to take care of, no job, and no family network to support her. At the thought of it, Elspeth felt her hands get clammy. If it were up to her, she would have her daughter and grandchildren home in an instant, but she was intuitive enough to know that Heather would have to come to the conclusion in her own time. No amount of encouragement would get her here any sooner.

Mother and son assessed each other across the room, each working through their own silent scenario for Heather's future. Finally, Elspeth stood up and walked over to the stove.

"She'll make the decision when it's right for her. I just don't want her to rush into anything and then regret it."

"Aye. Agreed." Murdoch wrapped a big arm around her shoulder and drew her into his side. "You're a rare breed, Mrs. MacDonald."

Elspeth felt herself flush and gently pushed her son away.

"Don't you have sheep to tend?" She poked him in the stomach and gestured toward the door. "Some of us have work to do."

Murdoch's deep laugh echoed in the room as he shuffled over to the door.

"I'll no' outstay my welcome then." He opened the back door, letting in a gust of frigid air. As he pulled on his muddy boots, Elspeth stood on the mat and waited for her customary kiss on the cheek.

He stamped his feet on the cobbled stone and leaned in toward her.

"It'll be all right, Mother. Don't worry. We'll give her a wee bit more time to come to her senses." He winked. "The kids would love this place, you know. Who wouldn'y want to grow up on the Isle of Skye?" Murdoch gave her a mischievous smile and walked away.

CHAPTER 5

Heather's phone was ringing. She pulled her eyes from the road and looked down at her handbag. Every time the phone rang these days, she jumped. Glancing in the rearview mirror, she pulled over to the side of the road to answer it.

"Hello. Is that Mrs. Forester?" It was a woman's voice.

"Yes, speaking."

"This is Vice Principal Honeywell, from Flint Ridge School."

Heather felt a knot forming under her breastbone.

"What's wrong? What's happened?"

"It's all right, Mrs. Forester. The children are fine. I just wanted to ask if you could stop by my office this afternoon?"

Heather exhaled. The twins were OK.

"Of course. But what's the problem?"

"It's Max. He was pulled from the playground today for fighting. It's the second time in two weeks."

As she processed the words, Heather felt nauseous. Max, fighting? She tried to speak but couldn't find her voice. She could not even ask if the other child had been hurt. What was wrong with her? She stared out the window at the passing traffic on the Dulles toll road.

Brett would have known exactly what to say. As she tipped her head and looked up at the sky, she wondered how many times he had flown over this very spot. There had been hundreds of approaches and departures when he had guided the wide-bodied aircraft in and out of Dulles. He would never have known that at some point in the future, way down below him, his useless wife would be sitting at the side of the road, mute and paralyzed.

"Mrs. Forester? We all understand what the children, and you, are going through. We want to be as helpful and supportive as we can, but we can't have him fighting." The woman's voice faded.

Heather took a deep breath and swallowed. *Get a grip. You can do this. You are an adult. You are his mother.*

"Right. Of course. I'll be there after school."

Heather hung up the phone and tossed it into her bag. She glanced in her rearview mirror and swung the car back out onto the highway.

What was going on with her son? Max had always been more reserved than Megan. He was a thinker, a loner, but never a fighter. He had become more and more withdrawn since Brett's death, and she had watched him gradually retreat into his own world as she stood by, helpless to hold on to him. She wanted desperately to comfort him, find the right things to say, but she came up short time after time. Megan was easy to mother, but Max's independent nature made it difficult at times, just as Heather was sure her own similar nature had made it hard for Elspeth and Matthew.

The traffic sped by as she continued on autopilot toward Reston Town Center. She had managed to snag a cancellation appointment with her hairdresser that had lifted her spirits, but now, as she approached the exit, she wanted to turn around and go home. What was she thinking, going to get her hair done? Her life was a mess, her son was in crisis, and she was concerned about how she looked.

Heather followed the flow of traffic, falling in with its momentum as if she were joining a school of fish, and before she realized it she was in town. As she turned the Volvo into the multistory car park, she scanned the rows for an empty space. It was a midweek morning, and already the place was jammed with cars. Finding nothing on the first floor, she turned up the ramp, climbing to the second level. Moving slowly down the line of cars, she made a deal with herself. If she found a space on this level, she would stay; if not, then she would take it as a sign and go home.

Heather guided her car carefully along the rows and just as she felt a tingle of relief at the lack of a space, her pass to go home, a car to the right of her began backing out.

"Damn." She slipped the gear lever into reverse and moved back to let it out. The man inside smiled and raised a hand as he pulled away, leaving her staring at the empty space. She sat for a few moments, her turn signal ticking inside the car, as she considered her next move.

Before long, another car pulled up behind her and flashed its headlights, the question clear: Was she staying or going? Heather leaned over and looked into the rearview mirror, catching sight of her eyes. New lines were etched around their edges, and a few lank tendrils of hair hung around her cheekbones. Yes. She was staying. She needed this.

Two hours later, she walked back toward her car. The stylist had done a good job tidying her up and had been sensitive enough not to bombard her with questions about her long absence. Her red hair shone, the freshly cut ends just touching her collarbones, and as it moved around her face in the breeze, she caught gentle wafts of the eucalyptus conditioner that she loved.

Inside the parking lot, feeling more in control than she had in several months, she slid the key into the lock and checked her watch. There was still time to go to the cemetery before her meeting with the vice principal, and then she would figure out how to deal with Max. The thought of her son, the thoughtful and tender little man she knew and loved, fighting in the playground took another stab at her diaphragm.

Things had been bad for months now, but this latest development with Max was deeply worrying. It was time to fix her family, and suddenly, with startling clarity, Heather knew exactly what she had to do to make that happen.

CHAPTER 6

Max and Megan sat in the back of the Volvo as Heather negotiated her way through the traffic. Megan chattered about her art class that day and what games her friends had played at recess as Max stared out the side window, his cheek pressed against the glass.

He had been silent since she'd met him at the school gate and told him that she'd spoken to Miss Honeywell. He hadn't offered much of a defense, saying only that the other kid, a boy called Alex, had called him a runt. When Heather questioned him about it, Max had said he didn't really know what a runt was, just that it was mean.

He looked none the worse for wear, and apparently the other child had not been hurt, either, but sensing that Max's emotions were hovering very close to the surface, Heather decided that it was best to leave any further interrogation until they got home.

The road was busy with the after-school surge, and the forecast for rain had been accurate. Big, fat raindrops battered the windshield as Heather increased the speed of the wipers and shivered.

"Are you guys cold?" She adjusted the heater on the dashboard and caught Megan's eyes in the rearview mirror.

"Nuh-uh." Megan shook her head and then plunged her hand into her school bag. "I have my gloves here, anyway." She looked up and met her mother's gaze.

The child had an old soul. In fact, Heather had often felt that both the twins had been here before. Her grandmother had talked about children who were born with the Sight, and Heather, having had a distinctly heightened awareness herself for as long as she could remember, smiled back at her daughter's comforting little face.

"Max?" She twisted around to see him. He leaned against the window, his hair falling into his eyes. He looked sullen, and his profile was defiant as he sat up straight and shook his head.

"Not cold." He looked at her and then turned back toward the passing traffic.

"We're almost home, anyway." Heather frowned at him and turned her attention back to the road. "When you've done your homework and we've had something to eat, I want to talk to you both."

Megan's face was buried in a book, but at Heather's words, she dropped the book onto her lap and looked up.

"What about?"

Max remained silent, his eyes boring a hole in the glass as he deliberately avoided her gaze.

"Something exciting." Heather forced a smile. "We'll talk about it later."

Megan shrugged and lifted her book up until her nose was obscured by the edge of the cover. Max had started to trace circles in the small patch of condensation his breath created on the glass.

"What's going on?" His voice sounded gravelly.

Relieved to hear him speak, Heather smiled over her shoulder at him. "Nothing to worry about, sweetheart. It's something good."

The rest of the drive home passed in silence. Once inside the house, the children deposited their bags and coats in the mudroom and then headed toward the staircase, the two sets of narrow shoulders jostling for the lead position.

"Hey. Be careful. Get changed and then we can make some cookies when you come down." Heather laughed at their antics. They were gently competitive, and she wondered if it was an inherent quality that all twins possessed. Whether it was to see who could finish their meal first, run up the stairs the fastest, get a better grade for a school project, or sing the loudest in the bath, the competition between them was good-natured but invariably present.

Megan won this bout, pushing in front of Max and pounding up the stairs. He yelled at her back.

"Cheater. You used your elbows."

Heather heard the laughter in his voice and felt the tension she had been holding under her diaphragm release. He was all right. He would be fine. She knew they needed to talk about what had happened in the playground, but for now she wanted to let him forget about it, have some fun, and eat a good dinner. Then she would tell them about her decision. It was time that they all had a plan to work toward, and as she tried to work out what to say to them, her nerves crowded her throat again.

"You mean we're leaving here?" Max's mouth fell. "Leaving Virginia? Leaving Flint Ridge, my friends, Aunt Chrissy and Uncle Frank?"

The twins both sat in their pajamas on the sofa in the family room as the fire flicked golden fingers of light across the wood floor. Heather, also in her pajamas, had made them all hot chocolate and sat opposite the children in Brett's favorite recliner.

"Yes. We're going to go live in Scotland. Near Granny Elspeth." Heather took a sip of her drink and forced the hot liquid down.

Megan thumped her cup down on the coffee table, sending a spray of hot chocolate across its surface. She sprang from the sofa and began jumping up and down.

"Granny Elspeth, Granny Elspeth. Will Charlie be there?" Her face was flushed with excitement, and her strawberry-blonde curls bounced on her shoulders as she sprang across the room.

Heather laughed. "Yes, he will, honey."

She knew that Megan adored her mother's dog. She'd bonded with him immediately when they had visited the last time, and it had been all Heather could do to resist Megan's continual begging for a puppy when they got home.

"Megs, can you sit down for a minute? I want to talk to you."

The little girl turned two more spins before hopping on one leg back to the sofa, where she threw herself down next to her brother.

Max stared at Heather, his mouth still hung open, and as she scanned his face, she was reminded that this could go one of two ways. She needed to tread lightly, as how she handled this conversation was critical to the success of her plan.

A few moments passed, the three of them suspended in a tense time lapse, waiting for Max to speak. Finally, he placed his cup down next to Megan's, folded his arms across his chest, and then closed his mouth deliberately. Heather steeled herself. This did not bode well.

"I want to ask you a question." Max looked over at her.

Heather pulled her feet up underneath herself and nodded. "Shoot."

"Is this because I was fighting? I mean, is this a punishment?" Heather heard the pain in his voice. "I won't do it again, Mom. I promise. He was just a mean kid and . . ." Max was leaning toward her, his arms now wrapped tightly across his middle as if he were holding in a wall of hurt. "I won't fight anymore." His eyes were glittering, and Heather was up in an instant. She moved over and sat next to her son, wrapping her arms around his resistant little frame. He pulled away from her, but she insisted, by the pressure of her grip, that he stay put.

"This is not a punishment, Max. Are you listening to me?" Max's dam gave way, and heavy sobs shook his shoulders as he leaned into her chest.

"But if we go—Dad will be left here." His voice was muffled.

The sound of his misery cut into Heather's heart like thousands of tiny slivers of glass shredding the muscle.

"Dad's not really at the cemetery, Max. He'll be with us, honey, in our hearts and in our memories. Daddy will always be with us wherever we go."

As she rocked him back and forth, she felt the tears on her own face leaving a cool track as they made their way down and hung under her jaw.

After a few moments, Heather felt her daughter's small arms circling her shoulders.

"Why is everyone crying?" Megan wailed. "We're going to live in Skye and be with Granny Elspeth and Uncle Murdy. Why are you crying?" Her little face was perplexed as she forced herself in between her mother and brother. "You're silly." She swiped at Max's cheeks with her fingertips.

Heather shook the hair out of her eyes and settled into the circle of her children's embraces. She wasn't sure how long they had stayed there before Max reached up a hand and touched her bangs.

"Your hair looks pretty, Mom." He sniffed and wiped the back of his arm across his eyes.

Megan looked up and nodded her agreement, and Heather felt a rush of love for her perfectly balanced little bookend babies, as she often called them.

"Thank you, sweeties. I had it cut today."

Max leaned away from her as Megan also disentangled herself from the clump of pajamas and slid to the other end of the sofa.

"You look like you again." Max smiled, his pink-rimmed eyes turning up at the corners the same way hers did when she smiled. "I missed you."

CHAPTER 7

Murdoch lifted the last bag of feed pellets from the back of the Land Rover. He flipped it up onto his shoulder, walked into the shed, and dumped it on top of the stack against the wall. Along with the hay he'd stored, he had enough provisions to get the adult flock through the worst of the winter months, when the pasture became too rough and sparse to sustain them. He stepped back and inhaled the tart smell of fresh hay and the musk of the damp ground underneath his feet. He loved everything about this place.

On Murdoch's twenty-eighth birthday, his father had been shocked when he'd told him that he wanted to leave his job at a bank in Portree and buy the croft that had come up for sale a few miles north of town. A local farmer named Davy Gunn had decided to sell after losing his family in a tragic chain of events. Gunn's wife had died a few years before, his daughter had emigrated to Australia under some kind of cloud, and then his only son, Daniel, had been killed in Iraq. Daniel had been in Murdoch and his best friend Fraser's class at school, and while they hadn't been close, they'd both known Dan as a quiet lad who excelled at sports.

Knowing that his son had been the only member of his family who could have carried on working the croft, which had been in the Gunn family for three generations, Davy had lost heart and decided to sell. One man's misery had turned into another's bliss, and, despite his sympathy for Davy's circumstances, Murdoch could hardly contain his excitement when he had spoken to Matthew about the prospect of becoming a crofter. Despite his surprise, and true to form, his father had soon rallied and lent him the money to get started.

Murdoch had read everything he could find on running a croft and caring for Scottish Blackface sheep, the small flock of the distinct black-and-white breed that he'd purchased along with the land. He had learned the intricacies of breeding for meat and, with sheer hard work, determination, and Fraser's help and advice, had paid his father back within four years.

They had been a close father and son, and the loss of Matthew still weighed heavily on Murdoch. Few days went by that he didn't think of his father and regret that he'd been taken from them prematurely. By the time Matthew had been diagnosed with pancreatic cancer, it had been advanced. There had only been twelve weeks from diagnosis to his passing, and while his death had come brutally fast, he had at least not lingered in pain.

Murdoch pulled the wooden door closed behind him and walked across the path to the low stone croft house. The house had felt like home almost as soon as his dirty boots were first abandoned at the back door nine years earlier. The wall was rough under his palm as he leaned forward over his knees and stretched out his back.

The view down toward Portree was flat and largely treeless, but the stark line of the land appealed to him. What you saw was what you got, and he appreciated that quality in his homeland—much as he did in people.

Behind Portree, east of the Trotternish Peninsula, far in the distance, he could just make out the outline of the Old Man of Storr. The large pinnacle of rock could be seen for miles around, and the massive ancient landside that had created the mountainous ridge had left in its wake one of the most stunning landscapes in the world. As far as Murdoch was concerned, with its lochs, mountains and moorland, and the clear blue waters of the Hebridean harbors, Skye was the epicenter of the world. There had been MacDonalds on the island since the twelfth century, and if it was anything to do with him, they would be here for many generations to come.

The idea that Heather might come back to Skye delighted him. It just made so much sense. He had missed her during the years of her absence, but as he stared out over his fields, he realized that he had not acknowledged just how much until Elspeth had mentioned her conversation with Heather that morning.

For Murdoch, home among family was exactly where Heather and the children should be now. It was obvious that the twins needed a father figure, and if they were here, close at hand, Murdoch felt that he could step into the breach. While he would never presume to replace Brett, he could at least be a male presence the twins could rely on. He had tried to talk to Heather about coming home when he had been in Virginia for Brett's funeral, but he had mistimed it, and it had caused tension between them for a while.

Murdoch worried about Max, in particular. When he had been in Virginia the previous summer, the little boy had barely left his room. With Heather not using the master bedroom and Elspeth taking the other guest room, Murdoch had slept on the floor in the children's bedroom, so he'd been aware of his nephew crying. It had broken his heart to hear it, and he had spent hours standing next to the bunk bed, patting Max's back until the sobs subsided and the little boy finally fell asleep.

Megan was a little doll. Deeply intuitive, with a sage soul, she had dealt with her own sadness over her father with such grace that it made Murdoch well up to think about it. Megan had taken care of Max during the darkest days, making him special sandwiches, giving him her favorite blanket, and deferring to him whenever he did venture to speak. It had made Murdoch feel quite humble. How did a seven-year-old gain such strength of character and depth of compassion when she herself was grieving? It was a mystery to him.

Far below in the field he could see the familiar black-and-white shapes of his sheep. The animals were thriving, and all being well, he would have a good year as a result. He whistled for Chick, his border collie, and soon saw the black strip haring toward him across the field.

"Come away to me now." He leaned down and ruffled the dog's neck. "It's been a good day, boy. A good day."

Murdoch opened the fridge and scanned the contents. He'd meant to get to the shops and stock up but had been too busy, and as a result it was looking rather bare. He grabbed a cold beer bottle, closed the door with a thud, and walked over to the old sofa that sat in front of the fire. Fraser was due to arrive in an hour for a game of cards. They were going to discuss the plan for selling their lambs to mainland farmers before the worst of the winter set in, and for taking part of the flock to market the following week. Murdoch was loath to part with any of his sheep, but he knew that he needed to rotate the flock, keep the stronger females, and plan for the spring—hoping for a good lambing season.

Chick lay in front of the fire. Murdoch allowed the dog to snooze there during the evenings but would send him to sleep in the barn when he turned in himself. He couldn't have the dog getting soft. Thinking about Chick out in the shed, sleeping but ready to spring to the flock's defense should he need to, he pictured Charlie, his mother's Lab, lying in her bed under the duvet like a naughty child. He smiled to himself and shook his head. His father would never have allowed it, but Elspeth needed the comfort these days.

As the flames licked up the sides of the logs, Murdoch was struck by the irony of having two widows in the family now. Life could be unjust. There was no more certain thing than that.

As he stretched his feet out toward the fire, he felt the heat permeate his thick socks. The children loved both Charlie and Chick. Perhaps when they came back to the island he could teach them both to call Chick, to learn the whistles and commands that sent the dog pelting across the fields and the sheep gathering together like iron filings on a magnet. He imagined his niece and nephew wrapped up in winter wool, whistling through their tiny white teeth. The thought made him smile as he closed his eyes to rest, just until Fraser knocked on the door.

CHAPTER 8

Chrissy sat on the sofa looking startled. The family room fire crackled, and as she waited for Chrissy to speak, Heather inhaled the tangy smell of wood smoke.

"Leaving. Are you serious?" Chrissy's wineglass was half-full and balanced on one slim thigh. Her impressive wedding ring glinted in the candlelight, sending a kaleidoscope of light across the cushion next to her. She still wore the all-business black skirt and creaseless silk shirt but had kicked off her shoes, and her slim ankles were crossed loosely on the coffee table. A few tendrils of dark hair had worked loose from the tight chignon, softening the more severe look of the morning.

Heather nodded. "Yes."

Chrissy took a swallow of wine and then blinked slowly.

Heather continued.

"I still need to do some research—find out about getting the twins into school, locate a house and stuff—but it's the only thing that's felt right since he died."

She watched her sister-in-law swallow the news with a mouthful of wine, her face seeming to contort around the information. With the words hanging between them, Heather felt bad for blurting it out this way, not fully considering the impact her revelation would have on Chrissy.

She had been a rock over the past few months, and Heather suspected that while the arrangement had been exactly what she needed from Chrissy, it was also something Chrissy had begun to enjoy. She loved to spend time with the twins, and Megan worshipped her—saying she wanted to grow her hair long, have a laptop, and be an attorney when she grew up. Chrissy would laugh and say, "Not on my watch, kiddo," which would send Megan into fits of giggles.

Heather wrapped her hands around her wineglass and swirled the dark liquid in circles.

"Wow. I'm not sure what to say." Chrissy's voice was thick.

Heather was suddenly flooded with doubt. What if this was a terrible decision? Was it totally selfish to take the kids away from their remaining American family? How would they adapt to Skye? It was the other side of the universe, as far as Max and Megan were concerned, and having visited only three times in their short lives, it might feel like living on Mars to their seven-year-old sensibilities.

As Heather mentally worked through the list of obstacles they could face, Chrissy leaned forward and placed her empty glass on the table.

"Well. I guess you need to do what you think is best for you and the children, but I can't say that it won't break my heart." Her eyes were glassy, and she ran a hand down her thigh. "It'll take some getting used to, but we can always visit. And you'll come back often, right? To see us?" Chrissy searched Heather's face.

"Of course. I would never keep them away from you, Chris. The kids adore you all. I just feel like I'm adrift—marking time. When you guys go to Atlanta, I'll be drowning here."

Chrissy stood and walked over to Heather's chair.

"Look. You're the best mom I know. If this is what you need to do, then I support you. I'll just miss you all so friggin' much." She leaned over and took Heather's hand. "You've become my sister, and I love you.

I'm sorry my stupid brother had to go and die. He always was a selfish asshole." Chrissy swiped her cheek and smiled.

Heather clasped Chrissy's fingers.

"You're the best sister anyone could ask for, Chris. I couldn't have made it, this—"

Chrissy raised a hand to stop her.

"No. You would have. It'd just have been tougher, and with a much lower consumption of wine." Chrissy squared her shoulders. "So. What do you need me to do? Research real estate over there? Find you a good real estate agent here? I presume you'll sell this place? How about moving companies? What about work—will you work, or just continue to enjoy a life of leisure?" Chrissy forced a laugh, stood up, and walked toward the kitchen.

Heather watched her elegant back as she moved, and a surge of love for this practical woman threatened to choke her. Heather was once again aware of her own disheveled appearance, having only graduated that morning from her pajamas into faded jeans, which hung loose around her diminished frame, and Brett's oversize Virginia Tech sweatshirt. At least her hair looked better. She rose and followed Chrissy into the kitchen.

The two women worked around each other, assembling a basic meal. Heather sautéed a pile of mushrooms in a heavy skillet, then threw two omelets together while Chrissy made a salad and cut garlic bread into thick slices. With a second bottle of wine, they settled back in front of the fire.

The TV flickered as they ate in silence. Once their empty plates were stacked on the table and the fire was settling into a heap of red-hot ash, Heather shifted in the armchair and turned off the TV.

"Are you OK, Chris?"

Chrissy nodded and yawned.

"I'll be OK. It'll just take a while to sink in." She stretched her long arms toward the ceiling. "What's your time frame for the big move?"

Heather was once again struck by the gravity of her decision. The implications of moving her little family back to Scotland were enormous, and hearing Chrissy refer to it made it frighteningly real.

"I don't know for sure. It would be good to get the kids into school for the new term, but I'm not sure how easy that'll be."

As she shifted forward in the chair, something moved in her peripheral vision. Heather swung her head around to see Max standing in his Spider-Man pajamas. His hair stuck out from his head in a sandy-red cone, and he was biting at the skin around his thumb.

"What school will we go to?" His voice was thick with sleep, and he stared at Heather.

Heather felt cornered. This was not the time to get into the details of all the changes they were facing.

"Maximus. What's up? Can't sleep?" She jumped up and padded over to her son.

"What school?" He pouted and pulled his hands back from Heather's as she reached for him. "Mom?"

Heather knelt down and gathered him into her arms.

"We'll talk about it all tomorrow, OK? You need to sleep, sweetheart. It's a school night." She felt his shoulder relax into her collarbone and smelled the fabric softener from his pillowcase lingering in his hair. "You're my champion, Maximus. You know that, right?" She leaned back from him.

The little boy nodded as his face broke into a yawn.

"You'll tell me tomorrow—promise?" His hooded eyes bored into Heather's. "I want to know before Megan, 'cuz I'm older."

She nodded and smoothed his wild hair back down at the crown of his head.

"I promise we'll talk about everything as soon as you guys get back from school. It's Friday tomorrow, so we'll have pizza and talk about what we'll do when we get to Scotland."

Heather lifted her son up against her shoulder and was startled at how long his legs had become, his feet dangling below her own knees as she carried him back up the stairs. Where was the time going?

She negotiated her way up the three steps of the ladder and carefully laid Max back in the top bunk. He curled up into the customary ball as she covered him and patted his back.

Seeing her son relaxing back into the warmth of his bed, Heather felt a surge of anger. Brett wasn't here to see this, to watch the twins become more themselves every day. He wouldn't see Max go on his first date, help him with a science project, see him graduate or get married. He wouldn't grill Megan's first boyfriend, object to her short teenage skirts, cheer as she got her degree, or walk her down the aisle. He would never cradle a grandchild, take a retirement vacation, or hold her hand again as they walked down the street. He would never do any of those mundane and precious things, and it incensed her. She was furious with life, with God, with the universe, and with all the forces that had taken her husband, her best friend, and her children's father. She cursed that goddamn blood vessel that had snapped the light out in Brett's eyes while he walked benignly on a treadmill. It was all just so bloody pointless and infuriating.

Heather wiped her face as Max's breathing settled into a smooth rhythm. Satisfied that he was asleep, she checked on Megan, who lay with her arms flung wide and a tiny smile on her face. This child was afraid of very little and had nothing to hide from the world. As Heather tucked the covers back around her daughter, Megan opened one eye and smiled.

"Don't worry about Max, Mommy. I'll take care of him." She lifted her head and accepted the kiss that Heather planted on her forehead.

"I know you will, Megs. We both will."

CHAPTER 9

The winter was closing in fast, and Elspeth was glad of her long sheep-skin coat as she trudged along the footpath on the Brae, heading toward the village. November was almost upon them, and the sky was heavy with rain. She glanced up and hoped she could make it home before the heavens opened.

Murdoch and his friend Fraser had been in the night before and eaten her out of house and home. She planned to take the car out to the supermarket later that afternoon, but for now she wanted to walk, get some fresh air, and pick up a few things from the newsagent along from the Forge.

As she ran through her shopping list in her mind, Elspeth was reminded of Murdoch sitting at the kitchen table the night before. He had tried to hide his spinach under the skin of a baked potato, but she had caught him out, scolding him as the three of them laughed. There was a childlike quality to her son that she admired, and in Fraser he had found a partner in crime. Even in their late thirties, the two men would laugh raucously at a prank they had played on some unsuspecting agricultural inspector or a neighboring farmer.

Murdoch and Fraser's crofts ran in long parallel strips along the hillside above Portree. They had known each other since high school and, despite their different interests at the time, had been great friends ever since. Fraser had spent most of his time with the children from Skye's farming families, as he was to inherit the croft from his father. Murdoch, on the other hand, had socialized more with the village children, those whose parents had businesses in Portree—shops, pubs, hotels, and bed-and-breakfasts. Regardless of which group they gravitated toward, all the islanders were accustomed to being surrounded by the influx of tourists, who would drive across the Skye Bridge from the Kyle of Lochalsh in the warmer weather, and many of whom would be dumbstruck at the notion that Skye had a language different from their own.

Elspeth had forgotten most of the Gaelic she'd learned when she had moved to Skye, except for a few phrases Matthew had repeated as he worked around the Forge. He had taught one to the twins that they'd repeated over and over as they marched around the kitchen table, until no one could stand it anymore. Brett had eventually threatened them with no TV for a week if they didn't stop. She smiled at the memory of Matthew chuckling conspiratorially in the conservatory with Murdoch at the chaos he had caused.

Elspeth tried to listen to BBC Radio nan Gàidheal now and then to see how much she could remember, but, disappointed in herself, she would quickly switch back to the English station.

She pulled her collar up closer to her jaw and put her head into the wind. The stripe of multicolored buildings that she passed overlooked the harbor. The tight row of frontages housed a café, the best fish-and-chip shop on the island, some gift shops, and a couple of charity stores where Elspeth often found bargain books. As she passed the familiar windows, another gust of wind raised the briny scent of the water.

Matthew had loved this time of year. He would often say that it was the rehearsal for winter, giving them time to get their Arran sweaters out of the cedar chest and oil their waterproof jackets, ready for the harsh conditions to come. He would pile wood up against the stone wall at the back of the Forge and then drive to the supermarket to stock up on cans, frozen food, dried goods, and batteries. She had often teased him, saying that it looked as if he were preparing for Armageddon rather than a change in the season.

Elspeth walked on, moving past two youngsters who were leaning against a wall outside the fish-and-chip shop, smoking. If she had been their mother, she would have said something about the damn cancer sticks hanging from their indolent mouths. Did they know what cancer looked like? How it could strip a person of everything that made them themselves in a matter of weeks—modern medicine be damned? She glowered at the young couple and then edged her way inside the door of the newsagent's.

It was quiet inside, with just two other people who appeared to be browsing at the magazine shelves rather than shopping with any purpose.

She pulled her gloves off and walked over to the counter at the back of the shop.

"Hello?"

Marjorie Davis, the shop owner and an old friend, was nowhere to be seen.

"Marj?" Getting no response, Elspeth picked up a small basket and circled the shop, grabbing the items she needed. By the time she had emptied her purchases onto the counter, Marjorie was walking in from the back office.

"Morning, Elspeth. It's a chilly one th'day." Marjorie's face was pinched, and she rubbed her chapped hands together. Her silver hair had a new, pinkish tinge to it.

"It is, Marj. Is that a new rinse?" Elspeth nodded at her friend's hair and pulled her purse out of her handbag.

"Aye. Not sure it was a good idea, though. It makes me look like my mother, the old goat." Marjorie cackled, her smoker's cough stripping any further words from her and sending her into a spasm.

"Are you OK there?" Elspeth reached across the counter and laid her hand on her friend's arm.

"Yes. Sorry about that. The damn damp is back, and there goes my chest." Marjorie thumped her sternum, wiped at her watery left eye, then focused on the counter. "So what's the news from the Forge? Anything new?" Marjorie lifted each item and punched the price into the register before packing a small plastic bag with Elspeth's purchases.

"Just the same stuff." Elspeth shrugged. "Murdoch misbehaving as ever—keeping me on my toes and out of food." She rolled her eyes theatrically as Marjorie chuckled. Elspeth noticed the marked quiver in Marj's hand, which had been increasing over the past year. She had been diagnosed with Parkinson's disease but seemed, by pure willpower and defiance, to be declining mercifully slowly.

Elspeth smiled at her friend. "We're quietening down now. Just two rooms occupied at the moment, and only one booked for next weekend."

"Seven ninety-five, please."

Elspeth handed a ten-pound note to her friend. Should she say anything about Heather coming home? Probably not. It wouldn't be wise to share the information, especially as nothing was confirmed. The island could be a veritable grapevine when there was news to be had, and Heather, being a private person, would no doubt be angry if she knew her mother had discussed her plans without her permission.

As if reading her mind, Marjorie looked up and asked, "How's wee Heather doing?"

Elspeth started slightly, then jammed the change Marjorie had handed her back into her purse. Marj had asked her a direct question, so what was she to do? Lie to an old friend? Elspeth leaned forward conspiratorially.

"Well, it seems she's thinking of moving home."

"Is that right?" Marjorie's face lit up and her voice rose an octave or two, making Elspeth cringe.

"Wheesht. It's not common knowledge yet, and nothing's confirmed, but she misses home, and the children are struggling over there without their dad." She shook her head and pulled a woolen glove onto each hand.

"I can imagine. Poor wee souls." Marjorie nodded. "They'll be needing to be among family now, more than ever. It sounds like a good decision to me, Elspeth. And won't you be chuffed to have her back? Have those grandchildren closer?"

Elspeth nodded. Her ears were burning, and she regretted confiding in Marj, as she'd known she would.

"You'll not mention it to anyone, will you?"

"Not at all. Cross my heart." Marjorie ran a wrinkled finger across her cardigan and winked. "It's in the vault."

Elspeth walked back to the Forge and unloaded her shopping. She had a weight in her chest that she was sure was guilt at having divulged her daughter's plans. When would she ever learn to get a grip on her tongue? It was so difficult to keep it in, though, when the thought of having her daughter and grandchildren back on Skye was making her bubble with excitement. Having given Murdoch a dressing-down for getting carried away and warning him not to push his sister on the issue before she had time to make her decision, here she was telling someone else. Shocking behavior.

She hung her coat on the rack in the hall and walked into the living room. An elderly man, a Mr. Lawrence visiting from Inverness, sat reading the paper. The fire glowed while soft violin music radiated from the CD player. Taking in the pleasant scene, Elspeth felt the sense of calm that she had woken with that morning return.

"Can I get you some tea, Mr. Lawrence?" She plumped a cushion on one of the leather armchairs.

"Oh, that'd be grand, Mrs. MacDonald. Thank you." The man smiled at her and turned the page of his paper as she padded away toward the kitchen.

When the bed-and-breakfast was quiet like this, she didn't mind making the occasional extra cup of tea or offering her remaining guests a whisky in the evening. These small gestures also seemed to make all the difference to the reviews she received on the travel websites that Murdoch monitored for her.

He was a good lad. As well as running his croft and managing the sheep, he always found time to help her with the technology that she found so confounding and irritating. When Matthew died, Murdoch had persuaded her that she needed a computer and a website, had helped her set it up, register the bed-and-breakfast with the right organizations, and find a photographer to take some pictures that did the old place justice. Although it had been a steep learning curve and a headache she could have done without, the website looked good now, and it had made a huge difference to the flow of business. Things had picked up to such an extent that Elspeth now hired a couple of local teenagers to help her over the summer months. Yes, Murdoch was a blessing, despite his mischief and bottomless stomach.

As she carried the tea tray into the living room, she heard the phone ringing. It had been three days since Heather had called, and each time the thing rang now, she found herself hoping that it was her daughter again.

"Here you go." She placed the tray on the small table next to the fire before trotting back into the kitchen to answer the phone.

"Hello. The Forge." She was breathless.

"Mum. It's me."

Heather's voice sounded different, as if there was more force behind it.

"Hi, darling. I thought it might be you." Elspeth slid onto a chair and lifted the spiraled phone cord over the table.

"Everything OK there?" Heather asked.

"Oh, yes. Just the usual—you know."

The suspense was killing Elspeth, but the least she could do now, after blabbing to Marjorie, was keep her peace and let Heather work this out on her own time.

"How're the children?"

"All good, thanks. We're fine, Mum. Listen, I've given this a lot of thought."

Elspeth realized that she was holding her breath.

"Uh-huh." She hoped she sounded nonchalant enough.

"So, would it be OK if the kids and I stayed with you for a while, just until I find a house?"

Elspeth felt her heart lift and her cheeks fold into a smile.

"Well, I don't know about that, now." She waited only a second or two before she let out a sharp laugh. "You know you don't have to ask, Heather. Of course you can." She nodded at her reflection in the window, noticing that behind her own outline the trees were now leaning dangerously, being buffeted away from the mountains.

"Thanks. We won't be under your feet for long, but I think the whole thing will be easier on them if we start at your place. They love it there."

Elspeth could hear Heather cover the mouthpiece of her phone and then speak to someone nearby. Her voice was muffled, but Elspeth realized that she didn't care what was being said. The only thing she cared about was the fact that they were coming home.

CHAPTER 10

Heather stood inside the closet in the master bedroom. Her side of the space was a mess, hangers askew and clothes dangling, some touching the floor and tangled in among the pile of shoes below. Her shelves were overflowing, sweaters stuffed in on top of T-shirts and scarves slung in knots around hangers. She scanned the bedlam on her left and then turned to Brett's side. His dark uniforms hung in a neat row, like a line of broad-shouldered flyboys on parade. His highly polished shoes stood to attention, and the shelf with his captain's hat pulled her eye. She remembered again the first time she had seen him. The hat had a way of melting her bone marrow, and seeing his warm eyes under its peak had sealed the deal.

She had been avoiding this task, but the decision to leave Virginia had now made it a hurdle that she had to get over. Chrissy had offered to help her, but Heather had refused. The thought of anyone else touching Brett's things was deeply disturbing to her. She had fleetingly worried that it had been a selfish move. Brett was, of course, Chrissy's brother, and she could have felt compelled to be involved, but Heather's heart had ruled her head on this point, and she was glad that Chrissy had quickly backed off.

The smell of shoe polish snapped her back to the present. The large black plastic bag she held in her hand dragged on the floor, and despite having been motivated to do this, Heather now felt overwhelmed.

She stepped over to the row of uniforms and lifted one dark sleeve to her nose. As she breathed in the citrus smell of aftershave, her chest constricted. Replacing the sleeve to the tidy lineup, she reached up and adjusted the hangers, ensuring that the gap between them on the rail was exactly even. Brett's obsessive tidiness had gotten under her skin when he was alive, but now, with so much else in her life in disarray, the order around her was necessary, comforting.

On the shelf to the side of the hangers was Brett's gym gear, sweat-shirts, T-shirts, and a pile of neatly folded jeans. She loved him in jeans. Casual clothes had suited his slender physique, and whenever he was not in uniform, she loved to see him in dark denim. He liked thick flannel shirts in the winter and would often layer them on top of each other rather than wear a sweater.

The light above her head cast a dull glow over the clothing, giving everything a yellowish hue. On the top shelf, above his captain's hat, was a shoe box. Heather squinted up at the box, not recognizing it as one she had seen before. Looking around, she spotted the small two-step ladder she kept in the closet. She discarded the plastic bag and pulled the ladder over. Standing on the top step, she carefully moved the box to the edge of the shelf, lifted it down, and knelt down on the carpet.

Inside were some papers folded into neat squares. She opened the one on the top of the pile to see a drawing that Megan had done for Brett on his last birthday. It was a roughly outlined plane with a stream of rainbow-colored smoke coming from the tail. The pilot was oversize and leaning out of the cockpit window. A banana-shaped smile, larger than the width of the face, was filled with white teeth. On the ground underneath was a house with two chimneys, and in the green of the garden stood two identical stick figures holding hands. A third, taller figure stood to the side in a triangular floral dress. To her knowledge,

Heather had never worn a floral dress, but it made her smile to think that this was how Megan saw her family.

She stared at the grotesque smile. Brett had been a happy guy, always half-full to her half-empty. Sometimes it had irritated her that he never allowed life to get him down. He would laugh at her and say, "What's the point?" Consequently, she sometimes felt self-indulgent if she let a bad mood get the better of her. Brett would be sympathetic up to a point. Then, when his patience finally began to fray, he would take the children out for ice cream or to see a movie to let her thrash around on her own.

She folded the picture back along the creases and pulled out another square. This one was of a car. It was red and very long, with six doors and six wheels rather than four. Max had said it was a limo, like he had seen on TV, and Brett had told him that it was an ace design. Max had scrawled his name in big black letters at the bottom of the sheet, pressing so hard that the paper was almost torn under the pressure of his intent. That was her Max to a T.

Underneath several more squares was an envelope. There was no writing on it, and even as she slid her finger under the flap, Heather was unsure whether she should look. What if this was private? The notion of Brett's right of ownership had not been buried with him, and he'd never told her about this box, never mind shared what was inside it with her. Perhaps she should leave well alone? Curiosity winning out, she opened the envelope and pulled out a selection of photographs. Some were old snaps they had taken on their honeymoon. They were faded, their edges curling inward. The two of them sat on the beach in Bali, tanned, firm, looking at the camera from their cocoon of newly wedded bliss.

Next there were a couple of candid shots that friends had taken of them at their wedding, standing outside the old mansion on the Potomac in Maryland. And then there were several of the twins as tiny babies, wrapped in blankets and cradled in her arms in the hospital on the day they were born. She was looking up into the camera, delirious with happiness, pride, and exhaustion after the twenty-nine-hour natural labor she had endured.

At the bottom of the pile was a single sheet of white paper wrapped tightly around one last photograph. As she unfolded the paper, Heather's heart was clattering in her chest. Two tiny knots of strawberry-blonde hair slid out onto her palm. The picture was of her, sitting in the garden with a pair of scissors in her hand. She had red-rimmed eyes and a tea towel full of hair clippings on her lap.

When the twins turned two, she had decided that she would give them their first haircut. Brett had been skeptical, saying she might find it difficult. He had suggested that perhaps they should go to a salon somewhere. Heather had resisted, saying that it was indeed a momentous occasion but that she wanted to do it herself, at home. She had cried the entire time she was cutting off their silky curls, and Brett had watched her, alternately laughing and comforting her as she sobbed behind her children's heads.

He had grabbed the camera and taken the picture as she sniffed and laughed back at him. She'd forgotten about this photograph, and seeing it now brought the moment back with such starling clarity that she began to tremble. She blinked her vision clear and carefully gathered the twists of hair, replacing them in the paper. This was too hard. She could not do this today, after all.

Heather stood up, her legs tingling as the blood rushed back to her feet. She held the box tight to her chest, reached out, and flipped off the light.

CHAPTER 11

In the week that followed, Heather had sprung into action. She had contacted a real estate agent and listed the house for sale, called an international moving company to give her a quote, and scrolled through websites of available properties in Portree. Her focus on practical tasks had made it easier to avoid second-guessing the decision.

The twins were at school, and she had worked all morning clearing out the basement and hall cupboards. Now she stood in the kitchen, assessing the checklist that sat on the countertop. Despite her false start a few days earlier, she had finally managed to empty the closet of most of Brett's clothes, taking much of it to the Salvation Army. She'd kept several items, including his Virginia Tech sweatshirt, a couple of flannel shirts, and his captain's hat. That she would never part with.

In the process of clearing out the closet, she had also found two pairs of cuff links deep inside his suit jacket pockets and, tucked into a corner of his sock drawer, his wedding ring. When it had been returned to her a few months earlier, she had put it away, unable to look at it without crying. Now the ring hung on a thin gold chain around her neck, and as she moved around the kitchen, it swung reassuringly between her breasts.

As she stared blankly into one cupboard after another, nothing she saw there interested her. Dishes and glasses and casseroles were suddenly just chinaware, and what did she care what plates they ate off when they got to Skye? She would buy new ones, plates that did not remind her of the many family meals they had shared around the kitchen table and Sunday picnics in the backyard. She would get new glasses—ones that she and Brett had not used to drink bottles of Sicilian wine while sitting opposite each other in the big bathtub, or that had sat on the patio furniture attracting fruit flies while the twins splashed in the paddling pool during the hot Virginia summers. She wanted none of that to slap her in the face with every new meal she prepared.

Slamming the cupboard above the stove closed, she glanced at the clock. If she left now, she could get to the store and then circle back in time to meet the school bus at the end of the street. She would see Max's anxious little face pressed up to the glass, searching for her. Megan, on the other hand, would be chattering to her friends, and sometimes Max would have to yank his sister's backpack to get her attention so that she would actually get off the bus with him.

Turning her back on the task at hand, Heather grabbed her handbag and keys and headed for the door.

Max dumped his bag in the mudroom and then slumped onto the sofa. He reached for the TV remote, and Heather raised a finger to stop him.

"Um, not yet, mister." She frowned. "Upstairs and change first, please." She pointed toward the stairs, where Megan's small back was already disappearing.

Max sighed and heaved himself out of the sofa.

"Can I get a soda?" he whined.

"May I have a soda, please?" She shook her head. "And no. You know we don't have soda. There's apple juice when you come back down."

She watched him tramp up the stairs, his narrow hips swamped by the baggy school trousers that were cinched in at the waist by a belt. Had he lost weight?

She had spoken to Elspeth that afternoon and told her that their flights were booked for three weeks' time. The reality of having a departure date was startling. The dark letters that she had scrawled on the calendar next to the fridge were as yet surreal to her. She looked at them again. November 27—Scotland. Scotland—home.

Murdoch had e-mailed her earlier that week, asking if she knew her dates yet, adding in a PS—followed by a smiley face sticking its tongue out—that she shouldn't tell Elspeth that he was asking again. Her brother's frequent communications were keeping her focused, but she knew that Elspeth would be angry with him if she felt that he was crowding her. To Heather, his excitement about their return to Skye was both endearing and mildly irritating.

Murdoch had suggested that she make this move months ago, but it had been too close to losing Brett and well before she was ready to consider it. She had been angry with him at the time, feeling pressured by his certainty that she needed to go home, when all that she could cope with was breathing in and out and not totally losing her mind. Now that they were finally going back to Scotland, and even though it made no sense to her, Heather felt that Murdoch, to a certain extent, had won. As the little sister, this didn't always sit well with her.

No sooner had she felt the flush of annoyance than she corrected herself. There was no doubt that Murdoch would be her greatest supporter when they got back, which could prove critical to this move working out.

CHAPTER 12

Elspeth stood at the door and looked into the bedroom on the top floor of the Forge. The two dormer windows looked out over the street but were high up enough that it was still a quiet room.

The twin beds were freshly made up with tartan duvet covers, and she had bought new towels for the children with their favorite cartoon characters on them. She had washed them twice, folded them in neat squares, and laid them at the foot of each bed. For Max it was Spider-Man, of course, and for Megan, Princess Merida from *Brave*. Her granddaughter's choice of heroine, a rebellious, redheaded Scottish warrior, had surprised Elspeth. The idea that the little girl, despite having been born and raised in America, found herself drawn to the quirky Gaelic princess who defied her parents and skillfully wielded a bow and arrow gave Elspeth an inordinate amount of pleasure. As she glanced at the Merida towels again, she smiled. Like mother, like daughter, sure enough.

Elspeth nodded to herself as she scanned the room one last time. The sharp smell of the windows, which she had cleaned with vinegar and lemon juice, the gleaming wood floor, and the freshly laundered bedding and curtains all said welcome to the senses.

She had asked Heather if the twins would like their own rooms, but Heather had said that they still preferred to share, at least for the moment. Elspeth suspected that that was more for Max's benefit than Megan's, but she felt comforted that they would be together, regardless.

She had made up the room next door for Heather, and the bathroom at the end of the hall smelled pleasantly of pine cleaner. There was nothing left to wash, polish, or prepare, and now all she had to do was wait the remaining seven days until her daughter and the twins arrived.

Elspeth chewed her bottom lip and felt a lilt of excitement, but then seconds later, beneath it, there was a twinge of anxiety. She must try not to bank on this new arrangement being permanent. While she relished the idea that her family would be reunited, there was a sliver of concern that nibbled at her, reminding her that Heather and the children might find this whole move back to the island too overwhelming. She must prepare for the possibility that they might leave again, and, with that in mind, she needed to protect herself.

Murdoch had popped in that morning for his usual breakfast and had been beaming. He'd had Fraser in tow, and they'd eaten a mound of eggs and bacon and half a loaf of bread. Seeing the two of them at her table took Elspeth back to their childhood, and she was flooded with memories of them as boys.

"It's crackin', Mother. Just a few days and we'll have them back." As Murdoch tucked into his eggs, his face had seemed ruddier than usual.

"Yes. It's great."

"So how long's it been since Heather lived here, Mrs. M?" Fraser spoke around a mouthful of egg. His fair hair was cropped close to his head, and his eyes were a startling blue. Paul Newman blue, Elspeth had always thought when she looked at the kind, open-faced boy, who had matured into an undeniably handsome man. Fraser stood as tall as Murdoch. Though he had a slighter frame, he looked Murdoch in the eye, which was a rare thing.

"Ten years. She met Brett in New York nine years ago." Elspeth remembered the call from her daughter telling her that she had fallen for a pilot. Elspeth had worried herself sick, knowing the reputation of pilots as sailors of the sky—a girl in every airport, et cetera. Thankfully, Brett had defied the stereotype.

"It'll be great to have her home." Fraser smiled and put his cutlery down on the empty plate. "That was great. Thanks, Mrs. M."

"You're welcome, Fraser." Elspeth reached across the table and picked up the plates. "How's your dad these days?"

Fraser drained his mug.

"Better, thanks. The stroke was mild, and his speech is back to normal." He nodded. "He's doing well with the physio. He'll be back on the croft any day now, telling me everything I'm doing wrong." Fraser laughed.

"Well, someone has to, pal." Murdoch stood up and walked to the sink. "Do you think we should throw a wee shindig to welcome them back?" He turned to Elspeth. "Nothing posh, just a few friends."

Elspeth shook her head.

"Absolutely not. I think that's the last thing Heather would want. I doubt she'll be in any mood to celebrate, Murdoch." Elspeth tutted and then frowned at her overenthusiastic son. "You are an eejit sometimes."

"Aye. You're probably right." Murdoch slung a meaty arm around his mother's shoulder. "You usually are."

Now, satisfied with her preparations, Elspeth closed the bedroom door and padded back down the stairs. Her last remaining guest was leaving that afternoon, and she had deliberately not accepted any new reservations for the upcoming weeks, sensing that her family would need the Forge to themselves in order to settle into a new routine. Also, aside from the fact that she was tired, as she always was at the end of a busy season, she was looking forward to having time to focus on Heather and children and to letting the bed-and-breakfast take a backseat for a while.

As she passed through the kitchen, she noticed that it was warm, the Aga throwing off a blanket of heat that filled the entire ground floor of the house. The fireplace in the living room popped, and a swirl of wood smoke meandered into the space as a movement ahead caught her eye. Someone was standing in the front hall—a tall man with a bag at his feet.

"Oh, sorry, Mr. Donaldson. I didn't realize you were waiting." She trotted into the hall and ran a flustered hand over her hair.

The small desk that she used in the reception area was tidy. A narrow vase of irises sat at its edge, and the laptop lay open. As she slipped behind the desk, the grandfather clock Matthew had inherited from his mother chimed loudly.

"Not a problem, Mrs. MacDonald. I was just enjoying the fire through there. You cann'y beat a real fire." The tall man smiled at her, his silver hair brushed back neatly over each ear. Glasses were balanced on the end of his nose, and his tweed jacket smelled slightly of mothballs—a smell that reminded Elspeth of childhood holidays spent on the Isle of Harris. Her father had kept two suits in their house there, and despite her mother airing them regularly, they'd retained a mild aroma of camphor that Elspeth had grown fond of over the years.

"Have you far to go today?" She searched for the right record on the computer.

"No—just to Fort William, then back to Glasgow tomorrow."

Elspeth nodded as he signed the credit card slip and shoved the smudged glasses back up his nose.

"Thanks for another super stay." Mr. Donaldson smiled. "You never disappoint."

Elspeth patted her chest.

"Well, thank you. It's always a pleasure to see you."

As she watched him back his car out of the driveway, Elspeth wondered whether he had a wife back in Glasgow. He came to Skye around the same time every year, stayed five or six nights, and spent his days walking on the moors looking for golden eagles. He had seen them more than once, and she had spent several evenings looking at the photographs he had taken of the rare birds and of the red deer that were seen in the more desolate parts of the island. He was a gentle man, and while he had never mentioned one, she hoped he had a nice wife to go home to.

CHAPTER 13

Murdoch shoved the last of the sheep back into the pen and closed the gate. Chick was circling the fence, his belly low to the ground. Murdoch whistled to the dog. It had been a long day, and as the sun was settling low over the horizon, he felt the brittle chill in the air.

Fraser was waiting for him to finish his work, and they planned on going to the pub in Portree to watch a football match in the bar.

It seemed to Murdoch that Fraser had become overly interested in Heather's return to Skye, repeatedly asking about her and the children, and even about Brett. The constant questions were beginning to annoy Murdoch, and he'd found himself, more than once, on the point of telling Fraser that it was none of his damn business. However, knowing that Fraser's intentions were good, Murdoch had stopped himself.

The phone in his pocket buzzed, and he turned toward the croft house.

"Come away to me, Chick."

The dog was quickly at his heel and followed him into the house.

Murdoch closed the heavy door behind him as Chick settled in front of the fire, which was now just a pile of ash, pale pink and winking gently at the back of the grate.

The croft house was warm, the thick stone walls retaining the remnants of heat that the fire had generated that morning before Murdoch had left. As he slid his boots off and dropped them at the door, he shivered, his skin transitioning into the comfortable air that surrounded him.

The phone buzzed again, and, pulling it out of his pocket, Murdoch glanced at the screen.

"Hiya, Wee Blister." The nickname he had given Heather when they were five and nine, respectively, had stuck. "Perfect timing. I just finished for th'day."

"Hi. I'm glad I caught you. I just wanted to ask you something about Mum." Heather sounded tired, and Murdoch tried to calculate what time it was in Virginia.

"What's up?" He walked around the sofa and flopped into the armchair. Chick raised his head, sniffed the air, then tucked his nose under a front paw.

"She's being a bit weird about us coming back. I wondered if she'd spoken to you about it?"

"What do you mean, weird?" Murdoch frowned.

"She just keeps saying, 'as long as you're sure' and 'if you think this is best' and stuff. Like she's trying to tell me I'm making a mistake." Heather sounded young. He could picture her pouting and then chewing the inside of her cheek.

"Nah. She's so bloody excited she can hardly contain herself. She told me a few weeks ago that she was a bit worried about you taking the kids away from their familiar surroundings. But she trusts you." Murdoch lifted one foot from the rug and curled his toes up, feeling the blood flooding back into the cold extremity. There was a hole in the end of the sock, and spotting it, he rolled his eyes. No wonder that foot had been freezing all day inside his boot.

"As long as she's not questioning my decision. It's hard enough doing this . . ." Heather's voice trailed.

"Just relax. It'll be fine. Get yourselves home, and the rest will take care of itself." He circled his foot above the table.

"Well, it's not long until we get there. The kids are excited and a bit nervous—about a new school and making friends, mainly."

"Aye, understandable. But they'll be fine. They're good bairns and they'll soon adjust. The locals'll love them. Those American accents will be a hit."

There was a moment's silence.

"That's what I'm afraid of. I don't want them to feel like novelties, like they stand out for all the wrong reasons."

Murdoch paused, formulating a response as he focused on his bare toe. He knew he needed to be careful here, not say anything flippant or dismissive.

"Well, it might take a wee while, but the novelty will soon wear off, and the children here will see them as the kind, clever little people they are." He waited.

"I hope you're right." She sighed. "Skye's home for me, but it's not home to the twins."

"Not yet, anyway." Murdoch pushed himself up in the chair. "But Skye'll get them in the end. You know it will." He laughed softly into the dimly lit room.

The Dockside Inn was around half-full. Several tables had been pushed together at one end of the pub for a large group, and as he walked past the long fieldstone bar, weaving around a couple of occupied tables, Murdoch spotted Fraser sitting near the fireplace.

"All right, my friend?" He pulled a chair out and sat down.

"Aye. Great. I got you one." Fraser nodded at a weeping pint glass that sat on the table.

"Cheers." Murdoch touched his glass to Fraser's, drank several gulps of ale and then wiped his mouth with his palm. "Steak pie, is it, or fish and chips th'night?" He gestured toward the menu.

As they talked about their sheep and the plan to sell part of each flock the following spring, Murdoch ate and watched his friend. Fraser was a good man, levelheaded and reliable. He had never asked for anything other than friendship in return for his help and initial advice when Murdoch had bought the croft. Murdoch had relied on him heavily at the start, as, despite all his studying of farming practices, he had been inevitably green. Fraser had been patient with him, guiding him through the first two farming years with a firm hand but without judgment or derision. Murdoch was deeply grateful to him, and as their friendship gathered years, so his respect for the man opposite him grew.

Fraser scanned the pub behind him as Murdoch pushed his empty plate away.

"You expecting someone?" Murdoch frowned.

"No. Not at all. I was just thinking about this place. What it'll look like to Heather after all those years in America." Fraser picked up his glass and drained the last inch of beer.

"It'll look like a pub on the Isle of Skye," Murdoch growled.

"Aye, I know that. But you know what I'm getting at, Murdo. I was just thinking that she might be disappointed. Skye's a small place, and she's seen the world now. Can someone really settle back here after experiences like that?" Fraser sat back and ran a hand over his close-cut hair.

Murdoch leaned forward on his elbows and shoved his empty glass to the edge of the table. Feeling bad for snapping, he controlled his tone.

"She's still the same Heather, and this is her home." He looked down at the tabletop and, seeing his opportunity, continued. "I know you've a bit of a soft spot for her, Fraser, but she's been through hell. You'll need to be careful not to overdo it when she gets here." He watched his friend's expression as Fraser's eyebrows shot up toward his hairline.

"I know what she's been through. I'm not a total prat, Murdo."

Murdoch noted the anxiety in the surveillance of his friend. Was Fraser right? Would Heather feel claustrophobic being back on the island after her jet-setting life in the States? To Murdoch, Skye was the epicenter of the world, and while he had traveled a bit, too, there was nowhere he would rather be than right here. Surely Heather would feel the same once she was finally back?

Feeling an unfamiliar weight in his chest, Murdoch coughed. He turned to see if he could catch the eye of the waitress.

At the far end of the bar, an older man sat hunched over his glass. His nose dipped down toward the bar top, and his hair was wiry and wild. Murdoch scanned his profile and the clamshell curve of his back under a dark jacket. This man had the look of someone who'd carried a heavy weight for many years. As Murdoch was about to look away, the man raised his head and glanced toward him. The clear eyes and broad face jolted Murdoch's memory. There had been something familiar about him, and now Murdoch could see clearly that this was Davy Gunn, the farmer who had sold him his croft. Murdoch instinctively raised a hand and waited for Davy to acknowledge him. The movement obviously catching his eye, Davy shifted slightly on the stool and returned the wave. Seeing an opportunity to give Fraser some space, Murdoch stood up.

"I'm just going to have a word with old Davy." Murdoch spoke to his friend's somewhat sullen profile as he craned to see the football match on the TV screen.

"Aye, fine." Fraser didn't turn around.

As Murdoch approached the bar, Davy Gunn left his stool and stood with a hand extended.

"I didn'y see you there, MacDonald." He smiled at Murdoch. "It's been a while."

Murdoch shook the large hand and nodded.

"It has indeed. More than a few years, Mr. Gunn. How've you been?" Murdoch gestured toward the bar, and the two men sat down on the vacant stools behind them.

"As well as can be." Davy dipped his chin toward his glass. "Can I get you one?"

"Oh, no, thanks. I've got one over there." Murdoch jerked his thumb in the direction of the table.

"Right. So how's the old place holding up? Sheep doing well?" Davy sipped his beer, his ruddy hand seeming to dwarf the glass.

As he had in the past, Murdoch felt bad for the old man. His family land was now in the hands of someone else, and having lived the farming life for a few years now, Murdoch was reminded how difficult it must have been for Davy to give it all up.

"It's all going well. You should drop in sometime, walk the croft with me." Murdoch smiled. "You could give me a few tips."

"From what I understand, you're doing fine." Davy nodded. "Is that ye'r pal, the Duncan lad over there?" He jutted his chin toward Fraser's back.

"Aye, that's him." Murdoch met Davy's eye. "I'd better get back. Looks like the match is picking up steam."

Davy shook his hand again, and Murdoch noticed that the older man still had a true farmer's grip.

The noise level in the bar was rising as the football match gathered momentum. As Murdoch sat down at the table, Fraser kept his focus on the TV and, it being obvious that the subject of Heather's return was now solidly off the table, they settled into the rest of the evening in a strained silence.

CHAPTER 14

Heather stood in the driveway and watched her breath puff toward the heavy sky. The house seemed small, almost indistinct now that everything that had made it home had been wrapped in paper and cardboard.

Eight days earlier, she had received a firm offer on the house that, when it came, had made her cry with both relief and despair. Not only was she now released from this place, but she was also to be separated from it forever. The home where she had lived her happiest life was soon to be closed to her and the twins. All her children's firsts had taken place here—first smiles, first words, first steps, first Christmases, first joys and disappointments. Nothing would ever replace those memories, and as she took in the dark, now empty windows, Heather knew that she would hold those mental pictures close to her heart for as long as she breathed.

Over the past three weeks, they'd had several garage sales, getting rid of much of the twins' baby paraphernalia. Heather had packed up tiny articles of clothing that she had, so far, been loath to part with: pink and blue onesies, miniature hoodies, and fluffy footed pajamas. She had also bagged up piles of the gauzy cloths that she used to drape over her shoulder as she paced the bedroom floor at night with one or other of the children on her chest, their little hands wound into her hair as she sang and rocked, whispered and cajoled them back to sleep.

She had donated boxes of early learning toys and baby books to the Salvation Army and had even sold the bunk beds and the climbing frame from the back garden to a neighbor. The small shipping container was packed with the few parts of this Virginian life that they could not part with.

The twins had selected their most precious toys, stuffed animals, and books to take with them, and each of them had picked out a sweatshirt of Brett's, along with several albums of photographs. They both had a set of the gilt airline wings that had been pinned to their father's uniform, which Heather had secured onto their winter coats for the journey.

As she stared at the familiar roofline, taking it in one last time, the car horn screeched, and her heart leaped into her throat. She turned around to see Megan grinning at her from the backseat of the rental car. Max was draped over the front seat, his feet floating dangerously close to his sister's chin as he pushed on the horn again.

"OK, OK. I'm coming." Heather patted the air as she walked back to the car. She opened the driver's door and saw her son looking up at her, his face a picture of mischief.

"Max, please get back into your seat, and enough with the horn. You scared me to death." She opened the door and got in.

Max slithered backward and settled himself into his own spot.

"Let's just go. It's so boring sitting here." The flash of mischief gone, his empty little eyes met hers.

"Right. We're off, then." She got in and then looked over her shoulder one last time at the place she'd called home for the past nine years. Their suitcases were in the trunk, and now all that was left to do in order to leave this all behind was to make it on to their flight.

Sandro, Brett's friend at the airline, had arranged to have them bumped up to first class for the transatlantic flight. Heather was relieved that they would have the extra room and more comfortable seats, which might even allow the children to sleep.

They had spent the past two nights at Chrissy's house in preparation for leaving. To Heather's concern, Chrissy had given each of the twins an iPad so that they could video chat with her and with their cousin, Philip, at college. It was overgenerous, but Heather could not bring herself to object when the children had been understandably ecstatic.

The good-byes with Chrissy had been agonizing, and Max and Megan had cried solidly for half an hour after leaving her house that afternoon. The swing by their old house had been at Max's request, and now, as she saw his sad little profile staring out the window, she regretted agreeing to the diversion. She should have stuck to her instincts and gone straight to the airport.

Megan was, as usual, nose-deep in a book, her little cloud of curls catching the light as Heather pulled out into the street. Her head ached, and as she pressed her fingertips into her temple, Max sniffed. She turned quickly to see him wipe his nose with the back of his hand.

"Maximus, you OK?"

He nodded and jammed his cheek against the window.

"I just want to go." His voice was husky.

"We're going, sweetheart." Heather focused ahead and then maneuvered the car into the lane.

"Mom?" Megan looked up from her book and sought her mother's eyes.

"Yes, honey?"

"Will Granny Elspeth and Uncle Murdy meet us when we get there?"

Heather nodded as she pressed her foot down on the accelerator, the house shrinking in the mirror as she watched.

"Uncle Murdy'll pick us up at the airport in Inverness. Granny'll be waiting at the house, on Skye. She's so excited to see us."

Megan smiled and then wound her fingers into a strand of hair over her ear.

"I can't wait to see Charlie. Can he sleep on my bed?"

Heather laughed as Max snapped his head toward his sister and then jabbed her with his elbow.

"He's not allowed on the bed, silly." Max smiled as Megan giggled.

With her usual flair, Megan had diffused the tension inside the car.

Heather, as she did numerous times a day, thanked the universe for her children, her perfect little bookends, who kept her breathing, gave her the strength to keep getting up in the morning, and made her believe that there was a future for them all, even without Brett.

Dulles was relatively quiet, and having sped through security, Heather and the children sat at the departure gate. The twins had their small backpacks at their feet, and she had bought them each a magazine and some trail mix. On one side of her, Max was thumbing through his magazine, and on the other, Megan was leaning against Heather's shoulder, her trainer-clad feet swinging wildly out from the seat.

"Sit still, darling." Heather reached out and placed her hand on the little girl's twitching thigh. Megan sat up straighter and smiled at her mother.

Heather kissed the top of her head and then looked up at the information monitor, calculating that they had twenty minutes until boarding. The seating area was quickly filling up with travelers, all searching for a small section of personal space.

As she let her gaze wander, farther down the concourse she spotted a familiar shape. A pilot, tall, wearing a dark blue uniform and cap, was walking toward the gate. Next to him were a copilot and then three cabin crew, each dragging small bags behind them and talking animatedly to one another. Heather's stomach lurched and a needle of pain shot through her left eye. The man came closer, and with each step her breathing became shallower. She tore her eyes away from him, focusing on her lap and then the top of Megan's head. Just a few more minutes, and he would be out of sight. She could do this.

Just as she thought the challenge had passed, she heard her name.

"Heather. Hey. Is that you?"

The voice was gravelly, vaguely familiar. She lifted her head and met the dark brown eyes staring at her from under the blue brim.

"How are you? I was so sorry to hear about Brett."

Heather took a deep breath and racked her brain for this man's name. She hoped her confusion wasn't obvious, but, seeming to understand, he scanned her blank face and then spoke again.

"It's Chris. Chris Maynard."

The man was leaning down toward her, his hand extended. On a reflex, she took it in hers just as her memory relinquished the information she sought. Chris had been a copilot at the same time as Brett. They had worked together in New York and then had joined United within months of each other. The two men had not been particularly close, so the connection had dwindled over time, and as they'd flown different routes, they'd had little contact once they were both based in Virginia. Heather remembered Brett saying that Chris was a good guy, but beyond that, she had little memory of him.

"Thanks, Chris." She forced a smile. "You piloting this one?" She nodded toward the gate.

"I am. I'll take good care of you all." He straightened up and nodded at Max's tousled head, still buried in his magazine.

Heather placed her hand on Max's back.

"Max, this is Chris. A friend of Dad's."

Max plopped the magazine onto his thighs and looked up. He licked his lips.

"Hey, buddy. You going to London?"

At the question, Max frowned and shook his head.

"No. To Skye."

Heather ran her hand down Max's back as he dropped his head back into his magazine, obviously finished with the interaction.

"Sweetheart, I told you. We're flying to London first, then taking another short flight to Inverness."

Max stared into his lap.

"We're heading back to the Isle of Skye. Time to go home." She looked at Chris and ran a hand through her hair.

"I'd have you come up to the flight deck, buddy, but we can't do that anymore." He looked down at Max's unresponsive head.

"Max. Chris is speaking to you." Heather felt her face flush with embarrassment at Max's obvious lack of interest in anything Chris had to say.

Max finally lifted his head and stuck his chin out.

"I've been up there before. With my dad."

The words were weighted, sharp, and strategically timed. Heather caught her breath.

"Max. That was rude." She pulled his right shoulder back, making him sit up straighter.

Chris met her eyes and shook his head, dismissing the slight.

"Of course you have. My bad." He winked at Heather as she smiled her apology.

"Well, I'd better get moving if you guys want to get out of here on time." Chris looked over at Megan, who was watching him and twirling some hair around her index finger.

Within fifteen minutes, they had boarded the plane, and as Heather buckled their seat belts, inhaled the familiar musty smell of the aircraft, and felt the spongy pillow behind her back, she wished there had been another way, any other way, for them to get home.

CHAPTER 15

Elspeth looked out the window, toward the street. The hedge along the driveway was tipped with white; the first frost of winter decorated everything in the garden that morning. Charlie, who was sleeping in front of the fire, jumped as a log slipped from the burning stack, spraying red-hot ash at the screen.

"They should be here by now, Charlie." Elspeth felt the slight flutter in her chest that always accompanied the anticipation of something pleasant. She had been watching the clock since Murdoch had called from the airport in Inverness. She hadn't wanted to call him back for progress checks, but now each minute was excruciating as she waited for the car to slide into the drive.

The kettle began to whistle on the Aga, and Elspeth walked into the kitchen just as she heard the familiar crunch of wheels on the gravel drive.

"They're here."

The dog lifted his nose.

Elspeth turned the heat off under the kettle and then skittered across the floor to the front door. As she opened it, she smoothed a hand over her already tidy hair.

Megan was tumbling out of the car as Max emerged from the far side, and then both twins were running across the front garden. They were taller than when she had seen them a few months ago, and Max had new shadows under his eyes. Megan was all legs, and as the children reached her, Elspeth opened her arms wide, accepting one little body under each wing as the twins wrapped their arms around her waist.

"Oh, come away in now. It's freezing out here." She hugged the children close. Behind them, Heather and Murdoch made their way toward the house. Heather was thin, pale.

Leaving Murdoch to handle the cases, Elspeth ushered the children inside. Gently disengaging herself from her grandchildren's grasp, she turned to Heather.

"Hello, love." She opened her arms, and Heather moved into her embrace. "Welcome back."

"Thanks, Mum. It's good to be home."

She felt a rush of joy to hear Heather say *home*. Elspeth had purposely not used the term in her welcome, but the fact that Heather had used it herself was definitely encouraging. She had been anxious about her daughter's decision to move back to the island, and now, as she watched the twins' energy permeate her living room—Max already sprawled on the sofa with a book and Megan, unsurprisingly, lying on the floor next to Charlie—Elspeth was reminded of the root of her concern. It was not that they would find the transition difficult, or that the children would find Skye confining. What really worried her was the question of whether eventually, after their presence became part of her everyday life, they would leave her again.

The children's coats were slung over the stair banister, and their shoes had been discarded at the door. Heather was in the kitchen with Murdoch, who was making tea. As Elspeth joined them, Heather was opening and closing cupboards.

"Cups are up there." Elspeth pointed.

"Right. It always takes a while to remember where everything is." Heather smiled over her shoulder at her mother.

With a tray of tea, biscuits, and some juice for the children, they settled into the living room, and soon Murdoch's huge feet were up on the coffee table. There was a large hole in one sock, and Elspeth tutted as she gently swiped his feet off the table.

"For heaven's sake, Murdoch. Give me those socks and I'll darn them."

Murdoch let out a laugh.

"Nob'dy darns socks anymore, Mother." He picked up his mug and dunked a gingersnap into his tea.

"Can I do that, Uncle Murdy?" Megan was watching, fascinated, as Murdoch expertly negotiated the softening biscuit into his mouth without letting any drop back into the mug.

"Aye, you can, pet. Grab a biscuit and come over here."

Heather and Elspeth watched, amused, as Murdoch pulled Megan down next to him on the sofa and showed her how to dip the biscuit exactly three times—just enough to soften it before popping it into her mouth. Megan giggled as a tiny trail of soggy biscuit clung to her chin.

"Almost perfect, madam." Murdoch poked his niece's ribs. "You'll soon be an expert dunker."

They spent an hour or so sitting in easy silence interspersed with chatter as the twins talked about the flight and the man sitting in front of them on the plane, who had gotten annoyed with Megan for kicking his seat. As the children's voices tinkled, Elspeth watched Heather wilting, her head gradually dropping back onto the cushion and then her breathing falling into the steady rhythm of sleep. Elspeth lifted a finger to her lips.

"Let Mummy sleep for a bit," she whispered. "Let's go and unpack your things."

Murdoch carried the bags up the stairs, and Elspeth showed the children to the room that she'd prepared for them. Megan immediately dived on the Merida towel and squealed.

"Merida, Granny. Thank you." She draped the towel across her back and spun in a circle.

Max lifted his Spider-Man towel up and smiled.

"Cool. Thanks."

Elspeth helped them unpack their suitcases and then sent Murdoch to put the bags up in the attic. The twins had asked for something to eat, and as they padded down the stairs, Elspeth noticed that Heather was no longer on the sofa.

"Murdo, take the children into the kitchen and make them a sandwich, please."

Elspeth opened the door to the small study off the hall that her husband, Matthew, had used as an office and retreat from the buzz of the B&B. Heather was sitting behind the narrow desk in the old leather swivel chair, thumbing through a photo album. She looked up at her mother with glassy eyes.

"Just looking at old photos. Look at these." Heather spun the album around on the desk, and Elspeth saw a series of three pictures of Heather and Murdoch sitting in bumper cars at a fairground. They had gone over to the fair in Fort William each year, and by the looks of these photos, Elspeth guessed that the children had been about seven and eleven, respectively.

Heather's hair was all but obscuring her face, and she was laughing up into the camera. Murdoch was, characteristically, sticking his tongue out, and he had two fingers held up behind Heather's head. Behind them, slightly out of focus, was Matthew in another car. He was grinning and pointing at the children, obviously directing Elspeth, the photographer, to capture their antics. Seeing his image brought a familiar wave of sadness, and Elspeth swallowed.

"That was a good day." She nodded. "I still miss him."

Heather looked up at her mother.

"How do you do it, Mum? I mean, get used to the absence." Her eyes were pink and full.

"Time. That's the only thing that makes it possible, sweetheart. Just time."

Elspeth sat down opposite her daughter, and they leafed through the rest of the album together. A lifetime of memories lay back-to-back in the leather-bound books that Matthew had spent hours poring over. It had been his pet project, and he had cataloged the years beautifully. If only, Elspeth thought, he had lived to see his daughter and her children come home. She knew that it would have made him extremely happy to know that his grandchildren would get to know the Skye that he had loved so deeply and completely.

CHAPTER 16

Heather closed the door quietly behind her and pulled on her welling-ton boots. They were frigid inside, having sat on the doorstep all night. Next to her, waiting expectantly on the step, were the boots Elspeth had bought the twins. Max's were covered in blue stars, and Megan's were bright yellow. The glaring absence of a fourth pair sucked the air from her lungs as she straightened up and zipped her coat closed.

She breathed in the dark morning and the smells of the island. The tang of the harbor brine and the sharp morning frost, mixed with wood smoke and burned toast, made her stomach ache with longing.

She had tiptoed down the stairs, leaving the rest of the household asleep behind her. It was five a.m., and jet lag had dragged her out of a vivid dream around three. She had been flying—soaring above Skye, seeing the landmarks she remembered as a child. She had floated over Portree, watching a fishing boat motoring back into the harbor, and then hovered above the rugged slopes of the Cuillins. She watched water cascading over Kilt Rock and next had circled the Skye Bridge. Turning west, she'd watched a golden eagle hanging in an updraft above Dunvegan Castle until she had thumped back down to earth, waking herself with a jolt. As she lay in bed, scanning the familiar and yet unexpected ceiling, she had put the odd, out-of-body sensation down to sheer exhaustion.

Now, exhaling into the dawn, she pulled her collar up close to her chin and headed for the waterfront. The Brae would be still this early in the morning, and she wanted to soak it in before anyone else could pollute the peace she craved.

A low mist hung over the water as she approached, her footsteps the only sound in the dark predawn. The row of buildings on Quay Street had lost their customary colors under a soft gray blanket of vapor. The ever-present row of small cars, dotted along the opposite side of the road, provided a barrier between Heather and the sea wall that dropped steeply away behind them into the black water. The masts of a couple of fishing boats speared upward, creating clean black lines against the purple-tinged sky.

Brett had loved this time of the morning on Skye. The last time they had visited, he had woken her up and dragged her, resisting, out into the crisp day. They had skirted the harbor and then climbed down onto the small beach at the far end of the bay, where he'd laid his jacket on the damp sand so that they could sit. As they watched the sun rise, he had whispered into her ear, his hand seeking hers.

"This has to be close to heaven, right here."

Now, as Heather moved silently along the curve of the sea wall, the memory twisted her insides. It was good to be back, but heaven had never felt farther away than it did right at this moment. Everything she saw in front of her was familiar, and yet there was a new, worn quality to it.

Suddenly a shadow caught her eye, and she squinted to focus on the shape of someone walking the same path as her, a few feet ahead. Disappointed at the contamination of her solitude, she pushed her hands into her pockets and shivered. Should she turn around, or perhaps just slow her pace enough to let the stranger create more distance between them? As she halted her progress, the person ahead seemed to sense her presence, the large head swiveling back over a shoulder. He was tall, like her brother, and heavy clothing was adding to his bulk, creating a formidable outline against the lightening sky.

Heather hesitated as the intruder turned to face her. The features were indistinct, but there was something familiar about the towering presence. Standing still, she watched as the figure started to walk slowly toward her. Rather than retreat, which would have been her instinct back in the States, Heather held her ground. She should not be afraid here. This was her home, and she had every right to be here.

"Morning."

"Morning." Heather's dry throat cracked the word in two.

The man continued his slow progress toward her.

"Good time for a walk." He raised a hand and slid the woolen hat off his head, revealing a shock of blond hair.

The hair, added to the features that were now revealing themselves to her, provided Heather with the final piece of the puzzle.

"Fraser Duncan, is that you?" She could hear the relief in her own voice.

"Aye." The man halted.

"It's me. Heather Forester." Jolted by hearing her name out loud, Heather felt her legs grow suddenly heavy. Taking two steps to the side, she grabbed the metal railing that topped the sea wall.

"God. Is it you?" Fraser, trotted over, closing the final few feet between them. "Wee Heather MacDonald."

His large hand was under her arm, and Heather felt herself sink into the support that it offered.

"Not got your sea legs back yet then, eh?" He steadied her for a few more seconds and then awkwardly pulled his hand away and jammed it into his pocket.

"Apparently not." Heather shrugged. "Jet lag, I guess."

Fraser looked down at her intently. His eyes were wide set and startlingly blue. His jaw had broadened over the years, giving him a

Norse-like appearance, and the mess of blond hair, while shorter, was as thick as she remembered. She had once—many moons ago, while Fraser and Murdoch had been babysitting her at the Forge—been allowed to plait that hair with tartan ribbon. The memory made her smile.

"Still no decent barbers on the island, then." She nodded toward his head.

Laughing, Fraser ran a hand over his crown.

"Naw. It's a do-it-yourself job. No time for fuss." He smiled, revealing a set of uniform teeth that any American would have been proud of. "When did you get home?"

At the word *home*, Heather felt light-headed. Was this home? Had Virginia been home? As Fraser's words settled on her like mist, Heather once again felt the weight of Brett's absence. He had been her home, and now, whether in Virginia, Skye, or Timbuktu, she doubted she would ever feel at home again.

"We got back yesterday."

"Aye. Right. Murdo mentioned that." Fraser sounded suddenly uncomfortable.

Heather sucked in a mouthful of briny air and waited for the inevitable.

"I'm sorry about your husband. I cann'y imagine how hard this all is." His large hand swept the gap between them.

The hot prickle of tears made her blink.

"Thanks, Fraser. Yes, it's been hard. Especially on the kids." The pat response that she had been wheeling out over the past few months sounded newly inadequate, insincere. Hard. Really? What she wanted to do was yell at the top of her lungs. *Screw this. Screw the damn blood vessel that stole my husband. Screw Skye and the rest of the world. Screw you, for still being alive.*

Fraser nodded and lowered his eyes to the ground.

"Where are you going?"

Heather pressed her eyes closed and tightened her grip on the railing.

"Just walking. I wanted to get out for some air before the village woke up." She opened her eyes and saw Fraser frowning as he pulled the hat back onto his head.

"Och, and I went and spoilt it for you."

"It's fine. I'm just trying to get my head straight before the twins get up and the craziness resumes." She shrugged.

"Well, I'll let you get on then." He scanned her face and then hesitated. "Unless you want some company?"

Heather shook her head.

"No, thanks."

Seeing his expression, she put a hand on his arm.

"Sorry. It's just . . . I'm not. I mean . . ."

"It's fine. I get it. You enjoy your walk and I'll see you soon, no doubt." Fraser took two steps backward. "Murdo'll have something up his sleeve, for a get-together."

Heather shoved her cold hands back into her coat pockets. She should have grabbed gloves on the way out.

"I'm sure he will."

Fraser lifted a hand in farewell and turned toward the village.

"Take care, wee Heather MacDonald," he called over his shoulder.

"Forester. It's Forester now." Heather watched as her brother's closest friend walked away from her, his broad back moving steadily forward into the mauve-colored morning.

"Where did you go?" Elspeth stood in the kitchen, wearing her Hail to the Chef apron that Brett had given her the previous Christmas. The twins sat at the kitchen table. Max's nose was in his iPad, and Charlie lay spread-eagled underneath the table with Megan's socked feet resting on his upturned belly.

"Hey, Mommy." The little girl smiled at her mother. "Granny's making potato scones."

Heather hung her coat on a hook behind the door and shuffled over to the Aga. Elspeth had turned back to the stovetop, where she expertly flipped several thin scones on the griddle.

"I just went for a walk. It's so pretty out there." Heather squeezed her mother's shoulder, padded around the table and sat down next to Max.

"What you doing, buddy?" She pressed her chin into the soft muscle of his shoulder.

"Nothing. Just playing Angry Birds." He shrugged and then shoved a stray curl out of his eye.

"We need to get you a haircut." Heather raked her hand through his hair.

Max pulled away from her. "Don't, Mom. Leave it."

Stung, Heather straightened and turned to face Megan.

"So what do you want to do today, Megs?"

Megan shifted her gaze from her brother back to her mother.

"Play with Charlie. Then can we go into town? Is the bookstore open today?"

Heather reached for the teapot and poured herself a mugful.

"What day is it?" She looked over at her mum.

Elspeth held a plate piled with golden potato scones. "It's Thursday, and the shop's open, pet." She forked two scones onto Megan's plate, then leaned over and gave Max the same. "Are you ready for some breakfast?" She took in her daughter's drawn face.

"Oh, yes, please. I'm starving." Heather nodded and pushed her plate out.

As they ate and talked, Elspeth refilled their mugs with tea. The children, having finished their scones, had gone into the living room to watch some TV. Heather wiped the last of the butter from her plate with her finger and stuck it into her mouth.

"Heather MacDonald." Elspeth laughed. "Shame on you."

Heather balked, irritated by her mother's slip of the tongue.

"Forester. It's bloody Forester." She felt blood rushing to her face.

"Oh, sorry, love. It's force of habit." Elspeth shook her head and tutted at herself. "Silly old woman."

Feeling bad for her outburst, Heather reached out and covered her mother's hand with her own.

"It's OK. I'm sorry to snap. I'm just tired."

Elspeth nodded and flapped a hand, dismissing the incident. Heather, feeling the need to heal the tiny wound that she had just created, picked up her mug.

"Guess who I saw down at the water today?"

Elspeth, obviously intrigued, leaned her elbows on the table and bit her bottom lip.

"Marjorie, from the shop?"

"Nope." Heather smiled.

"Um, Murdo?" Elspeth tried again.

"Nope." Heather shook her head.

"Eh—give me a clue?" Elspeth shrugged.

"Tall, blond, and glaikit as ever." Heather rolled her eyes.

"What was Fraser Duncan doing down there at that time in the morning?" Elspeth laughed and then stood to gather the empty plates.

"Oh." Heather pulled her mouth into a grimace. "I didn't think to ask him. Suppose that was a bit rude, really." She looked over at her mother, who was stacking the plates into the dishwasher.

"Och, I wouldn't worry about Fraser's sensibilities. He'll live." She smiled back at her daughter and then held the kettle under the tap, refilling it. "More tea, love?"

"Always." Heather nodded and stretched her feet out under the table in search of the warm dog. "Where's Charlie?"

"With the children. As ever."

"Is Murdo coming for breakfast?" Heather looked up at the big clock that hung on the chimney flue above the Aga. It was 7:10—late for her brother to show up, from what she understood.

"No. Not th'day. He thought you might sleep in and didn't want to wake you. He'll be by for his dinner tonight, though. Just you try to keep him away." Elspeth chuckled as she poured steaming water into the teapot and then replaced the lid.

The two women sat in companionable silence, drank tea, and passed sections of the newspaper back and forth across the table. The muffled noise of the TV from the living room, the ticking clock, and the soft tapping of tree limbs being blown against the kitchen window were mesmeric, and Heather soon began to feel her eyelids grow heavy.

"Would you mind if I crashed out for another hour or so, Mum?" She folded the paper and laid it next to her mug.

"Of course not, pet. You go and rest. I'll keep an eye on those two." Elspeth nodded toward the living room. "When you wake up, we'll take them into the village for a wee wander."

"Thanks, Mum. What would I do without you?" Heather stood up and walked behind her mother's chair. She leaned down and planted a kiss on top of the soft gray hair. "You are my rock."

Elspeth reached up and patted Heather's cheek.

"Off you go now. Sleep."

The bedroom was cool as Heather slid back under the covers. The duvet was heavy with down, and soon she could feel the heat of her body permeate the cold sheet underneath her. On an impulse, she reached across to the empty side, running her fingers over its icy vacancy. She still wasn't used to having the bed to herself. Brett had refused to buy a king, saying that she would be too far away from him. She had loved to wake up and turn over to see the curve of his side, his long legs protruding from the covers, and hear the soft rumble of his rhythmic breathing. Knowing that it would wake him, it had been all that she could do not to reach out and touch his thick dark hair, curl up against his broad back, and soak in his presence.

Now, next to her, the covers lay flat and the pillow was smooth, undented. The sight of it was like staring at the sun, so she closed her eyes tight and turned her back on the emptiness. She needed to sleep, and then she would be ready to face the first day of their new lives on Skye. Whatever else she did not know, she knew that this was where she and the children needed to be—for now, anyway.

CHAPTER 17

The old Land Rover bumped along the rutted road between Achachork and Portree. Murdoch had been distracted all day, wanting to call the Forge and see what was going on, envious of the time that his mother was spending with his sister and the twins. But he had resisted, and now, after a long day and a quick shower, he was heading over for dinner.

The flock had been fractious that afternoon, and Chick had had to circle and herd them more than once. Murdoch wondered if the sheep were picking up on his mood, being made anxious by his haste to get through the day's tasks, or perhaps they were divining that bad weather was on the way, as he had often noticed the creatures could.

He hit a pothole, and his teeth chattered in his head.

"Shit," he growled.

Fraser had sounded odd when they'd talked, and Murdoch was sure it was because of him warning his friend not to crowd Heather. It was clear that there was a definite attraction, on Fraser's side.

It had started when they were all in their teens and Heather was already looking beyond the bounds of Skye for a job. Fraser had asked her out a couple of times, and in an unconscious and yet typically callous teenage way, Heather had laughed. She'd said no and then asked Fraser if he thought she was going to be happy to spend the rest of her life on Skye, chasing sheep around a croft and peeling turnips for pies. Murdoch recalled that Fraser had tried to brush off the rebuff, but he knew that Heather's harsh words had hurt his friend.

As he pictured Fraser's injured expression in the pub, Murdoch felt bad, but he still hoped Fraser would take the warning to heart.

Even before his father had died, Murdoch had relished the role of protector of his little sister. When they'd first met Brett, Murdoch had given him a harder time than Matthew had, grilling him on his career plan, his intentions, and his ability to support Heather. She had been incensed, giving Murdoch the evil eye as he made Brett squirm. Later that evening, she had accosted Murdoch in the kitchen of the Forge and thumped his chest with her fists.

"Don't bugger this up for me, Murdo. I mean it."

He had seen her eyes flash in a way that he hadn't since she was a youngster.

"I love him."

There had been no doubt in Murdoch's mind that his sister was in love. His mission had been purely to ascertain whether this Yankee pilot felt the same.

The following night, Brett had asked him to go to the pub for a drink. Murdoch had agreed, and as the two men walked into the village, Brett had addressed every concern of Murdoch's, closing down his arguments gently but firmly. He said he had every intention of proposing and that, aside from his having talked to Matthew already, he would also like Murdoch's permission to ask Heather, that same weekend, to marry him.

Murdoch had been disarmed by the candid American and, not being able to come up with any more plausible objections, had finally slapped Brett on the back and told him to go for it.

Heather's obvious happiness was proof of her good decision. However, he had missed his sister over the years, and despite his fondness for Brett, he had silently held him responsible for separating him from his sibling.

Heather and Brett had visited Skye when the children were only a few months old. Seeing the two tiny creatures with their tight fists, raspberry mouths, and soft curls, Murdoch had been captivated. He knew then that if he hadn't previously been a fan of the implications of Heather's marriage to Brett, these little angels had exonerated his brother-in-law of all selfish intent.

Murdoch focused ahead. The road was dark, and the Land Rover's headlights jumped with the holes and mounds of the track. He would soon turn onto Home Farm Road, and then the rest of the journey would be smooth sailing. His croft was only three miles from the Forge, and he drove this route so often he swore the car could make it on autopilot.

Chick was doing his best to stand up on the backseat, panting so close to Murdoch's ear that he could smell the dog's breath.

"Sit down, boy. Sit." Murdoch spoke over his shoulder. "You'll come a cropper if you don't sit, lad."

Murdoch looked in the rearview mirror and saw the dog drop down and lie low across the backseat.

"Good boy."

He knew that the children were dying to see Chick, and he had promised to bring him along for the evening. Chick and Elspeth's dog, Charlie, were old friends, and while they didn't get the two dogs together often, it was always an easy meeting when it happened.

Megan had immediately gravitated toward Charlie, but Max had formed a close bond with Chick on a previous visit. Murdoch had been amazed to see his dog cross the Forge kitchen and sit at the little boy's feet. Chick never sat with anyone other than Murdoch, and while he was momentarily taken aback, he was also in awe of the dog's ability to recognize a troubled soul, or one simply in need of companionship.

Murdoch knew that Max wasn't coping as well as Megan since losing their father. Not that his little niece was any less affected, but she had the ability to look outward, soak in the support of the people around her, and share her moments of sadness. Max, on the other hand, kept everything inside, isolated himself, and withdrew from the very same support network that Megan relied on. Murdoch hoped that by having Max here, close to him, he would be able to coax the boy out of his gloom. Murdoch had promised to show him how to whistle to Chick and work with the sheep, and Max had said that would be cool.

As he turned onto Home Farm Road, Murdoch shook his head. *Cool, neat, awesome.* He would need to remember to use some of that Yankee language if he wanted the children to feel comfortable. No sooner had the thought crossed his mind than he shook his head again. It would perhaps be better to teach them some of the local patter, to help them fit in with the other children at school.

The lights of Portree were now visible, and soon he was pulling the car into the Brae, heading for the Forge. As he negotiated his way along the waterfront, Murdoch glanced at the stretch of businesses on his right. The little shop where his mother's friend Marjorie worked still had its lights on. On an impulse, he pulled over and switched off the engine. He could pop in and get some sweets for the kids.

Marjorie was sitting behind the counter with her back to the door. A small TV warbled on a low shelf, and she was staring intently at some dancers twirling around a big ballroom.

"Hiya, Marj. What're you watching?" His voice boomed over the sound of the TV, and Marjorie jumped. Spinning toward him, her wizened hand flew up to her throat and she began to cough.

"Oh, jeepers, Murdo. You scared the life oot'a me." The coughing came in spasms and, feeling bad for scaring her, Murdoch went behind the counter into the kitchen area and filled a glass with water.

"Here you go, Marj. Sit down, woman. You're fit to choke." He patted her wool-covered back, and eventually the racking coughs subsided. "Are you OK?"

Safely back on the customer's side of the counter, he looked at her pastel-colored head as it quivered.

"Aye. Thanks, Murdo. I'm fine."

"You should keep an eye on the door at night, Marj."

The little woman pulled the edges of her cardigan closer and swept a wrinkled finger under each eye.

"Well, I was watching *Strictly*, and I thought I'd just as well finish it down here than up the stair." She winked at Murdoch. "I wasn'y expecting anyone to come in."

"I just popped in for some sweets for the twins. Maybe a bottle of Irn-Bru, if you have any?"

Marjorie nodded to the left as she sipped some water from the glass.

"Over there, pet. Next to the Jaffa Cakes."

Murdoch lifted the large plastic bottle from the shelf, then picked up a bag of Maltesers and a bag of Murray Mints.

"That'll do it." He smiled at his mother's friend, who had regained her equilibrium.

"So how's wee Heather and those lovely bairns? Such a tragedy." She shook her pinkish head as Murdoch held out a note to her.

"Och, they're fine. They'll settle down, and the change will do them all good." Murdoch nodded.

"Aye. A change is as good as a rest, right enough. Give them my love, won't you, Murdo? Will they be coming in to see me?"

Murdoch gathered up the items and shoved the change into his pocket.

"They surely will. Tomorrow, no doubt, once they've had a chance to get their bearings."

As he climbed into the car, he noticed that Chick had hopped over the central console and was sitting comfortably in the passenger seat. The dog had licked a patch of condensation off the side window.

"Ah, it's like that, is it?" Murdoch laughed as he pulled the seat belt across himself. "Can you do the rest of the windows while you're at it?"

Elspeth had laid the kitchen table with her favorite tablecloth. The Aga was heavy with pots, and something smelled wonderful. Murdoch put the drink and sweets on the counter and, hearing voices, padded through to the living room.

"Anybody home?"

Megan jumped up from the carpet, where she was lying with her head on Charlie's stomach.

"Uncle Murdy." She was quickly in his arms, her warm cheek pressed against his cold one.

"Well, hello to you, too." He chuckled as the little girl planted a kiss on his forehead and then wriggled back out of his grip to resume her position on the floor.

Elspeth and Heather were sitting at either end of the sofa. His mother was knitting, and Heather was staring at the TV.

"Hiya." Heather heaved herself out of the sofa and walked over to him. As he hugged her, he was shocked to feel a xylophone of ribs under his forearms. The heavy coat she had been wearing the previous day had obviously camouflaged her thinness.

"God, we need to get some meat on those bones, Wee Blister." He pushed her gently back. "There's nothing of you."

Heather self-consciously pulled her thick sweater down over her hips as Elspeth got up from the sofa behind her.

"You leave her alone, Murdoch MacDonald." Elspeth gave him a wide-eyed warning as she passed, and then patted his chest. "She'll get herself sorted without us nagging her."

Murdoch turned to see Max lying on a cushion beside the fire. Chick was already next to him, and his nephew absently stroked the dog with one foot as he held an iPad over his face.

"So, Max. No welcome for your favorite uncle?"

The little boy lowered the tablet and sat upright.

"Sorry. I'm playing a game. Want to see?"

Murdoch settled himself on the floor, and while Elspeth and Heather served the dinner, uncle and nephew were soon lost in a world of trolls, magicians, and flying carpets.

CHAPTER 18

A week later, having spent time adjusting to the time zone, going for walks in the hills, and exploring Portree, the twins had started school. On the first morning, Megan had been quiet in the car, and Max sulked when Heather asked him if he had remembered his dinner money.

"I'm not a baby, Mom." His bottom lip protruded as he rolled his eyes at her.

As was happening more frequently these days, Heather saw herself in his reaction, and she recoiled. Had she looked like that when Elspeth had chided her or reminded her of some basic task? She suspected so.

After a stilted conversation, reflective of their collective nervousness, Heather had been reluctant to simply drop the twins off outside the school, so she had parked the car and walked them inside the gate. Then, to Max's obvious embarrassment, she had begun to hug them in the busy playground. After an awkward few moments, with the surge of children around them watching, she almost cried with gratitude when a young teacher came out to meet them and suggested that Heather take the children into their classroom to say good-bye.

The day had dragged without them, and when she picked the twins up that afternoon, it cheered Heather up to listen to Megan's detailed account of the day. Max, on the other hand, contributed very little.

Back at the house, while Megan chattered on, Max had focused very deliberately on his iPad. Heather silently locked eyes with Elspeth above his tousled head when, eventually, he had shoved his earbuds in to further remove himself from the conversation.

That evening, as Heather cooked for them, Max had talked a little about his classroom, mentioning the white rats in the cage at the back and the mobile of the planets that hung from the ceiling in the corner. Then, having eaten his dinner, he unceremoniously announced that he wanted to tell her something.

"What is it?" Heather smiled at her son, hoping for a nugget of information about something that he'd enjoyed that day.

"Tomorrow you can just drop us off, and we'll walk from the gate, like the other kids." He'd glared at her over his soup bowl, and Heather felt the intended sting in his words. She knew that she had embarrassed him that morning, but walking inside the classroom with them had been as much for her as, she thought, it had been for them.

"Fine, Max. If that's what you want." She swallowed her hurt and lifted their empty plates, aware of Megan watching her back as she left the room.

On the subsequent days, she walked them to the gate and left them there, the twins waving as they trotted into the building, surrounded by so many other little heads that she quickly lost sight of them.

By the end of their first week, Megan had made a special friend called Rosie, whom she had invited to the Forge for tea the coming weekend. She'd also told Heather that she wanted to join Highland dancing classes. Max had been predictably noncommittal about his first week. When she pressed him, he had grunted.

"It's OK, but the kids in our class are weird."

Heather had been unable to get anything more out of him, and rather than press it, had backed off, hoping that in time he would open up. However, as the days passed, he became even quieter than usual, verging on sullen, only coming to life when playing outside with Megan or when Murdoch appeared with Chick.

Seeing her son struggle but choose not to confide in her about his worries ripped tiny holes in Heather's heart. She wanted to wrap him in her arms, make new friends for him, fight his battles, and clear the path for him to once again be the happy little boy she'd known less than a year before. Whenever she tried to talk to him about school, he set his mouth in a way that she recognized as her own. When that happened, there was no point in continuing to ask questions.

She had been concerned about the twins' ability to integrate into the local school, for various reasons. Aside from the things she imagined that every parent worried about—whether they'd make friends, whether they'd find the new curriculum difficult to adapt to, and so on, she was also afraid that they'd stick out for being different. She knew how cruel children could be to anyone who didn't fit in, and Max and Megan had much going against them in that regard. Their accents were distinctly American, their clothes were different from most of the village children's, and they used American words for things, not always understanding the local vernacular—all of which she knew could leave them open to teasing.

Each morning, as she watched them disappear into a group of other children, she pressed down her anxiety, marveling at their brave little souls and how they were coping with all the changes that she'd subjected them to since Brett's death. As she reflected on everything that had happened over the past nine months, Heather realized that the fact that they'd so recently lost their father now seemed to have taken a backseat to all the other obstacles that stood between them and feeling at home on Skye. As she struggled not to feel overwhelmed for them, Heather found herself wondering, increasingly, if she had done the right thing by bringing them back.

It wasn't just the twins who were struggling to find their place on the island. As the days passed slowly and her sleepless nights lingered, Heather had begun to feel more and more like a barnacle on a rock. She stood out, harsh against the gentle backdrop of her surroundings. She was a parasite, feeding off the environment but not contributing to its sustainability. Life on Skye had gone on in her absence, and yet time had also stood still.

She had attempted to talk to the other parents at the school gate a few times but had made very little progress in connecting with anyone. Some of them had been tentatively friendly but had made no bones about the fact that they considered her an outsider. She had even overheard one of them referring to her as "the American," which, while it didn't necessarily surprise her, had set her teeth on edge. As she nursed her hurt, she told herself that she was, jagged barnacle or no, most likely more of a true local than many of these people. Their attitude toward her was not only hurtful but also frustrating. Her response had been to withdraw from them completely, and now, when she dropped the children off, she would smile from a distance but not cross the road to talk to anyone. Even though she recognized that she was effectively behaving the exact same way that Max was, she couldn't help but want to isolate herself.

Having been home a few days, Heather had called Kirsty, the one school friend who still lived on the island and whom she'd kept in touch with over the years. They'd arranged to meet for coffee in the village and Kirsty had seemed pleased to see her, but, as the conversation turned to America, Kirsty's eyes had gone blank and her responses had become monosyllabic. Afraid that she was whining or, worse, being perceived to be bragging about her life in the States, Heather had clammed up. She'd spent the remainder of their time together peppering Kirsty with questions about her husband and children, who were a few years older than the twins. When the hour and a half was up, Heather had bolted from the café. The knowledge that she probably wouldn't hear from Kirsty again for a while had left her feeling profoundly lonely.

It struck her as strange that when she walked around the village she didn't see more faces that she recognized. For a small community where she'd spent the majority of her life, there seemed to be little to connect her to the past, aside from her family.

CHAPTER 19

Halfway through the second week of school, Heather was wrapped up in a coat and hat and was walking into the brisk wind on the shore near Portree when her cell phone rang. She had received so few calls on the new phone that the ringtone startled her, and she rummaged through her coat pockets in search of it.

"Yes, hello?" She felt the familiar patter of nerves that any ringing phone provoked in her now.

"Mrs. Forester?"

"Yes, speaking."

"This is Mr. George, head . . . school."

Heather felt a jolt under her ribs as the voice crackled inconsistently in her ear.

"Yes, Mr. George. What's wrong?"

"Your son, Max, hit a boy . . . playground, and knocked him over. Your daughter . . . to pull Max off when . . . hit her in the nose with his elbow." There was a pause. "Mrs. Forester . . . you there?"

The icy wind that blasted her face forced her eyes closed. Could this be happening again? What was Max thinking?

"Mrs. Forester?"

"Yes, I'm here. Is Megan OK?" she shouted into the phone. "You're breaking up."

"She's fine now. She . . . a little nosebleed, but . . . school nurse managed . . . stop it quickly." The voice was distant, and the intensity of the wind was causing her to miss a word here and there.

Heather opened her eyes and turned her back to the water as the wind buffeted her toward the road that ran behind the beach.

"I'm having a hard time hearing you Mr., em, Mr. . . . ." Damn, what was this man's name?

"Mr. George." He sounded irritated now. "We'd like you . . . and pick the children up please . . . perhaps we can make an appointment . . . come in and talk to us?"

Heather pressed the phone closer to her face, as the wind was stealing her voice. Even with the half sentences she had picked up, she knew exactly what had happened.

"Right. I'll come now." She switched off the phone and paced across the narrow strip of sand, scanning the road beyond for Elspeth's car, which she had borrowed. The green Ford was parked only a few feet away, and she focused on its roof as her calves burned from the tug of the sand.

Max sat on the sofa in the living room and stared out the window. Heather perched on the edge of the coffee table, her elbows on her knees.

"Max, I'm talking to you." She shifted her hips.

"Uh-huh." Max chewed on his cheek and swiped a hand across his eyes.

"Honey, you need to tell me what happened." Heather reached out and touched his hand. Max snatched it away and tucked it under his leg.

She could see his chin quivering, and the idea that she might make him cry was torturous.

"I can't help you if you won't talk to me." She leaned back. "You need to tell me what's going on."

Max sniffed and started to chew on the skin around his thumb.

"C'mon, buddy. I won't be mad. I just want to hear it from your side." She ran a hand down each thigh and waited.

"The kid was a jerk." Max spoke around his thumb.

"What did he do?" Heather kept her voice level, afraid to rush him.

"He said mean stuff. That I had weird hair and that Megan and me were orphans." Max's eyes glittered, and Heather felt the stab of the word under her rib cage.

Max continued. "I told him that he was dumb and that orphans have no parents. I said we have a mom, and he just shoved me here." Max thumped his chest with his fist.

"Then what happened?"

"Well, I hit him in his stomach and he fell backward."

"Yes." Heather waited.

"Then I sat on him, and he hit me over and over on the arms. Lots of other kids were there shouting, and then Megs came over. She pulled my arm and I told her to go away." He dropped his gaze to his knees. "But she kept on pulling, so I tried to push her off, but I hit her in the nose."

A tear slid over his bottom lid, and Heather instinctively reached into her pocket for a tissue. Not finding one, she leaned over and wiped it away with her fingertip.

"It was an accident, Mom. I didn't mean to hurt Megs." His face crumpled as Heather moved onto the sofa next to him and gathered him in her arms.

"I know you didn't mean it. But you can't lash out at people, Max. You need to try not to get so angry." She rocked his stiff little frame.

After a few moments, Max pushed away from her arms.

"But he was jerk." He gave an almighty sniff and shook the hair from his eyes. "He deserved it." There was the familiar defiant set to his chin.

Heather laced her fingers and sat back against the cushion. How should she handle this? Brett would tell her to step away and think it through, but she had an appointment with the headmaster the following afternoon, and she needed to get things straight in her mind before she talked to him.

"I'm going to go see the head tomorrow, Max. I want to be able tell him that you're very, very sorry, that it'll never happen again, and that you'll apologize to the boy you hit." She watched his profile as he grimaced and shook his head.

"No. I won't." He frowned.

"Max."

Max jumped up from the sofa and rounded on her.

"You're supposed to stick up for me, be on my side. Dad would've been on my side." His eyes were streaming now, and Heather made to get up, but he stepped backward and held up his hands and then screamed at her. "Don't touch me. I hate you. I hate it here. I want to go home." He turned and ran toward the stairs.

"Max, you come back here." She was up and following him.

"Leave me alone. I just want to go home and live with Aunt Chrissy."

Heather stood at the bottom of the stairs and watched him take them two at a time and then disappear around the top of the landing. She stared into the empty space where he'd been, his anger seeming to have left a vapor trail behind him. Her heart was clattering, and her chest was throwing off so much heat that she grabbed her shirt and flapped it against her sternum. Deciding not to follow him right away, she turned and sat on the bottom step. As her heart returned to a normal pace, her own dam broke. Hot tears coated her cheeks, and as she clenched her jaw in order to keep quiet, she struggled to catch her breath between sobs. What was she going to do? Had this whole thing been a terrible mistake?

Heather shoved Megan's bloodstained shirt into the washing machine along with a few other white items from the basket. Max was still upstairs in his room, and Megan was in the living room, sitting on Murdo's lap while they watched TV. Heather was aware of Elspeth hovering behind her, and while she knew that she should tell her mother what was going on, she just wanted to be left alone to cope with yet another drama involving Max.

"Can I help?" Elspeth spoke to her back.

"No. I'm fine."

Elspeth moved across the utility room and began folding some towels that she had pulled from the dryer.

"Is Max OK up there?"

Heather felt her face heating up as she poured powder into the drawer and then slammed it closed.

"He's fine. He needs to stay up there and think about what he did." She spun around and flashed her mother a warning glare.

"All right. I was just asking." Elspeth held her hands up in front of her chest. "But he's just a wee boy, Heather. He's hurting."

Heather felt a needle of pain under her shoulder blade, and she pressed her eyes closed. She didn't want to see Elspeth's soft face, the questioning eyes, or the telltale judgmental dipping of the chin.

"He hit another child today, Mum. That's the third time in just a few weeks. I can't let him get away with it this time." She spoke deliberately and then opened her eyes to see her mother staring at her, her mouth slightly open.

"You didn't tell me that."

"I don't tell you everything that goes on in our lives."

Heather heard Elspeth draw breath.

"I know that. But punishing him, rather than talking to him . . ." Her mother took a step toward her.

Heather felt something click in her jaw, and then she exploded.

"Jesus, Mum. I can't get him to talk to me. It's not like I haven't tried. Just back off, OK? I'm the mother here." Heather saw her words pepper Elspeth's face.

Elspeth swung around and lifted the pile of towels up against her chest, and Heather could see her mother's narrow back trembling.

"What's going on?" Murdo stood in the doorway. Megan was clinging to his back with her legs, clad in pony-patterned tights, wrapped around his waist.

"Mommy?" Her eyes flicked between her mother and grandmother.

Heather's voice wouldn't come as Elspeth turned around and, laying the towels down, opened her arms. "Come on, toots, time you were in bed."

Murdoch leaned over to allow his niece to slide off his back. "Off you go, pet. I'll see you tomorrow." He ruffled her hair.

Heather watched as Megan padded across to Elspeth and then slipped her hand into her grandmother's.

"'Night, Mom." Megan glanced anxiously over her shoulder as they left the room.

"Good night, sweetie. I'll be up to tuck you in." Heather felt the cinch of regret for her outburst tight across her chest.

Murdoch hovered in the doorway, his silence audible. Heather met his gaze and saw utter disapproval.

"What?" she snapped.

"Nothing, Wee Blister." He shrugged.

"No. Say it." She glared at him.

"Are you sure?" He held her gaze.

"Yes. Go for it. It's open season on my parenting skills, so go ahead."

Murdoch shook his head, turned, and walked back into the kitchen. Frustrated at his leaving rather than having it out, Heather punched the "Start" button on the washing machine and followed him. When she walked into the room, he was at the sink filling the kettle.

"Sit down." He spoke over his shoulder.

"I don't want tea." She heard the pout in her voice as she pulled out a chair and sat at the table.

"Well, I do."

Heather watched him making two mugs of tea, her anger simmering as she anticipated the potential lecture coming her way.

Murdoch sat down opposite her and shoved a mug toward her.

"Just in case you change your mind."

"So, have at it." She held her hands out. "I can take it."

Murdoch sipped some tea and then placed the mug carefully back down on the table.

"You shouted at Mum." He eyed her. "What happened?"

"She made out that I wasn't trying to talk to Max about what happened at school." Even as she said it, her reasoning began to lose ground. "She implied that I shouldn't punish him." The hole was getting deeper.

Murdoch nodded, waiting for more. "Uh-huh."

Heather ran through the confrontation with her mother in her mind. She knew that she had overreacted, but having to admit that to her older brother still felt like defeat. They had had very few disagreements as children, or even as teenagers, so this was territory that she'd only navigated occasionally. Their most significant falling-out had been over her decision to leave Skye and move to Edinburgh. It had taken Murdoch a few days to forgive her and take her calls, and the time that they hadn't been talking had been purgatory for Heather. Even now, after all the years and events that had passed, and despite her fierce independence, there was a large part of Heather that dreaded his disapproval.

As she looked at his broad face, her remaining anger evaporated.

"Oh, God. I know." She shook her head. "I was a bitch."

Murdoch sipped more tea.

"She just pushed the wrong button." Heather shrugged.

"Aye, apparently." He eyed her. "You need to calm down, though. She didn'y deserve that."

Heather felt her anger flooding back.

"Calm down? For Christ's sake, Murdo, do you have any idea how much I'm dealing with? I'm drowning here." She shook her head. "The last thing I need is a lecture from you—all sanctimonious."

Murdoch tutted and then thumped his mug onto the table.

"We know what you're dealing with, and we're here to help, every day. But you're not the only one who's coping with stuff, Heather."

She started at his use of her proper name.

"Mum and I know exactly what you've been through, you and the kids. If we could've changed any of that for you, we would." He leaned forward on his elbows. "But who has been taking care of Mum, and everything else here, day in and day out for the past two years?" His eyes flashed. "Yours truly." He jabbed a thumb at his chest. "And I'm happy to do it, but just don't think you're the only one who's handling tough stuff." He slammed back against the chair.

Heather felt the air leave her lungs. Murdoch had never spoken to her this way, and neither had he ever given her any hint of discontent about being around for Elspeth since Matthew's death.

"But it was your choice to stay here, Murdo." She searched his face. "Nobody made you."

"Aye, and that's what I'm saying. Nobody made you leave, and nobody made you come home, either. We both made our choices, and now we're all dealing with life, as a family." His voice returned to its normal mellow timbre. "We need to work together, not snipe at one another, if this is going to work." He swept an arm around the room.

Heather wiped her eyes and reached for the mug in front of her. Her brother had, as was his style, hit the nail on the head. She was the one who had taken the leap, of her own volition. If this new arrangement was going to work, they all needed to pull together, now more than ever.

"Just settle down, Wee Blister." He frowned. "Now, tell me—what happened at school, exactly?" He laced his hands behind his head and waited.

CHAPTER 20

The following afternoon, Heather parked in front of the school. She was nervous, as if she were being hauled up in front of her own headmaster, two decades ago. She twisted the rearview mirror and took in her reflection. Her hair was freshly washed and she had put on some light powder and mascara, sensing the need to present herself as a together mother, one who had everything under control. As she assessed her drawn face, she wondered if these people would see that underneath the carefully applied makeup, she was exhausted, terrified, adrift, and floundering—here, in the one place where she was supposed to feel at home.

The headmaster's office was glacial. There was a distinct smell of roast beef, and as she sat down, Heather wondered why all school offices seemed to smell the same. Mr. George, a short man with a ruddy complexion and thick glasses, had offered her a cup of tea, which she now regretted not accepting.

Anxious to get this conversation over with, she cleared her throat.

"I'm very sorry for what happened, but from what I understand from Max, the other boy provoked him." She crossed her legs and linked her hands over her knee.

"Well, I suppose you could say that." Mr. George assessed her from behind his desk. "But we can't have children resorting to violence, irrespective." He tapped the spoon on his cup and laid it in the saucer.

"I'd hardly term it *violence*." She didn't want to sound defensive, but *violence* seemed too harsh a term for a playground clash.

"That kind of aggression is not tolerated here, Mrs. Forester. Regardless of what might've been acceptable in America." His dark eyes flashed.

Heather's ears filled with a dangerous rushing sound. *Calm. Calm. Don't screw this up.*

"I beg your pardon?" She uncrossed her legs and leaned forward.

Seeming to sense that he had perhaps ventured into dangerous territory, Mr. George patted the air.

"I meant to say that we understand that things are different in America. We just have to make sure that your children know what's expected of them here." He smiled, a twisted little smile that was calling at Heather to reach out and wipe it off his red face.

"Max isn't settling in as well as we'd hoped. He's withdrawn and rarely joins in in class. He is prone to sulking and is sometimes impolite to his teacher." He nodded decisively as he lifted the teacup from the saucer.

"Impolite?" Heather's leg was shaking now, under her elbow. "What exactly do you mean?"

"He doesn't take criticism terribly well." Mr. George swallowed some tea. "He's a little immature for his age, we find."

The last shred of Heather's composure snapped.

"Immature?" Her voice was gravelly. "Mr. George. You do understand that my children are seven years old?"

He nodded. "Well, of course."

"Do you know what they've been through recently?" Heather dug her elbow into her thigh to stop her leg jerking. "They've lost their father and come several thousand miles from the place they've lived their entire lives. They've moved to a place they're unfamiliar with and that they don't fully understand yet." She swallowed. Damn him, she would not cry. "They're coping with more than most adults would struggle with. Max may be lonely, sad, and even angry—which he has every right to be—but he is far from immature."

Mr. George glanced down at his desk. "Yes, we do understand." He placed the cup back in the saucer. "We want to be of help, Mrs. Forester."

"Well, it sounds to me as if you've written Max off." Heather's voice cracked, and she dug her fingernails into her palm.

"Och, no, not at all." He shook his head dismissively and then pushed his glasses farther up his nose. "I'd like to bring in Max's form teacher to talk to you, if you're agreeable?" He smiled, revealing a set of mismatched teeth. "She has some thoughts on how we can help Max find his feet."

"Fine." Heather nodded and then lifted her handbag onto her lap to search for a tissue.

A few moments later, the young woman who had met her in the playground on the first morning walked into the room.

"This is Miss Bell, Max's teacher." Mr. George watched as the woman pulled a chair over next to Heather's.

Heather walked back toward the car. The rushing in her ears was abating, so she dipped her head and focused on the keys in her hand. She needed to hold it together, just until she got into the car—then she could let go. She thumped down into the seat and jabbed the keys into the ignition. Glancing in the mirror, she saw Miss Bell standing outside the gate as if waiting to wave her off. While the young woman had been soft-spoken and more understanding than Mr. George, Heather hadn't warmed to her.

There was a distinct scent of judgment coming from both of these people that had incensed her. It was as if they considered her children subpar in some way, simply for having a different background. Heather had listened to them talk and had stood up for Max without being unreasonable. She had accepted that he had behaved badly, and Mr. George had taken her assurance that she would deal with Max, and that this kind of thing would never happen again, on the understanding that Max apologize to the little boy. Heather had then insisted that the apology be reciprocated, as the other child had obviously provoked Max. After some tutting and a discussion with Miss Bell, the headmaster had reluctantly conceded the point.

The Ford's engine caught, and she slammed the car into reverse and then swung her head over her shoulder, ready to back up. As she pressed down on the accelerator, the car lurched forward, and a sudden jolt sent her head jerking away from the headrest. Heather's stomach flipped as she turned and looked ahead at the car she had hit. It was a low two-seater, some kind of sports car, she guessed, and no doubt expensive. Her legs began to shake again.

She unlatched the seat belt and stepped out of the car, glancing back at the gate to see if the young teacher was still there, witnessing her humiliation. Mercifully, she had gone, and as Heather walked around to the front of the Ford, she felt her eyes prickle. She leaned down to assess the damage to both vehicles as tears plopped onto the tarmac below. What the hell next? Did the universe have something against her? After everything she'd been through, this stupid mistake could be the last straw.

Having written her name and phone number on a piece of paper and tucked it under the windscreen wiper of the other car, Heather pulled away from the school. She glanced at her watch. It was nearly five fifteen, so she should head straight home to relieve Elspeth, who'd been watching the children. Instead, at the junction where she should have turned left toward the Brae, the car seemed to steer itself toward Achachork. She needed someone to talk to, but as she turned onto Home Farm Road, still feeling hurt by Murdoch's reproach of the previous day, it was clear that he was not the person she wanted.

As the road opened up in front of her, the car rumbled past Murdoch's driveway and then climbed the hill, going farther up onto the moor. Before long, she saw the long metal gate that she was looking for. She swung the car onto a patch of gravel, glanced at herself in the rearview mirror and hoped that Fraser was home.

CHAPTER 21

Murdoch stared out across the moor. Far to his left, Chick was circling a group of sheep, lassoing them into a clump of white and black wool. He whistled, but the high-pitched peal was instantly torn away by the wind. He signaled to the dog and whistled again, and this time Chick responded by doubling back to gather a stray ewe.

It had been a couple of days since his confrontation with Heather, and he was beginning to worry, because he hadn't heard from her since. He had left a voice mail for her the previous morning, but, as he'd chosen not to go to the Forge for his usual breakfast for the past two days, either, he supposed he, too, was contributing to the silence. As he watched the dog manipulate the flock, he resolved to call her again and settle any residual bad feeling.

Fraser had been elusive, too, for a couple of days, which was odd. Even if they didn't see each other every day, they usually talked on the phone. He pulled his hand out of his pocket, peeled back his sleeve, and checked the time. He'd finish up here, then give him a call and see if Fraser was up for a meal or a drink that night.

Fraser walked into the pub and, spotting Murdoch at the bar, raised a hand. Murdoch nodded back and pushed a pint glass toward his friend as he approached.

"Cheers, mate." Fraser shrugged his heavy jacket off and slid onto the stool.

"So, what's new?" Murdoch sipped his beer and addressed Fraser's reflection in the mirror behind the bar.

"Nothin' much. I lost a ewe yesterday. Looked like a fox, or maybe a dog." Fraser took a long draft of beer.

"Oh, sorry."

"Aye, it's a shame." Fraser nodded. "I'll need to keep an eye out."

Murdoch reached for the bar menu.

"Eating?" He addressed Fraser over his shoulder.

Fraser nodded. "Uh-huh."

Murdoch scanned his friend's profile. There was something different about him. Fraser seemed uncomfortable, not his usual relaxed self.

"Everything OK, pal?" Murdoch closed the menu and slid it back across the bar.

"Aye, all good."

Fraser's face was slightly flushed, and the way he was avoiding meeting Murdoch's eyes made it obvious that there was something he wasn't saying. Murdoch swiveled around on the stool and faced him.

"So, what's going on?"

Fraser placed his glass down on the beer mat.

"It's nothing, really. Just that Heather came to my place the other day." He hesitated. "She'd been to the school, about Max. Sounds like she took a bit of a beating."

Murdoch let the statement settle on him. Heather had been to see Fraser, but neither had mentioned it. He stared at his friend. He knew that she had been going to the school, and that's why he'd left her the message asking how it had gone. The fact that she hadn't called him back, but she'd driven past his door and been to see Fraser, cut deep, shaking him.

"She came to yours?"

"Aye, just for a cuppa. She needed to talk, and then with the car . . ." Fraser halted.

"What car?" Murdoch snapped.

"Your mum's car. She borrowed it and then bumped someone outside the school. Nothing major—but I think it was the last straw. She was awf'y upset." Seeming to sense dangerous ground, Fraser turned back to the bar.

Murdoch clenched his jaw. He shouldn't be angry. Even knowing it was childish to be jealous, he still was. He was Heather's rock. He was her go-to person for support. He was her brother. Why had she gone to Fraser? Gathering himself, he turned to his friend.

"So, what happened to the car?"

"Och, just a wee scrape on the bumper. I told her to take it to Healy's in the village. Angus'll sort it out with some T-Cut." Fraser shrugged.

"What about the one she hit?" Murdoch's voice was low.

"She left her info on the windscreen. She said it was a tiny dent. Shouldn't be too much of a problem. Your mum had put her on the insurance."

Murdoch felt his neck muscles tensing. Was this turn of events his fault? Had he been too hard on Heather when they'd argued? Was she being petulant in turning to Fraser, or had he, Murdoch, pushed her away with his own outburst? Regardless of what had created this new distance between them, he needed to fix things.

"Thanks for helping her." He hoped he sounded genuinely grateful, but Fraser swung around and looked startled.

"Hey, it wasn'y anything. She just needed to talk." Fraser's face was red.

"And she chose you." Murdoch bit down on his tongue. He hadn't meant to sound like a petty kid. Seeing the impact of his words on his friend's face, he immediately felt like a fool. "Look, there's so much going on at the moment, we've hit a few bumps since they all got home. We're sorting it out, though. I mean it—thanks." He reached out and put his hand on Fraser's shoulder.

At the contact, Fraser seemed to relax.

"No bother. You're all like family. Anything I can do." He smiled at Murdoch and then turned gratefully to the barman, who was asking what they wanted to eat.

CHAPTER 22

The third morning that Murdoch had not come in for breakfast was a Friday. Elspeth was making toast for the twins while Heather read the paper at the table. Elspeth was worried about her son's unusual absence, and when he had called her the previous afternoon, he'd sounded odd. He said he was getting some paperwork done for the next trip to market and would be by in a couple of days. Despite his assurances, she knew her boy, and she also knew that Heather had been somewhat sheepish since their argument. As she placed a plate of toast in front of each child, Elspeth eyed her daughter.

"So, are you seeing Murdo today?" She lifted the teapot to check its weight.

"No. Probably not." Heather stared at the paper.

Opposite Heather, Megan was biting into her toast.

"Why isn't Uncle Murdy coming for breakfast anymore?"

"Your mouth is full, Megs." Heather shot her daughter a warning glance.

"Thorry." Megan grinned, revealing a swath of chewed-up bread.

"Ew, Megs, you're gross." Max leaned over and elbowed his sister as she giggled.

Having finished her mouthful, Megan tried again.

"So why isn't he?" When Heather didn't reply, she looked over at Elspeth. "Granny?"

Elspeth stared at Heather, waiting for her to take up this tricky gauntlet, but Heather made no move to answer the child. Exasperated, Elspeth sat down opposite Megan.

"He's busy with some work on the croft, pet. He'll be coming back soon." She reached over and tucked an errant curl behind Megan's ear.

Max's head shot up, and his eyes flicked over to his mother, whose head remained buried in the paper.

"That's not true," he spat. "He's not coming anymore because Mom yelled at him."

At this, Megan's face fell. She dropped her toast onto the plate and turned to her mother. "Mom?"

Heather slowly folded the paper, and then Elspeth saw her blink deliberately. She looked up at Elspeth, asking for help, but this was Heather's situation to deal with. Elspeth was still stinging from her daughter's rebuke of a few days ago, and backing off was exactly what she was going to do now. She shrugged, passing the baton back to Heather with her silence.

"Uncle Murdy and I had a little disagreement, but it's all OK now." Heather forced a smile.

"Then why isn't he coming around anymore?" Max frowned and then tore the crust off his toast.

"He will. He's just busy." Heather sighed.

"You're a liar." His eyes flashed. "You made him leave 'cuz you were mean."

"Max. Don't speak to your mother like that." Elspeth couldn't contain herself. Max had pushed it too far.

"Mum, it's OK. I've got this." Heather held a hand out, palm down. Her voice was controlled and her eyes clear. "Max, you just got yourself grounded for another day. Now please finish your breakfast and get your shoes on." She turned to Megan. "Eat up, honey, and get ready to go, OK?" Megan nodded sadly and popped the last bite of toast into her mouth as Max shoved his chair away from the table and stomped to the coatrack.

"I hate you." He hissed over his shoulder. "And I hate this stupid place." Grabbing his shoes, he flung the door open and then, stepping outside in his socks, he slammed it behind him.

Megan's eyes were wide as she glanced between her mother and grandmother.

"He doesn't mean it." She shook her head. "He's just sad."

Elspeth felt her heart tear a little. She reached out and wrapped an arm around Megan's tiny shoulders.

"We know that, love. Don't you worry. Everything'll be fine. You'll see."

Heather's eyes glittered as she stood up. She bent down and kissed the top of Megan's head.

"Love you, Megs."

Elspeth did some laundry while she waited for Heather to come back from dropping the children off at school. The scene at the breakfast table that morning had been heartbreaking, and now, whether it was interfering or not, she intended to talk to her daughter about what was going on between her and her brother. This was still Elspeth's home, after all, and she had every right to live in it peacefully.

Fifteen minutes later the car pulled into the driveway, and then Elspeth watched as Heather's outline appeared behind the glass panel in the door. She seemed to be hesitating outside, perhaps sensing that Elspeth had something on her mind. Eventually, the door opened and Heather came in. She slipped her shoes off, hung her coat on the rack, and walked into the kitchen.

"The kids get off OK?" Elspeth forced a smile.

"Yeah, they're fine." Heather sounded tired, defeated. "Listen, Mum. I'm sorry about that, earlier. He just oversteps sometimes." She moved in close and wrapped an arm around Elspeth's waist. "Testing me, I suppose." She squeezed her mother tightly.

"I understand. It's not exactly unique behavior, you know." Elspeth leaned her head over and rested her cheek against Heather's.

"No, I don't suppose so." Heather's minty breath felt cool on her face as Elspeth turned into her daughter's embrace. She wrapped her arms around Heather's bony frame and pulled her close.

"You and Murdo need to sort things out. It's difficult enough for the children without the two of you falling out." She spoke into Heather's hair.

Heather nodded against her shoulder and then pulled away.

"I know. I'll call him today." She smiled and then brushed her copper fringe away from her forehead. "It's daft, really, but I went to see Fraser after I pranged your car. I haven't told Murdo, and I think he'll be angry." She looked very vulnerable as she retucked her shirt into her jeans, and seeing a shadow of a much younger Heather, Elspeth's exasperation evaporated.

"Why would he be angry?"

"I always go to him, you know, when I've got a problem. But after what he said about Dad, I felt like I shouldn't always use him as a safety net." She turned toward the table.

"What did he say about Dad?" Elspeth felt a flutter in her chest as she watched Heather walk over and begin to straighten the chairs.

"Oh, nothing. He said something about me leaving and coming back, and some stuff about nobody making me." Heather was avoiding Elspeth's gaze, a clear indication that she was covering something up.

"What exactly did he say?"

Heather lifted her head and met Elspeth's eyes. "Look, it doesn't matter now. We just needed to clear the air, that's all. We're fine, Mum. Honest." She smiled.

Sensing that she would get no more information, Elspeth sighed.

"Well, just call him. This has gone on long enough." She nodded decisively and turned away. "I mean now—call him now."

CHAPTER 23

The following morning Heather stood at the window, waiting to see Murdoch's Land Rover appear. The dense hedges that ran along the driveway buckled, leaning in toward the house, as a crumpled paper bag skidded across the browning lawn. Winter was settling in.

The twins were playing a noisy game of snap at the kitchen table, and Elspeth had gone to the supermarket to stock up on soup-making supplies. Megan had picked up a nasty cold and so Heather intended on keeping her close to home over the weekend.

Heather had called Murdoch the night before and asked him to come over and had been relieved at the normalcy of his voice when he answered the phone. She was grateful that he didn't ask why she hadn't returned his calls, but instead had asked after the children.

"If Megan's confined to barracks, why don't I come and get Max in the morning? He can spend a few hours wi' me and see Chick."

"That'd be great." She had hesitated. "Murdo, I'm sorry about the other night."

He'd only waited a second or two before tutting.

"Och, forget it, Wee Blister. We're past it."

Heather felt relief seep into her bones. She hadn't slept well since they had argued, and she needed this unaccustomed rift to be healed. As she waited for him to say something more, despite knowing that she should probably leave well alone, she felt compelled to ask him about his remarks, which had been swirling around her head for two days.

"What you said about Dad dying, and about you taking care of everything here. I really didn't—"

He cut her off. "Look. We both said too much. Just forget it now, OK?"

His tone had been clear. The subject was closed.

As she focused on the empty driveway, Max trotted up behind her and unexpectedly slid his hand into hers. She felt his cool fingers under hers.

"Mom?"

"Yes, love."

"Is everything fixed, with Uncle Murdy?"

"Yes. It's fine." She squeezed his fingers and then pulled him close to her side. "I love you so much, Maximus. You know that, right?"

He nodded against her ribs.

"I'm sorry if I don't do everything right, buddy. Sometimes I make mistakes . . ."

Max pushed away from her. "You're hugging too hard. I can't breathe." He looked up at her and smiled.

Murdoch burst in the door, along with a gust of wind.

"God, it's bitter out there." He slammed the door behind him, crossed his arms, and then slapped his biceps. "Would freeze the brass—"

"Murdo!" Heather held up a warning finger and then gestured toward the children at the table.

"Oh, right." He grimaced as Megan trotted over and launched herself at him.

"Hey, Uncle Murdy."

"Get away from me, you—you're contaminated." He pulled his thick sweater up over his nose and gently pushed her away as Megan, laughing, tried to climb his thick limbs like a tree.

"No, no, it's the Black Death." Murdo picked her up by the arms and swung her away from him.

Heather rolled her eyes.

"You'll make her sick."

"She's sick already." Murdoch laughed as he lowered his giggling niece to the ground. "Now just simmer down, or I'll be in trouble." He winked at her.

Heather let Megan's laughter settle on her. The sound provided her with basic sustenance. Murdoch seemed to have the ability to bring it out in them, while she seemed to be gifted at taking it away. As she watched her daughter trip around behind her brother, Heather wondered if all single parents felt this way. She was a single parent now. It wasn't something she had ever put into words before, and the reality of the label bit into her.

She was sure that playing the bad guy wasn't a job any parent relished, but, to compound things, now she had no wingman to share the burden. When Brett had been alive, they had traded off coming down hard on the children. Heather had necessarily taken on the role of disciplinarian when Brett had been away flying. She'd established routines and ground rules, and the household had run smoothly in his absence. Then he would come home and immediately break the rules she'd set, making exceptions, letting the children get away with things that she didn't allow. It had driven her crazy, and she'd often taken him to task for it.

"You can't act like an overindulgent visiting uncle, Brett. You're their father."

She could see his hurt expression, even now. But as general discipline went out of the window whenever he came home after a few days away, she had wanted to shed the mean-mommy black hat as quickly as possible.

"I just got home. Why do I have to ground them for something they did while I was away?" he would growl.

"Because I'm the bad guy the entire time you're not here. I need to wear the white hat, too, sometimes."

She knew it was unreasonable to expect to hand things off so quickly, but she needed Brett to take his turn at saying no, too.

Now, as she watched Murdoch settle at the table and lean his big sandy head in close to Max's smaller one, she would have let Brett break every single rule, and then break them again, just to have him here with her.

Max and Murdoch had left for the croft an hour before, and Elspeth had started to wash a pile of leeks. Megan pouted, her raw little nose glowing, when she realized that Max was going to spend the morning with their uncle. But Heather had been firm, her black hat in place.

"Megs, you're ill. You need to stay home with Granny and me, otherwise you'll not be well enough for school on Monday. Do you want to miss country-dancing practice?"

Megan's lip quivered as she shook her head, but then, rather than join her grandmother in the kitchen, she had slunk up the stairs. Now, checking her watch, Heather realized that had been half an hour ago.

"I'm going to see what she's up to."

"OK, love."

Heather walked along the top floor hallway and could hear Megan's voice, soft, as if she were whispering. She imagined her telling her ponies a story or perhaps singing along to something that she was listening to on her iPad, but as she reached the bedroom door, she heard Chrissy's voice.

"Honey, you need to tell your mommy."

Heather stopped abruptly outside the bedroom door as Megan whispered again.

"I don't want to make her sad."

Heather reached for the door frame, careful not to make a sound.

"She'll understand, Megs. She loves you so much, and she wants you to tell her when you feel bad."

Megan sniffed, and it was all Heather could do to stay still, but something kept her rooted to the spot.

"Have you been to see our house?" Megan's words were interspersed with watery sniffs. "Is someone else living there now?"

Heather felt light-headed.

"I think so, sweetie." Chrissy's voice was soft.

There was no sound for a moment or two, and Heather imagined Megan staring at Chrissy's image on the screen.

"I miss my room." Megan's voice cracked.

Heather felt a stab of pain, but still she didn't move. While it was agonizing that Megan had chosen Chrissy to tell, at least she was telling someone that she was unhappy.

"I know, Megs. But you have a new room now, right?"

"Yeah. Max and me, we share. It's OK. Granny got me Merida towels."

"Well, that's cool, kiddo." Chrissy used the nickname that had always been guaranteed to make Megan smile.

"When are you coming?" Megan sniffed again.

"Soon, honey, I promise. I'll talk to your mom this weekend about some dates, OK?"

"OK."

"And Megan?"

"Yes."

"It's not good to be sad by yourself. You need to tell Mommy, sweetie. Do you promise?"

"OK."

Heather released the unconscious fist that she had been making. Megan was now crying softly. As she stood frozen to the spot, Heather listened to her daughter say good-bye to her aunt and was crushed by guilt. Her sweet little girl had been hiding her own unhappiness, protecting her from her homesickness and putting a smile on her face rather than come to her mother for comfort. To compound her guilt, Heather had been relying on Megan to help her with Max, to make allowances for him, even though she was just a child herself, and all the while Megan had been hurting and struggling silently. She had turned to her aunt, talking to her online, more than three thousand miles away via a seven-inch screen, rather than seek out her mother, press her head into her lap, and ask for help.

Heather felt her legs begin to quiver. What kind of parent was she? What kind of mother would not have seen that happening under her nose? She released her grip on the door frame. What had she done to her little family, dragging them here and making them miserable? She'd brought them to a place that should have been a sanctuary for them all, and yet, even she didn't fit in anymore.

Swallowing against the sudden threat of nausea, she pulled her shoulders down, gently pushed the door open, and stepped into the room.

"Megs, honey. Are you here?"

CHAPTER 24

Elspeth shifted in the armchair next to the fire. Everyone was out, and she had the Forge to herself for the first time in weeks. The silence was soothing, and even as she acknowledged the relief of it, she felt bad about feeling that way.

It had been two weeks since Heather and Murdoch's argument, and she was relieved that they seemed to have sorted things out. Murdoch was coming for breakfast again, often with Fraser in tow, and the children seemed to be more settled, as if they were gaining confidence in their place on Skye. In fact, their presence had begun to pervade the entire house, their clothes filtering down from their room and being left strewn on the furniture. Small pairs of shoes had started creeping from the hall into the living room, board games were now piled up behind the sofa instead of being put back on the shelf in the office, and homework formed a permanent layer of paper on the kitchen table.

Elspeth sipped her coffee and inspected the room. Having walked and fed Charlie and then put some laundry into the machine, she'd gathered various shoes and put them back under the coatrack, moved Max's backpack and jacket from the stairs and hung them on hooks, tidied Megan's artwork into one pile at the end of the table, and even retrieved and folded Heather's sweater, which had been stuffed behind a cushion on the sofa.

Nestling the mug in her lap, Elspeth felt its warmth against her thighs. Charlie was curled at her feet, and with the room being somewhat back in order, she relaxed against the cushion and leaned her head back. She disliked disorder, but Heather seemed to thrive on it. As she shook her head against the soft leather, Elspeth realized that the children obviously took their lead from their mother in that regard.

Heather had always been a messy pup. Whenever they had crossed swords in the past, it had inevitably been over one of two things—her defiance or her mess. She had been a headstrong child, and Elspeth had seen that develop into a deep-set independence that sometimes left her feeling superfluous in her daughter's life. She had tried not to be petulant whenever Heather would launch herself into some new project or interest and not mention it to Elspeth. It had caused tension between them in the past, just as the chaos that was pervading her home was beginning to now.

She glanced at the clock on the mantel, closed her eyes, and exhaled into the warm room. She had another hour before the troops got back, so a short nap wouldn't be a bad idea.

The door flew open, and as it hit the wall, Elspeth jerked awake, her heart racing. The coffee cup had slipped down her lap and with the jolt, the dregs of cold liquid sloshed onto her trousers. Instantly angry, she jumped up from the chair.

"For God's sake, you lot," she shouted toward the noisy group, "you're like a herd of elephants." She brushed at her legs and turned toward the kitchen.

Behind her, she heard a moment of silence and then whispering. Heather was telling the children to settle down and they were giggling under their breaths, obviously amused by Granny's outburst. The fact that they found it funny made Elspeth all the angrier. Having rubbed roughly at her trousers with a tea towel, she thumped the mug into the sink and went back into the living room.

In the doorway were Megan's trainers, which Elspeth pointedly kicked to one side. Inside the room, Heather had dumped two shopping bags on the coffee table, knocking some magazines onto the floor. Max lay in front of the fire flipping through a book, his coat having been thrown over the back of the armchair where Elspeth had been sitting. As she watched, Megan squealed and began chasing a barking Charlie around the room. Heather, seeming not to notice any of the mayhem, looked at her phone. Elspeth felt her temples begin to throb. This was too much.

"Enough!" she shouted at Megan. "Stop, Megan. Leave Charlie."

Heather's head snapped up.

"I've just tidied up, and now look at this place." Elspeth swept her hand around the room. "It's a disaster area."

Heather shoved her phone into her back pocket and walked over to Megan, who was standing behind the sofa, her mouth slightly open. Max was now sitting upright on the fireside rug, staring at Heather for a cue as to what to do next. No one spoke as Elspeth tried to slow her breathing down.

"Sorry. We'll tidy up." Heather was moving Megan toward the door and gesturing to Max to get up.

"Yes, you will. Because I'm tired of doing it for all of you." Elspeth was spent. She hadn't meant to be spiteful, but this was the last straw. She was too old for this.

Heather ushered the children into the kitchen and then told them to go upstairs. As she walked back into the living room, she gathered up the children's belongings. Silently, she lifted the bags from the coffee table and scanned the room before heading toward the staircase.

"Heather, come back." Elspeth now felt the crush of regret, as she'd known she would.

"It's OK, Mum. We'll go upstairs for a bit. Give you some space." Heather spoke over her shoulder as she mounted the stairs. At the sight of the narrow back moving away from her, Elspeth felt the prickle of tears. Damn. That had not been what she'd intended to happen.

Two hours later, Heather padded into the living room. Her hair was pulled up in a tight bun, and her face looked freshly scrubbed. She wore a pair of baggy sweatpants tucked into thick socks and an oversize sweatshirt with the letters *VT* on the front. As soon as she saw it, Elspeth remembered it as having been Brett's.

"Hi, Mum." She sounded sheepish.

"Hi, love." Elspeth put her book down and made to get up.

"No, sit. I'll make us some tea." Heather patted the air and walked out of the room.

Elspeth felt her heart quicken. Heather looked so vulnerable and tired. What had she, Elspeth, been thinking, shouting at her family that way? Unable to wait for Heather to come back, she stood up and followed her into the kitchen.

Heather's back was to her as, on tiptoe, she pulled mugs down from the cupboard.

"I'm sorry. I didn't mean to lose my temper like that." Elspeth swallowed over a walnut. "I just got such a fright and . . ."

Heather turned to face her. Her expression was calm and her eyes dry and focused.

"No, I'm sorry. We're a lot to take in, and sometimes I forget you're not used to all this." Heather stretched her arms out, the sleeves of the sweatshirt hanging over her small hands. "We're noisy and messy and bring all kinds of chaos with us." She shrugged. "It won't happen again." She looked at Elspeth and waited.

Elspeth felt her heart skip. She had made them feel unwelcome, and that was the last thing she'd intended to do.

"I enjoy your chaos. Well, most of it." She smiled. "I love you all so much. I'm just a bit set in my ways, I suppose."

Heather stepped forward and slipped her arms around Elspeth's waist.

Elspeth hugged her daughter.

"But that's no excuse for shouting at you. I'm sorry, love. You know you're all welcome here for as long as you want, don't you?" She leaned back and took in Heather's expression. There was something different about the set of her jaw.

"Heather?"

"I think it's time we started to look for our own place." She smiled. "We don't want to outstay our welcome, and to be honest, the kids need more space, too."

Elspeth felt a jab to her middle. Had she done this? Made them want to leave?

"Heather, I didn't mean that you should go. God, I didn't mean . . ."

"No, Mum. I absolutely know that. But I've been thinking about it for a week or so. We need to move out sometime, and the sooner the twins and I have our own place, the sooner they'll feel like this is really their home." Heather smiled, and Elspeth sensed the truth in her daughter's words. Rather than look petulant or hurt, Heather appeared to be clearheaded and even happy about the decision, and for that, Elspeth found that she was undeniably grateful.

CHAPTER 25

Elspeth lifted the heavy shopping bags into the back of her car. The twins had hung on to the trolley all the way around the supermarket, grabbing things and asking her what they were or if they could please have them. She'd refused some of their requests but had capitulated on many.

She had picked them up from school, as Heather had gone to meet an estate agent about a cottage that was for rent nearby, in Peiness. Elspeth had seen the details of the house, and it looked perfect. While she was feeling mildly sad about the prospect of them moving out, she couldn't deny that she was hopeful that this cottage could be the answer to their current living situation.

She watched as the twins buckled themselves into the car seats that Murdoch had installed in the back of her old Ford.

"You all in safely?"

"Yep." Megan smiled.

"OK. Let's go home and get the dinner started. Mummy said she'd be home at five, so we have time to bake some biscuits, if you like?" Elspeth smiled encouragingly at Max. She knew he liked to roll his sleeves up and join her in the kitchen.

"Can I make the ginger ones?" His hopeful eyes met hers.

"Of course. Those are easy-peasy." She grinned. Hoping this show of interest might open the door to further conversation, Elspeth got into the car and twisted the rearview mirror so that she could see Max's face.

"So, what did you do in school today?"

Max sniffed and then wiped his nose on his sleeve.

"Max?"

He looked up and met her gaze.

"Some stupid experiment on the weather." He spoke around the edge of a finger he was gnawing.

"Don't do that. You'll make it bleed." Megan reached out and pulled his hand from his mouth.

"Get off. You can't tell me what to do," Max snarled at his sister. "Little Miss Bossy."

Megan recoiled, her eyes widening, and Elspeth thought she could see them begin to fill up.

"Max. That wasn't nice. Say you're sorry to Megan, please."

Max mumbled an apology. Megan nodded silently and then turned to look out the window.

The drive back to the Forge was quiet. The children stared fixedly out of their windows, and despite Elspeth's attempts to engage them in conversation, they remained silent.

She was still worried about Heather, who seemed to go from being pensive and withdrawn to overly cheerful, her voice brittle and forced. She was taking early-morning walks, and Elspeth had encouraged the activity, as her daughter seemed to be enjoying the time alone at the start of the day.

The previous evening, Elspeth had urged her to go out for a drink with Murdoch, Fraser, and Jenny, her friend Marjorie's daughter, who was visiting from Inverness. Jenny was an architect and was sweet on Murdoch, and Elspeth suspected the feeling was mutual, despite the distance and the time between Jenny's visits. Heather had refused to go out, saying that she didn't want to leave the children at night in case they woke or had nightmares. Elspeth did not take offense at the dismissal of her ability to cope with a nightmare—rather, she recognized it as Heather's avoidance of a social scenario.

With the car safely tucked away at the end of the drive and the shopping bags piled on the countertop, Elspeth watched as the children clattered up the stairs. Backpacks were discarded halfway up the staircase, and shoes, coats, and scarves lay strewn around the living room. As she scanned the mess, she sighed. She would have them tidy up when they came back down. For now, she needed to get the meat into a pan so that dinner wouldn't be too late.

After half an hour, the stew was in the oven. As she laid the table, the unusual silence became concerning, so Elspeth went upstairs to check on the children.

Max was lying on his bed with his feet tucked under the extra quilt that was folded at the end. He held his iPad high above his head, and Elspeth assumed that he was reading something.

Megan sat on the floor. Her pony toys were lined up neatly along the bottom edge of her bed, their backsides tucked under the long coverlet and their heads facing out into the room. She held a pink pony on her lap and was carefully combing its glossy mane.

"Are you coming down to bake some biscuits?" Elspeth stood in the doorway and addressed Max. "We have time."

"Sure. Now?" Max dropped the iPad onto the bed, and to Elspeth's pleasure, he sat up and smiled at her.

"Yes, now. If we hurry, we can get them finished before Mummy gets home."

Max stood up. He had pulled a dark blue fleece on top of his school shirt, and Elspeth didn't have the heart to tell him to change.

As he passed her, she reached down and wrapped her arms around her grandson's bony frame.

"I'm so glad you two are here." Max did not resist her embrace. "Come on, tykes, let's bake."

Max extricated himself from her arms and turned to his sister.

"Last one down's a dork."

Megan squealed, and before Elspeth knew it, they were all three headed for the stairs in a knot of feet, arms, and hands.

With Elspeth in front, the children shoved each other and laughed as they trotted down the first stairs. Megan then managed to slip in front of her grandmother, and Max, who was trapped behind, eager not to let his sister win the race to the kitchen, pushed at Elspeth's back, trying to get around her.

"Be careful, you two." Elspeth tried to slow the alarming momentum that carried her forward and threatened to unbalance her. "Stop. Slow down, children," she shouted, but before the words were out, she felt herself disconnected from the stair under her feet. Max had shoved past her, and as she tried to lift her left leg to place it on the lower step, it was lassoed by something. Her ankles felt hobbled as she grabbed blindly for the banister, her body falling forward, heavy and out of control.

The first stab of pain was to her right ankle as it twisted awkwardly underneath her. Next was a tearing in her knee as it gave way, sending her right shoulder out into thin air. Elspeth reached out to touch the wall, trying to stop herself barreling forward. The frail effort of her arms was no match for the weight of her body, and as her side slammed onto the stair, her torso flipped over, sending her into a somersault. As she rolled, she felt the hard lips of each steps against her back, her side, and her thighs and the graze of carpet on her cheek. As her pelvis finally smacked onto the ground in the hall, a laser of pain shot down her left leg.

She was aware of someone shouting and tried to focus on the sound. It was a child, afraid, panicked. The voice grew dimmer as the pain in her back built. It was so bad that it threatened to take her breath away with each blink of her suddenly leaden eyelids.

"Granny Elspeth. Granny?" Megan was at her side, her face pale and her eyes like saucers. "Are you OK?"

Elspeth felt the bone in her hip grind as she tried to shift her leg out from underneath her. She let out an involuntary yelp, and her grand-daughter burst into tears.

"Oh, Granny. You're hurt." Megan knelt close and swiped at her cheeks as Elspeth ran a mental inventory of her pain.

Her ankle and knee throbbed. Her left leg was probably broken, and the pain in her back could mean even worse. Afraid to move and potentially pass out, leaving the twins alone, she pushed down a wave of nausea and reached for Megan's hand.

"Sweetheart. Get Max, and get the phone from the kitchen. Can you do that for Granny?" She felt light-headed. She must not faint.

Megan nodded and sniffed.

"Max. Max, where are you?" Megan stood and shouted into the hall behind her. There was no sign of her brother.

"I can't find him." She looked down at her grandmother.

"OK. Never mind. Just get Granny the phone, pet. Hurry now."

Elspeth dialed Heather's number and waited as the phone connected.

"Hi, Mum. I'll be about half an hour. Sadie is taking me to see another cottage, up near Achachork."

Elspeth felt bile rise in her throat.

"Heather, listen. You need to come home now. I've had a fall." The words sounded so matter-of-fact, so stark.

"What's happened? Are you all right? Where are the kids?"

Elspeth heard the panic in her daughter's voice.

"I'm all right, love, but I can't move, so I need you to come, now. The children are fine." She scanned the room for any sign of Max.

Megan sat on the floor next to her, her small hand lying lightly on Elspeth's shoulder.

"I'm on my way. I'll call an ambulance. Hang on Mum, I'm coming."

Heather ran up the driveway. The ambulance lights were flashing, casting an orange glow across the side of the Forge. The back door was open, and she could hear static and then someone talking on a radio. The kitchen was empty, so she followed the noise into the front hall. Her mother was being lifted onto a stretcher, and as the two paramedics moved her, Elspeth whimpered in pain.

Megan stood across the hall with her back up against the grandfather clock. She was transfixed, ashen, and Max was nowhere to be seen. Heather crossed the space and pulled Megan into her arms.

"It's all right, sweetie. Mummy's here now."

Turning back to her mother, Heather paled.

"Mum. Oh, my God. What happened?" She reached Elspeth's side and lifted her hand from the thin blanket that covered her.

Elspeth had an oxygen mask on her face, which she shoved away with a shaky hand.

"Fell down the stairs. An accident. I'm OK." She gasped between words.

"Keep that on, love," the paramedic instructed Elspeth, and then with a nod, he directed Heather, with Megan still clinging to her, into the kitchen.

"It seems she fell down the stairs. Looks like she got her foot caught in a backpack." The young man pointed toward the hallway and shrugged. "Spider-Man."

Heather nodded, not totally registering what was being said.

"Is she badly hurt?"

"From what we can see at this point, a broken leg, possibly pelvis, and maybe some bruised ribs. She'll need to be checked for internal injuries, so we're taking her to Broadford Hospital. You and your daughter can come in the ambulance, if you want?" The man looked down at Megan, whose head was buried in her mother's side.

Heather nodded again.

"I just need to find my son, then we'll all come." She looked around the hall.

"Max?" She called his name and then gently peeled Megan from her side. She tried again. "Max, honey?"

There being no response, Heather turned to the paramedic.

"Have you seen my son?"

The man shook his head.

"I didn'y see anyone else. Just the wee girl." He inclined his head toward the door. "We've got to go now, miss."

Heather felt a lead weight settle on her chest. Where was Max? Perhaps he was hiding up in his room, scared by all the activity.

"Megs. I need you to put your coat on and then stay here and wait for me. I'll be two minutes. I'm just going to go up and get Max. OK?" She turned toward the stair, where the blue-and-red Spider-Man backpack lay at the bottom, the strap ripped from one edge and the contents strewn across the floor.

"He's not up there," Megan whispered.

"Where is he, then?" Heather leaned down and took Megan's shoulders in her hands. "Megan?

Megan swallowed.

"I think he ran outside when Granny fell. I called him, but he didn't come." Megan shrugged as a fat tear rolled down her cheek. "I'm sorry, Mommy."

Heather felt as if her heart would crack through her sternum.

"It's not your fault. I'll find him, and Granny will be fine."

She sat Megan on the sofa in the living room and then pounded up the stairs. Galloping along the hallway, she checked each room as she passed. Not finding her son, she mounted the stairs to the top floor two at a time. Chances were he was in his room with earphones on, or perhaps hiding under his quilt.

"Max. Maximus, are you here?" Trying not to sound angry or panicked, Heather fought to control her breathing. There was no response. No sound of any kind. As she ran into the twins' bedroom, cold silence greeted her, and Max's iPad lay on his bed.

"Max!" She yelled into the silence and then held her breath, waiting for anything that would burst the bubble of terror that had engulfed her.

Silence. She turned and ran full pelt back down the stairs. Where could he have gone? She had to go to the hospital, but she couldn't leave the house until she found Max. As she trotted through the living room, she waved at Megan.

"Stay put. I'll be right back." The little girl, now wearing her coat, nodded silently.

Back outside, Heather ran around behind the ambulance. Elspeth lay motionless on the stretcher as one of the paramedics slid a blood pressure sleeve around her arm.

"We have to go. We can't wait any longer." The young man looked over at Heather as the radio on his shoulder crackled.

"I can't find my son. I can't find him." Heather felt the mounting blackness of the evening closing in on her.

Elspeth lifted her head from the pillow and shoved the oxygen mask aside.

"Stay. Find him. I'm all right." She coughed and lay back as the paramedic lifted an IV bag and hooked it on to a stand beside the stretcher.

"Right. Let's go." He spoke to his colleague.

"I'll be there as soon as I can, Mum. I won't be long. I'll call Murdo." Heather patted Elspeth's hand. Then the paramedic gently pushed her aside so that he could close the double doors.

She watched the vehicle backing down the driveway, her heart being torn in two at it leaving without her. She should be with her mother, and yet, where was Max? Had he run off into the night, terrified by the commotion? As the blinding headlights disappeared behind the hedge, Heather ran through the nightmare scenarios that suddenly filled her head. He had been hit by a car, or perhaps fallen over and knocked himself out. He was lying by the road somewhere, hurt, where she couldn't get to him. He was lost, somewhere in the night, afraid and alone.

Snapping back to the moment, she pulled her phone out of her pocket and searched Murdoch's number. Her hands shook so violently that she had to make a fist with one and then the other in order to dial. She could not imagine how much pain her mother was in, but worse than that, she could not imagine the agony of losing Max. That would, without question, be her undoing.

CHAPTER 26

Murdoch pulled the Land Rover into the hospital car park. His heart was racing as he slammed the door and ran toward the entrance. Heather had sounded traumatized when she called, and while he was anxious to see his mother, the idea of Max having run away was tearing at him. Heather had been crying, and the sound of her fear had curdled his blood. He knew she couldn't take much more before she crumbled into a shadow of the sister he knew. Where had the child gone?

Having checked in at reception, Murdoch slumped into a chair to wait. The room was dimly lit, and opposite him a woman was asleep, lying across three chairs against the wall. Elspeth was apparently in the X-ray department, so he would have to wait for her to come out before they could tell him how badly she had been hurt. He slowed his breathing and glanced around the room, looking for a vending machine. He always got hungry when he was nervous, and who knew how long it would be before there was any news on his mother's condition.

With a Twix and a can of Coke in hand, Murdoch settled himself in one of the hard plastic seats. As he tore the wrapper off the chocolate bar, he stared down at his mud-caked boots. Elspeth would have scolded him for the mess that he had dragged inside, and the thought of her tutting and wagging her finger at him stole his untimely appetite. He threw the chocolate away in a nearby bin and slid the unopened can into his coat pocket.

An hour later, worried that they had forgotten about him, Murdoch was about to shout hello when a nurse in pale blue scrubs walked toward him.

"Mr. MacDonald?" She was round faced and fair skinned with glasses pushed up into her mass of curly hair.

"Aye. That's me." Murdoch blushed.

"Your mother is out of X-ray and in a room. Would you like to see her?" She shifted a pile of clipboards up against her stomach.

"Yes. How is she?" He was suddenly self-conscious, newly aware of his mud-spattered trousers and mucky boots.

"She's resting. We've given her something for the pain and set her leg. She'll probably sleep until the morning now." The nurse smiled up at him. "She was lucky, really. A broken femur and pelvis, a couple of bruised ribs, some scrapes and bruising, but no internal injuries, thank goodness."

Murdoch swallowed. *Lucky* wasn't the word he would have used to describe that catalog of injuries, but he supposed it could have been much worse.

Elspeth lay still. Her leg was in a cast from the hip to the ankle, and her face was flushed in sleep. Murdoch sat down as carefully as he could in the spindly chair at her bedside. He watched as his mother's eyelids fluttered, and he hoped that she wouldn't wake up and be in pain. He had never been good at handling other people's pain. A memory of seeing his father in his last days stabbed at him. Matthew had been stoic and had tried to keep the mood light, even when his family knew that he was in agony. Murdoch had cracked jokes about how they would go on the mother of all pub crawls when he was up and around again, and his father had smiled and nodded, letting his son hide from the reality of his good-bye.

Murdoch shifted in the creaking chair.

"Sit still, can't you?" Elspeth spoke without opening her eyes.

"Och, sorry, Mother. I didn't want to wake you," he whispered.

"I was awake anyway. Just resting." She turned her head to him and smiled. "So, I've made a bit of a pickle of myself."

Murdoch reached out and lifted her hand in his great paw.

"Aye. You've done a great job, woman." He let out a low chuckle. "I've told you before not to do cartwheels down those stairs."

Elspeth's smile faded as quickly as it had come.

"Did she find Max?"

"I need to call her again and check. I'm sure she did. Don't worry."

Murdoch glanced at the clock on the wall opposite the bed. It had been almost two hours since he had spoken to Heather, when he had told her to call the police. There had been no updates since.

"Call her. Now. Go. I'm fine here, and she needs you." She shooed him toward the door.

Murdoch walked out into the corridor to make the call. Heather answered on the third ring.

"Hi. Did you find him?"

"Oh, Murdo. No. I can't breathe. I can't . . . he's gone." Heather was choking through sobs, and the sound of her fear was deafening.

"I'll come."

"What about Mum? What's happening?" Heather coughed into his ear.

"She's resting. A broken leg and pelvis, some cuts and bruises, but the nurse says she was lucky." He peered back into the room. Elspeth had closed her eyes, and her chest rose and fell rhythmically. He hoped the medication was kicking in and she was indeed asleep this time. Not only did he not want her to be in pain, but if she was awake, she would inevitably be worrying about Max and Heather, which would not help her at all.

Fifteen minutes later, he walked into the kitchen at the Forge. Heather was at the table with a female police officer, and another policeman stood at the door to the hall, talking on his phone.

Murdoch nodded at the policeman and walked behind Heather. He knelt down at her side and put an arm around her back.

"I'm her brother. Any news of Max?"

The policewoman was holding a small photograph of Max and Megan taken in Virginia. She shook her head.

Heather sniffed. "No. They're looking all along the Brae and into the village. They said I should wait here in case he comes back." She searched Murdoch's face for guidance.

"Aye. That makes sense. Where's Megan?" He stood and planted a kiss on top of his sister's head.

"She's asleep on the sofa in the living room." Heather spoke quietly as tears ran down her face and over her top lip. "Can you check on her?"

Murdoch nodded and padded away.

Megan was lying with her head on a cushion, her diminutive frame creating a small mound under a tartan blanket. Her hair was tousled and splayed over the cushion, and her hands were curled up under her chin like paws.

Murdoch lifted an additional blanket from the basket behind the sofa, leaned over, and gently laid it on top of his sleeping niece.

"Uncle Murdy. Did they find Max?" Her big eyes were open, and a tiny, uncharacteristic frown line crept down toward the bridge of her nose.

"Not yet, pet. But it won't be long." He brushed the hair away from her face and tucked the blankets tighter around her back.

"Are you going to look for him?"

"Aye. I'm going to go and help the policemen. I'll get Chick, and we'll keep looking until we find him. Don't you worry."

Megan nodded. Then, as he straightened up to leave, she reached out and grabbed his hand.

"I think he was afraid. He was afraid because he hurt Granny." Megan's eyes were watery.

"What do you mean, he hurt Granny?" Murdoch knelt down next to the sofa and held Megan's hand.

"He pushed her, by mistake, and then she fell because of his back-pack." Her eyelids looked heavy. "Mommy is always telling him not to leave his bag on the stairs." She eyed her uncle. "Do you think he's hiding?"

Murdoch stood up and ran a hand over his hair.

"He might be. He shouldn't be afraid, though. He didn't mean to hurt Granny, and when we find him, we'll tell him that. OK?" He looked down at his niece.

Megan nodded and slid her hand back under her chin.

"Love you, Uncle Murdy." She yawned and closed her eyes.

In the kitchen, Heather had a steaming mug in front of her and a blanket around her shoulders. The female officer was sitting opposite her, and Heather was describing Max's clothes as the woman wrote in a notebook. The other policeman had left the room, and the back door was ajar. Heather was ashen as she lifted the mug to her lips.

"So, Mr. MacDonald. When was the last time you saw your nephew?" The policewoman indicated the chair next to her.

"This morning. At breakfast." Murdoch remained standing, looked across at Heather, and widened his eyes. Did they really think he had something to do with this?

As if reading his mind, Heather placed her mug down and shook her head.

"My brother came for breakfast around seven. He left at seven forty-five, and then I took the children to school." Her face was dry now, and her eyes flashed. "They were fine when I left them, and then my mother picked them up this afternoon. As I've said, I had an appointment in the village."

Murdoch registered the edge in her voice.

The policewoman's gaze swiveled back and forth between the siblings, and then she closed her notebook and addressed Murdoch.

"Please understand. We need to ask these questions as part of our inquiry. It's routine, and nothing's implied by it."

Heather visibly softened.

"I know. I'm sorry. It's just that it seems as if we'd be better off out looking for him rather than sitting here, with you asking his uncle when he last saw him." She swallowed. "It feels futile." She looked at her brother. "My mother fell down the stairs because she tripped on Max's backpack. That we know for sure. He probably panicked and ran, because he knew he had done wrong. I know my son, Officer."

The young woman stood up and carried her empty mug to the sink.

"Well, I suggest you keep your phone with you, but try to get some rest. We'll be in touch if we learn anything new."

Color flooded Heather's face, and Murdoch, sensing the impending verbal explosion that his sister was prone to, trapped her hand underneath his.

"Thanks, Officer. I'll see she gets some rest."

As the police car pulled out of the driveway, Murdoch turned to see Heather putting on her coat.

"Where are you going?" He closed the kitchen door.

"To look for him. He can't have gone far, and it's freezing out there." Her face was freshly wet.

"Just slow down, Wee Blister. I think you should stay here with Megan and let me look for him. I'll go and get Chick and Fraser. We'll split up to cover more ground. If we find him, I'll call you right away." He watched as his words sank in. "Megan is scared, and when she wakes up, she'll need her mum."

Heather seemed to be letting the logic of what he was saying settle on her. Then she walked over to him and gripped his arm.

"You need to find him, Murdo. I just can't . . ."

"I know. I'll find him. I will."

CHAPTER 27

Heather looked down at her phone for the umpteenth time. It was close to one a.m., and she hadn't heard from Murdoch for a couple of hours. The temptation to call him again was agonizing, but she placed the phone back on the coffee table and pulled the blanket tighter around herself and Megan, who now lay with her head on her mother's lap. Charlie was in a tight curl at her feet. His heavy head was on her foot, and each time she moved, he twitched his ears but didn't lift it.

She looked down at the painful perfection of her daughter's face, a reflection of her twin brother's. Her peachy skin was luminous in the firelight and her hair like spun copper. The gossamer tresses rolled into soft, natural curls that Heather could slip her little finger inside. Megan's mouth was slightly open, and her lips moved with each exhale of minty breath. Lurking under her eyes, the dark pink smudges from where she had been crying were the only things marring the angelic countenance.

Heather ran a hand through her hair and sighed. Max had been gone for nine hours now, and the idea of him being outside without the proper clothes was torturing her. What if someone had passed him on the road and abducted him? All the grotesque thoughts of what might have happened continued to plague her as her eyes swept the familiar and yet now oddly discomfiting room. As she stared into the orange glow of the embers, her sternum tight and her throat raw, Heather heard Brett's voice in her head.

"He's OK, honey. He's going to come home."

Heather let out a whimper and pressed her eyelids closed. It was almost impossible to breathe when she considered that Max, her little alter ego, one of her precious bookend babies, might not come back to her. She could withstand pretty much anything but that.

Megan stirred at the noise her mother had made and opened her eyes, as Charlie pricked up his ears and climbed stealthily onto the sofa.

"Is he back?" Megan lifted a small fist and ground it into her eye.

"Not yet, honey. Uncle Murdy's looking." She smiled at her daughter.

"Did the police come back?" Megan pushed herself up to a sitting position and curled into Heather's side.

"Not yet. They're still looking, too." She dragged the blanket over and rewrapped Megan in it.

Megan yawned.

"Will he be in trouble when he gets home? He didn't mean it, you know."

Heather shook her head.

"He won't be in trouble for Granny's accident, but he shouldn't have run off, Megs. We never do that when we have a problem—right? We talk about it, we face it, and then we fix it, together."

Megan nodded silently and nuzzled in closer, her shoulder blade fitting into Heather's armpit.

"Can I have a drink?"

"Sure. What do you want?" Heather stood up from the softness of the sofa and shivered. She needed to put more wood on the fire before it went out.

It was bitterly cold outside. The wind ripped at her coat as she loaded the old copper bucket with six long logs and carried them inside. Slamming the kitchen door behind her, she hefted the wood to the fireside. Even in the few moments she had been outside without gloves, her fingers had become red and stiff with cold. Her mind went back to Max's gloves on the kitchen table and his hat slung over the back of a chair.

As she pulled the fireguard aside and piled new logs onto the embers, she once again took a mental inventory of what he was wearing—his gray school trousers, a cotton shirt, and the fleece that Megan had told her he had put on when he got back from school. Thin socks (because he hated the scratchiness of wool) and the black leather school shoes that offered little to no protection from the elements.

An image of him lying still in a ditch with blue lips and stiff limbs made her stomach churn. She shoved the guard back into place and rushed out to the small bathroom off the hall.

With her cold hands on the even colder porcelain, she leaned over and vomited, her empty stomach collapsing in on itself, looking for something to expel. She couldn't think about Max being hurt. She simply could not think it.

Megan was dozing when Heather returned to the living room with a cup of hot chocolate. Charlie had inched his way up next to her daughter, and his black snout was close to Megan's face. A day earlier, the proximity of the dog's mouth to her daughter's might have bothered her, but now it was in some way comforting.

"Here you go, sweetie." She placed the cup down on a coaster. "Sit up and have your chocolate."

Megan complied, bundling the blanket around her hips as she reached for the cup. She dug the fingers of one hand deep into Charlie's coat and, with the other, picked up the hot drink and blew on the surface.

"Max will be so cold. He didn't have his coat."

Heather settled herself next to her daughter.

"Do you remember if he said anything to you before he left?" Heather pulled a corner of the blanket over her own thighs.

"No. He heard Granny shout when she fell, and then I went to help her. She asked me to get Max, but he was gone."

CHAPTER 28

Murdoch's Land Rover bumped along Home Farm Road for the fourth time. The headlights flashed ahead, revealing nothing but a few pools of water that had accumulated in the potholes and the occasional prick of yellow as the beams reflected off some night creature's eyes. He and Fraser had split up, Fraser taking the roads north of their crofts and Murdoch focusing on the ones south, between Achachork and Portree. He knew that his nephew couldn't have gone too far, especially as he didn't know his way around the island. The only places Max had been so far were into the village with Elspeth and Heather, back and forth to school, and out to Murdoch's croft, which was three miles from the Forge—too far for Max to have made it on his own in the dark.

Murdoch peered into the darkness and bit down on the inside of his cheek. He had dropped the ball. He should have seen something like this coming. Max had been hovering close to the edge for weeks, going back and forth between being quiet and being totally uncommunicative. The fight incident at school had been yet another setback. What kind of father figure did he hope to be if he couldn't focus on the kids and see what was happening? He shook his head.

Chick sat on the passenger seat. Seeming to sense the urgency of their unusual nighttime foray, the dog was alert, his nose pressed up against the cold glass, his ears pricked forward.

"Keep 'em peeled, boy. He's got to be here somewhere."

Murdoch slammed his foot onto the brake as a small deer ventured out into the road up ahead. Chick lurched, his front legs tensing against the forward momentum, and then he widened his stance to steady himself.

"Sorry, lad. Didn't see that."

The dog sniffed the air and then resumed his watch out the window.

Murdoch's phone rang, and he fished it out of his pocket.

"Anything yet?" It was Fraser.

"Nope. Nothing. I'm back on Home Farm Road. Where are you?"

"I'm up on Shepherd's Road. It's so bloody dark, though. I keep thinking I've seen him, then it turns out to be a fox or something."

"Aye. Me, too. I'm going to call Heather again, see if the police have been back to the Forge." Murdoch indicated left at a junction even though there was no one behind him in the blackness. "Thanks, pal. Really appreciate this." His voice wavered.

"Don't mention it. How's your mum?"

"She's sleeping. I called the hospital a while ago. They said she'll be out until the morning. A blessing, really." Murdoch frowned.

"True enough. Well, call me when you've spoken to Heather, OK?" With that, Fraser was gone.

Heather's phone only rang twice before she answered. The police had called her to say that they had not seen or found anything yet. They were planning on waiting until morning, then forming a search party, with officers and local volunteers, to walk the moor from Portree to Achachork.

When Murdoch had spoken to her, Heather had been sobbing, saying that Max might not survive the night if he was out in the cold, and Murdoch knew that to be true. Only a few years ago, a lone hiker had become disoriented out on the moor, and some local walkers had found him frozen inside his tent two days later.

Murdoch shook the grisly image from his mind and headed back toward the Forge. From the sound of things, Heather needed some company and a dose of reassurance before he set out for the next wave of searching.

He walked into the kitchen at two fifteen a.m., and Heather was pacing the floor with her phone at her ear.

"What do you mean? Where was it?" Her voice was rough, and her eyes were glazed over.

"What's happening?" Murdoch mouthed.

She closed her eyes tight, shook her head, and then her knees buckled as she slid down the kitchen cabinet onto the floor.

Murdoch bent and took the phone from her trembling hand.

"Hello. Who's this?"

"It's Sergeant Finlay. Is Mrs. Forester all right?" The concern in the man's voice surprised Murdoch.

"She's OK. I'm her brother. What's going on?" Murdoch had no time for pleasantries.

"I was just telling her that we've found a shoe. It's black leather, a boy's shoe that could possibly be her son's. One of our patrol cars was heading back to the station, and an officer spotted it on the Brae."

Murdoch felt a wave of cold move from his chest up to his face.

"Can you bring it here?" His voice was low.

Heather now hugged her knees and had begun rocking. He moved over and sat down next to her.

"Yes. I'll be there in a while."

Murdoch put the phone down and cradled Heather in his arms. Her breaths were coming in short bursts, and while there were no tears, he could feel her shuddering.

"Breathe, Wee Blister. It's just a shoe. It doesn't mean anything, and we don't even know if it's Max's." Even as he said it, he knew that he sounded less than convincing.

Heather abruptly shook her head and jumped up from the floor.

"No. Murdoch, it is his, I know it. He is dead. Max is dead." Her voice pierced the quiet of the room.

"Wheesht, Heather. You'll scare Megan." He cast a glance over his shoulder to check the door to the living room. Seeing no movement, he turned back to his sister. "Stop it now. Do you hear me?" He was up on his feet and following her progress around the kitchen table. Catching up to her, he pulled at her resistant arm.

"Hear me, Heather MacDonald. Max is not dead." He locked his arms around her, until gradually she stopped pulling against him. "Do you hear me?" He whispered now and looked down at the top of her copper head. She nodded slowly, and he released his grip on her. She stepped back.

"It's Forester, dammit." Heather wiped her nose with her sleeve and then ran a shaky hand down her jeans. "Forester." Her eyes flashed angrily at him as she yanked her sweater down at the sides.

"Sorry. Forester. I know that." Murdoch was relieved to see the anger. "We'll find Max, and this time tomorrow we'll all be sitting at Mum's bedside, eating her grapes."

CHAPTER 29

Murdoch had reluctantly left Heather at six thirty a.m. to return to the croft. Just an hour earlier she had disintegrated when Sergeant Finlay brought over the shoe, which was undeniably Max's. The sight of his sister folding at the waist, her unkempt hair hanging toward the ground, had shredded his heart. Murdoch had spent half an hour trying to reassure her and keep her keening down, so as not to wake and terrify Megan.

Now, he strode across the field heading for the croft house. His heart was pattering wildly and despite the cold, a line of sweat trickled down his back. He'd been home for less than two hours, but the urgency of needing to be gone again had had him running between the fields and the barn to get his work done. Chick had been fractious, pelting off at tangents to the sheep and needing to be called repeatedly. The dog, deeply in tune with its owner, was obviously sensing Murdoch's tension.

Fraser and he had agreed to each speed through the basic minimum on their crofts and then regroup at Murdoch's place before heading in to the police station. Murdoch wanted to see Sergeant Finlay before they went back out to continue their search. The sergeant had rallied a group of villagers to join his officers and march the moor to look for signs of the boy if Max hadn't been found by nine a.m. They would set off at ten a.m. from the Brae and work north, cutting broad swaths across the land until it got dark. As Murdoch pictured a line of fluorescent jackets moving through the coarse grass, shoulder to shoulder, combing the undergrowth, he had to swallow down bile. Could it be possible that Max would be found, lying frozen, unconscious, with broken bones, or worse? Murdoch couldn't think it. He shook his head to rid himself of the gruesome images.

Scanning the field behind him, he jammed the big key into the cottage door and locked it. Whatever he hadn't managed to get done would wait.

Megan sat at the kitchen table. Her face was puffy. Heather hadn't had the heart to make her go to bed, so they'd lain together on the sofa all night, watching the fire glow. She had tried to sing to Megan, but her voice wouldn't come, so the little girl had sung instead—working though her seven-year-old repertoire several times as Heather stroked her hair. Megan had eventually slept while Heather stared at the clock on the mantel, willing the hands to stand still. If time didn't move forward, then Max had been missing for less of it.

"Mommy, it's burning." Megan's voice was raspy, and Heather jumped, startled out of her daydream.

"Damn. Sorry honey." She grabbed the blackened slice from the toaster and tossed it into the sink.

Megan was now at her side.

"It's OK. I'm not very hungry anyway."

Heather looked down at her daughter.

"I'll make you some more, Megs. You need to eat." She cupped one pink cheek.

Heather had called the hospital an hour earlier to check on her mother. She'd been relieved when the nurse had told her that Elspeth had had a good night and was still sleeping. As long as Elspeth was asleep, she wouldn't have to deal with this nightmare, which was one thing less for Heather to worry about.

As she moved around the kitchen, absently making fresh toast and wiping surfaces, Heather's mind was flooded with images of Max. She tried not to focus on the grotesque, but the pictures kept coming.

Murdoch had left for a while but had promised to come back as soon as he could. She stared at the clock. Eight thirty. By her count Max had been gone for sixteen hours now. Sixteen hours with no coat, one shoe, and the cold eating into his soft skin. Stop—she needed to stop. Max was coming home. There was no other way forward.

As she watched Megan eat, Heather heard the unmistakable crunch of wheels on the driveway. She spun on her heel and sprinted to the door.

"Is it Max?" Megan's voice was bright behind her.

She flung the door open to see Murdoch getting out of the Land Rover. He looked flushed, tired. His chin was dark, as was the skin under his eyes.

"Any news?"

He walked past her into the house.

"Nothing yet. Fraser and I are off to look again now. I was just at the police station. Finlay's got a group together to start walking the moors at ten." He looked down at her. "You OK? Any updates on Mum?"

Heather followed him into the kitchen, where Megan was on tiptoe putting her plate in the sink. She trotted over to her uncle, who scooped her up onto his hip.

"Mum's sleeping. Had an OK night." The effort of speaking drained Heather's remaining energy, and she sank onto a chair. Whatever strength she had left, she had to focus on bringing Max home. That was all she could do.

"How are you, toots?" Murdoch squeezed Megan then dropped her back to her feet.

"OK. Tired." She yawned. "Is Max coming back today?"

Murdoch glanced over at Heather.

"We'll make sure he does."

She heard the quiver in her brother's usually robust voice.

An hour and a half later, Heather pulled up outside the shop and helped Megan out of the car.

"Aunty Marj has got some games for you to play and will make you lunch, OK, sweetheart?"

Megan nodded, lifting her bag of coloring pencils from the backseat.

"How long will you be away?" Her voice was little more than a whisper.

"Not too long. I'm going to go and help Uncle Murdy look for Max, and then we'll come back and get you."

"Before it's dark?" Megan's eyes were glassy.

"Yes. Before it's dark. I promise." Heather dragged her finger across her chest.

"OK." Megan sniffed. "But Marj smells of cabbage."

Despite herself, Heather laughed.

"Megan Forester. That's rude." She smoothed the little girl's hair and took her hand.

As they walked into the shop, Marjorie was coming toward them.

"Och, there you are. I've been waiting for you, young lady." Marj winked at Heather. "We've got lots to do."

Heather smiled gratefully at the older woman.

"Thank you Marj, really. This is . . ." She halted.

"Off ye' go and don't worry. We'll be fine here." Marjorie waved Heather away.

"'Bye, Mom." Megan lifted a gloved hand and mustered a brave smile. "Tell Max I've missed him."

At the far end of the Brae, a large group of people were gathered around a policeman in a bright orange vest. He was handing out copies of a photo of Max as he talked. Heather looked for Murdoch's outline among the clutch of unfamiliar faces. She spotted him at the far side of the circle, talking to Fraser. The sight of the two men gave her a tiny lift as she skirted the group and made her way toward them.

She stood on tiptoe and hugged Fraser.

"Thanks, Fraser."

He held her tight for a few seconds then, surprisingly, kissed her cheek. Heather felt a jolt to her middle as she stepped back from his embrace.

"No problem. Wouldn't be anywhere else, th'now." He blushed and raked a hand over his hair before cramming a thick wool hat on.

Murdoch was next to her.

"Megan OK?"

"Yes, she's with Marj. I felt bad leaving her, but . . ." Heather swallowed.

"It's best. She'll be fine."

The policeman had stopped giving his instructions to the group and was now watching her. Feeling self-conscious, Heather cleared her throat.

"When do we start?" She met his gaze.

"We're ready to go now." Sergeant Finlay addressed the group. "We'll break up into groups of four and spread out across the moor. It's very important that we stay close and keep an eye on one another, in case anyone finds something. If you see anything, stop and raise your hands above your head like this and blow your whistle." He pointed his thick arms to the sky.

Several of the people gathered tested their whistles, while others pulled on bright-colored vests over their coats. Heather scanned the faces. To her surprise, Kirsty was standing near the sea wall railing holding a photo of Max. Heather felt her throat tighten as she walked toward her old friend.

"You're here?"

Kirsty shoved the photo in her pocket.

"Of course. How could I no' be?" Kirsty squeezed Heather's arm through her thick coat as Heather swallowed a sob.

"Thank you." Her voice gave way as Kirsty folded her into a hug.

"You'd do the same for me, Heather."

She nodded against the rough wool of Kirsty's coat.

"I would."

Heather wiped her face and turned to see Murdoch talking to another man. As she looked at the profile, it was vaguely familiar. He was short and had thick glasses on. His waterproof coat scraped the tops of his boots, and as Heather squinted she recognized him as Mr. George, the headmaster of the twins' school. Next to him, wearing a fluorescent green vest, was Miss Bell.

Heather felt her face hot against the chilly breeze that was skidding across the briny water lapping below the sea wall. The more she looked at the people around her, the more they came into focus. There was Marj's brother, Donald, talking to Kayla, the young waitress, from the café. Behind them were the MacLeod brothers from the hotel in Portree, and next to them was one of her father's friends, Jim Robertson. As her gaze slid from one to another of the volunteers, she realized that there were more familiar faces than strangers among them.

Heather made her way through the crowd, pressing gloved hands, accepting hugs and whispering her gratitude to these people who had gathered to help find her son. As she moved among them, she became increasingly ashamed of herself for having felt so totally alone. The sight of all these shadows of her former life, this community that cared enough about her and her family to come out and do this, was nothing short of humbling.

CHAPTER 30

The line was moving slowly, rows of boots picking carefully across the bumpy terrain of the moor. Murdoch glanced to his side, where Fraser was intent on the ground around his feet. They'd been out for six hours now, and the light was beginning to fade. So far there had been no sign of Max or anything relating to him. As he kicked a large clump of grass, Murdoch felt the sharp irony of being both worried and relieved by that fact. While all he wanted was a clue as to the whereabouts of his nephew, as long as they hadn't found anything significant, or concerning, there was a higher chance that Max was still out there, somewhere.

Heather had left the group a few minutes earlier to go and pick up Megan. He had assured her that he'd call if anything turned up. The prospect of Max being outside for a second night was twisting his gut into knots, so he couldn't imagine how his sister was feeling. The fear had been stark in her eyes when she'd left, making him more determined than ever to find the boy and give her some relief. As he leaned down to pick up a crumpled plastic bag, Sergeant Finlay appeared at his side.

"We're going to call it a day." The policeman was frowning. "It's starting to get dark, and we need to get back and regroup."

Murdoch nodded. "Aye. I suppose so." He glanced to his right and caught Fraser watching them. "I think I'll stay out awhile longer, see what I can see."

Finlay wiped his forehead with a handkerchief and replaced his hat.

"Well, don't take any risks. It's getting cold, and we'll be back out at the crack of dawn. You should try to get some rest." He smiled at Murdoch kindly.

Fraser had made his way over and was listening to Finlay. "I'm staying with Murdo. We'll keep looking."

"OK, lads. Keep your phones with you and call in anything significant." Finlay turned and beckoned to the groups who were collecting on either side of them. "Let's go, everyone. Back to the meeting point."

Murdoch watched the crowd disperse as people made their way back toward the road. The sight of them walking away was disheartening, but as the night had begun to draw in around them, he knew it made sense. He shivered inside his heavy coat.

Fraser had moved away to his left and was bending over something in the grass.

"Anything?" Murdo called to him.

"Nah. Just an old lighter." Fraser held the object on his palm then jammed it in his pocket.

"Not sure how much longer we can see out here." Murdo stepped over a rock. "Even with the torches."

Fraser nodded. "Aye. We maybe should head back and check on Heather?"

Murdoch nodded. The prospect of seeing his sister but having no news for her weighed heavy on him.

"I suppose so. Wish we had something to tell her."

The two friends wove their way across the darkening moor and back to Fraser's car. The drive to the Forge was short and, feeling deflated, Murdoch was grateful for the silence.

Ten minutes later, Fraser pulled up at the driveway.

"I'll no' come in, Murdo. Give her my love."

Grateful to his friend for his thoughtfulness, Murdoch patted his shoulder.

"Thanks pal. Will you come to my place in the morning?"

Fraser nodded. "Aye. I'll get the morning rounds done and I'll be there at six. OK?"

"Fine. See you then. Get some kip." Murdoch climbed out of the car and headed for the Forge.

Megan was reading a book on the sofa, and Heather stood with her back to the fire. Her eyes were vacant, and her hair was matted, as if she'd been lying down. She stared at him, wordlessly begging for something to hang on to.

"No news, Wee Blister." He watched her face crumple. "But we're heading out at first light to start looking again." He slung an arm around her shoulder. "We'll no' give up till we find him."

Heather was trembling and leaning heavily against his arm. He felt her legs buckle, so he scooped her up under her armpits and moved her to the sofa. Settling her next to Megan, he kissed the top of his niece's head.

"Hi, toots."

"Hi, Uncle Murdy." She smiled at him. "You look tired."

Murdoch shrugged his coat off and tossed it over the arm of the chair.

"Aye, I am, pet. I need a drink and something to eat."

He turned to his sister.

"Have you eaten today?" Seeing her drawn face, he knew the answer.

Heather shook her head.

"I'm going to make us all some sandwiches. How about that?" He winked at Megan, who had pushed herself up from the sofa.

"I'll help you. I make good sandwiches."

"Great. I need a decent sous chef." Murdoch draped a tartan blanket around Heather's shoulders, put more logs on the fire, and then followed his niece into the kitchen.

Megan stood on a small stool at the counter. She was spreading butter on thick slices of bread.

"Is this OK?" She looked at her uncle. "Mommy doesn't like butter, but I do."

Murdoch smiled.

"Ladle it on, pet. Butter's good for you."

As they assembled a basic meal, Murdoch fielded Megan's questions.

"What if Max doesn't come home tonight? What if he was kidnapped? What if he hurt himself or he's lost and can't find his way home? What if someone bad finds him and takes him away?"

As he tried to reassure the child, Murdoch battled his own feelings of dread.

He stacked the plate of sandwiches and the teapot onto a tray, and as he turned, Heather was standing in the doorway. The blanket had fallen away from one shoulder and dangled down her back. She was picking at the skin of her thumb.

"Megs. Can you take the cups through?" She smiled at her daughter, and Megan, seeming pleased to hear her mother speak, lifted three mugs from the counter and skipped past her into the living room.

Murdoch watched Heather's face contort. He expected more tears, but instead she stared at him, dry-eyed.

"If he's out tonight again, in this cold, what are his chances?" She bit at her thumbnail. "Honestly."

Murdoch felt a tightening in his chest. The chances of a seven-year-old boy making it through two nights in the open, at this time of year, were slim. He knew that Heather was aware of the dangers of the moor, but he also knew that if he was brutally honest with her she would come undone in a way that he might be unable to cope with.

"He's a bright lad. He could've found some shelter and just be biding his time." He watched her lift the blanket and wrap it around herself. She watched him and waited for more. "Someone could've come across him and taken him in." The moment he said it, he wanted to take it back, knowing where her mind would go.

Heather's eyes snapped on.

"Shit. What if some pervert has him? Oh, my God. What if . . . ?" She leaned against the door frame.

Murdoch set the tray down and crossed the room.

"He's more in danger of getting trampled by an angry ewe. This is Skye, not New York." He tried a smile.

"How the hell do you know?" she shouted at him, her eyes wild. "Bad people exist everywhere."

Regretting his attempt at humor, Murdoch placed a finger across his lips.

"Shh. You'll scare Megan."

Heather seemed to register the warning and clamped her mouth shut.

"I need to go out with you tomorrow. I can't sit here. I need to look for him." She pulled her shoulders back and locked eyes with him, daring him to disagree.

"OK. I'm sure Marj can have Megan again." He nodded. "We're setting off as soon as it's light—around eight thirty."

"Fine. I'll call her now and see if we can drop Megs off then." She turned into the hall.

Murdoch realized that he hadn't asked after his mother in a few hours. Having set the tray down on the coffee table, he pulled his phone from his pocket. No missed calls, so no news from Finlay or anyone else. Heather was watching him.

"Have you checked how Mum's doing?" he asked as she accepted the steaming mug he held out. "Should we call?"

"I did. An hour or so ago. "Heather placed a sandwich in front of Megan and sat down next to her daughter. "She's OK. I said I'd go and see her in the morning."

"OK. Well, I'll need to go home tonight, so I can get the sheep taken care of early, before Fraser comes down. Maybe tomorrow you can drop Megan off at Marj's, then pop in on Mum before you join us?" He bit off a huge chunk of sandwich.

Heather picked at the crumbs on Megan's lap. "Yes. I can do that." She nodded. "Poor Mum. I won't know what to tell her." She stared into space.

"The truth." He shrugged. "She's too clever for anything else."

CHAPTER 31

Having spent another night on the sofa, Heather stood in the shower. The hot water pelted the top of her head, and as it ran down her back she pictured it taking all her negative thoughts with it, sloshing them into the sewer system where they belonged. Two nights in the cold. Two nights in the dark, scared, lost, alone. Max's face floated in front of her as she reached for a towel and scrubbed her face dry.

Megan had slept curled up against her back, with Charlie as a pillow. The dog seemed reluctant to leave the little girl, even to go outside. Heather hadn't even tried to get him off the furniture. He was sensing their collective need for comfort, and she was grateful for that.

Marj had agreed to take Megan from eight a.m., and the hospital had said that, under the circumstances, they'd make an exception and allow Heather in before visiting hours. She was looking forward to seeing her mother and dreading it at the same time. She knew that Elspeth's clear gaze would demand the truth, and Heather was afraid to say out loud that there was still no news of Max. As long as she held her fears inside, they would perhaps remain unfounded.

Twenty minutes later, having dropped Megan off, Heather walked on unsteady legs through the doors of the hospital.

By eight thirty a.m. Murdoch and Fraser were back on the moor, a mile above Portree. Finlay's group of volunteers was a little larger than the previous day, and Murdoch recognized more faces from the farming community. Sergeant Finlay's plan was to work farther north than before, heading up beyond Achachork. While Murdoch felt that they could be casting the net too wide, he had acquiesced, trusting the seasoned policeman's experience. Before long they'd be approaching his own croft and then Fraser's land. Could the boy have gone that far?

Off to his right Fraser was talking to old Archie Ferguson, a farmer that Murdoch saw regularly on market day. He lived west of Fraser and had a large flock of Blackface. His croft was impressive, with expansive views over Portree and out to sea.

Fraser seemed intent on whatever the older man was saying and then, turning, trotted over to Murdoch.

"What's up?" Murdo pulled off his gloves.

"Archie says that when we get up there, we should spread out, over toward his place. There are a couple of barns that might be worth searching." Fraser shrugged.

"Good idea." Murdoch flicked his gaze to the group on his left. "I could go now."

"I was thinking the same thing. You'd be back in less than an hour." Fraser nodded. "I'll stay here, and we'll keep in touch by phone if anything turns up."

Murdoch saw a flash of orange in his peripheral vision.

"Will you tell Finlay where I've gone, if he misses me?"

"Aye, sure. Away ye' go."

Murdoch paced across the moor. His car was another ten minutes' walk, and he'd calculated that it would take him ten or fifteen minutes more to get over to old man Ferguson's land. With a plan in action, such as it was, the notion of being proactive lifted his spirits. If Max had been thinking straight, he'd have found shelter somewhere, and a barn full of dry hay would be a good spot to hunker down overnight. Just as the image of Max sleeping soundly under a pile of hay comforted him, Murdoch frowned. An island child would probably know how to find shelter from the harsh cold, but would his American nephew?

Having reached the Land Rover, Murdoch headed north on Home Farm Road. The beauty of the sunrise over the familiar terrain was lost on him as he focused on the fields, looking for any telltale shape or movement. Soon he had passed his own croft and was heading toward Fraser's, looking for the road that would take him west. As he spotted the turning up ahead, Murdoch frowned. Surely this was way too far for Max to have made it on foot, and with one shoe?

Ahead of him he saw a wide gate with a heavy chain slung around the post. There was no padlock, so he lifted the chain, pushed the gate open, and drove through. He'd been here once, many years earlier, with his father. Archie was a keen card player, and Matthew had enjoyed their spirited games of canasta at the pub. When Ferguson had broken his ankle in a farm accident, Matthew had taken Murdoch along to visit.

As he maneuvered the car along the rough lane, Murdoch spotted the dark roof of a barn to his left. He pulled the Land Rover over and jumped out. The heavy wooden door was ajar, and as he pushed it open, his heart was thumping.

"Max. Are you here? Max."

He stepped inside.

"Max?" he bellowed into the dark space. Bales of hay were stacked high on either side and ahead of him. The scent was sharp and fresh, and as he pushed his way toward the back of the barn, he felt spears of hay jab his arms and face.

"Max?"

There was no sound. The boy wasn't here.

Having checked every corner of the building, Murdoch got back into the Land Rover. The other barn had to be closer to the croft house, if memory served him correctly. The lane twisted to the left, and as he drove over several potholes, Murdoch glanced at the passenger seat and wished he'd brought Chick with him.

The second barn was lower to the ground. The stone walls squatted under a rusty metal roof, and a small door was set deep in the side wall. Murdoch switched off the engine and made his way over to the building. This was his last hope. If Max wasn't here, he'd have to go back to the search party and report his failure to Fraser.

The narrow door was stiff in its frame. Murdoch leaned down and put his shoulder to the wood. It opened slowly, scraping over the stone threshold. Murdoch's eyes took a few moments to adjust to the darkness, but gradually the sacks of grain piled against each wall revealed themselves to him. There was a small, dirty window in the back wall with only one pane of glass still intact. As he moved through the space, Murdoch felt cold air, sucked into the space by the open door behind him, blast his face.

"Max?" He rubbed his eyes. "Max, are you here, son?"

The wind whistled through the gaps in the window, and Murdoch shivered.

"Max?"

Back at the car he checked his phone. No messages. Had this been a fool's errand? Could he have been more use combing the moor with the group? He dialed Heather's number, wanting to keep her updated and to see how Elspeth was doing. After four rings her heard Heather's voice mail message. Damn. He'd forgotten that the hospital wouldn't allow the use of cell phones inside. Next he dialed Fraser.

"Hi, Murdo. Any luck?" Fraser sounded breathless. "There's nothing on this end."

Murdoch grimaced his disappointment.

"Nothing here, either." He paused. "I tried calling Heather just now, but her phone's off. How close are you to the road?" A plan was formulating in Murdoch's mind.

"About ten minutes. Why?"

"I want to keep Heather away from the moor. I think it's best if she stays with Mum while we're looking." Murdoch waited.

"I was thinking the same thing."

Murdoch heard Fraser put his hand over the mouthpiece and speak to someone.

"Finlay was saying that we're going to move up toward Home Farm. So what do you want me to do?"

Murdoch considered the idea he'd had and wondered if Heather would see through it. Deciding that he didn't much care, he continued.

"Can you go to the hospital? Just tell her that you were passing by on your way to the police station or something. Tell her that Finlay says finding nothing is better than the alternative, and we're going to keep going. Tell her that he suggests she stay in the village, in case we need someone at base camp, so to speak."

Murdoch caught his reflection in the side mirror. His hair was wild and his eyes darkly shadowed. The lines of his jaw and the intensity of his eyes reminded him sharply of his father.

"Won't she think it's odd?" Fraser sounded hesitant.

"She might, but it's worth a try." Murdoch shrugged.

"Well, I'll give it a go." Fraser coughed. "I'll call you once I've seen her."

Murdoch started the engine and steered the car farther up the lane, looking for a place to turn around. As he spotted a widening in the road ahead, a flash of white drew his eye. Intrigued, he guided the car carefully through a gap in the trees.

Ahead of him, a mildew-covered caravan was tucked under the canopy of a large oak tree. Long grass pattered either end of the mobile home that had once been white but was now several shades of green.

The roof sagged in the middle, and a small set of metal steps led to a split door that hung unevenly in its frame. A light glowed from the small frosted window set in the side of the van, indicating that there was life within. Murdoch pulled the car to a halt and took in the scene, momentarily unsure of what to do next.

His nerves were jangling as he walked over to the vehicle. There was no discernible sound coming from inside, so Murdoch climbed the steps. Feeling them bend and shift under his weight, he rapped hard on the upper door then jumped back to the ground—creating space between himself and whomever was inside.

"Who's it?"

The gruff voice startled him.

"Eh, it's Murdoch MacDonald," he shouted at the closed door.

After a few moments of silence, just as he was preparing to knock again, the door flew open. Davy Gunn stood on the step looking down at him. His hair was disheveled, and his heavy cord trousers hung loose on his large frame. He wore two wool sweaters and muddy boots.

"MacDonald. What're you doing here?"

Shocked to see Davy in this odd context, Murdoch hesitated. "I—I didn't know you lived here?"

"Aye. I do." Davy was watching him. "So what can I do for ye'?"

Murdoch felt his face warming.

"I'm sorry to disturb you, Mr. Gunn, but I'm looking for my nephew. Well, the whole village is out looking for him. He ran away two days ago and we're—"

Frowning, Davy held his hand up.

"Is he about this high?" He flattened his palm next to his ribs. "Curly hair?"

Murdoch heard a rushing in his ears.

"Aye, that sounds like him."

Davy stepped back.

"Come in, man. The child's here."

Murdoch's stomach lurched as he mounted the steps, dipped his head under the low door frame, and walked into the caravan. The light was dim inside as he followed Davy past the narrow galley kitchen. A camping chair sat in front of a small Calor gas stove, which was giving off oily fumes. At the back of the van on a low platform that ran along the wall behind a table, Murdoch saw a figure curled up in a sleeping bag. The face was turned toward the wall, but the copper curls were unmistakable.

Max wasn't moving. Murdoch felt his heart flip-flop as he leaned over and, not wanting to startle the little boy, whispered.

"Max? It's me, Uncle Murdoch."

Max rolled over, and his eyes met Murdoch's. He looked tired, but as a smile split the grubby little face, Murdoch felt himself release the breath he'd been holding.

"Are you OK, pal?"

Max sat up on the narrow platform and stretched.

"I'm OK."

Murdoch opened his arms, and Max crawled up into them. As his nephew clung to his neck, Murdoch could smell the mustiness of the caravan, mixed with wood smoke and damp earth, in the boy's hair.

With Max clinging to him, he turned to see Davy standing back, next to the stove.

"How—I mean—how did he get here?" Murdoch hoped that he hadn't sounded accusatory, but Davy was instantly defensive.

"Showed up last night around nine," he snapped. "Last thing I expected when I was out walking the dog was to see a wee boy, wearing one shoe, wandering around." Davy sniffed. "What on earth was he doing out there alone?" He looked at Murdoch and frowned. Not waiting for an answer, he continued. "I brought him home, fed him a tin of baked beans, and put him to bed." He gestured toward the sleeping bag. "He told me his name was Max, but that was about all I could get out of him."

Max released his grip around Murdoch's neck and slid to his feet. The boy looked well enough, if filthy, and as Davy lifted a pan onto the stove, Max pushed past Murdoch and stood next to the older man.

"Thank you for finding me." Max extended a hand. "And thanks for the food, and for letting me have your sleeping bag."

Davy leaned down and shook Max's hand and then cleared his throat gruffly.

"You're welcome, lad."

Davy glanced at Murdoch.

"I've no phone, so was waiting for morning to take him in to the police station." He stuck his chin out toward Max. "I'd no idea folk were out looking for him."

Murdoch suddenly felt light-headed—he guessed from a combination of exhaustion and relief. He reached out and steadied himself against the side of the van.

"You look like death, MacDonald. Do you want a cup o' tea? I think Max might've left one biscuit in the tin."

Max sat in the passenger seat as Murdoch dialed Heather's number. His hands were shaking, making it hard to manipulate the phone. As soon as it went to voice mail again, he tutted, remembering that he couldn't call her at the hospital. Next he dialed Fraser, hoping that his friend would be somewhere he could reach him.

Fraser picked up.

"Hello?"

"Where are you, Fraser?"

"Outside the hospital. What's up?"

"I've got him. I found Max." Murdoch felt his throat thickening with emotion as he looked over at his disheveled nephew.

"Oh, thank Christ." Fraser's voice was gruff. "Is he OK?"

Murdoch nodded. "He seems to be."

Max smiled at him and buckled the seat belt across his waist.

"I can't reach Heather. Can you go and tell her?" Murdoch started the engine.

"Aye, of course." Fraser hesitated. "You're sure you want me to?"

Murdoch caught the hesitation.

"Sure, sure, go and tell her. She doesn't need five more minutes of worry over this one." He reached over and jabbed a thumb into Max's arm.

CHAPTER 32

The sun had risen, sending splinters of pink across the gray sky outside the window, and as she shifted in the bed, Elspeth winced. The corridor outside her room was silent, and the smell of what she presumed was breakfast being cooked was far from pleasant. Her back was aching from lying in the same position for so long, and while she had been awake and in significant pain for over an hour, she had yet to press the bell for the nurse. She hated to be a bother and so had tried ignoring the hot needles that stabbed along her thigh.

She had woken at five fifteen, horrified that she had been asleep while her grandson was still missing—out in the cold, alone, and undoubtedly terrified. She had waited until nearly six before calling Heather to see if there was any news. Heather had said that she was coming in to visit her, but as yet, there was still no sign of Max.

Elspeth glanced at the clock on the wall. It was a little after seven, and she was desperate to know what was going on. The worry and suspense were excruciating, much more so than the striking ache that was taking over her entire lower body.

Mercifully, within a few moments, the nurse came into her room, and Elspeth confessed her level of pain. The nurse administered some medication, and despite her wish to stay alert, Elspeth was soon drifting toward sleep again.

There was a thump, and Elspeth's eyes flew open. She cast her eyes around the room. The curtains weren't familiar, and why did her leg feel like lead?

"Mum. It's me."

Elspeth turned to see her daughter standing next to the bed. Her face was drawn, and she had dark smudges under her eyes.

"Heather. How are you, darling?" Elspeth reached for Heather's hand.

"Oh, Mum." Heather's eyes filled as she perched on the edge of the bed. "I'm losing my mind. I can't breathe." She dropped her face into her palm.

Elspeth felt the stab of pain to her leg that Heather's weight on the bed had provoked but clamped her mouth closed.

"Just hold on to me. They'll bring him back," Elspeth cooed. "Murdo and Fraser'll not stop until they find him."

As Heather raised her head, the extent of her daughter's torment was painfully clear.

Elspeth shifted awkwardly; the pressure of the blanket trapped under Heather's thigh was becoming unbearable.

"Sorry, Mum." Heather, registering what was happening, stood up. "Can I get you anything?" Heather slipped off her coat and tossed it over a chair.

"No, I'm fine. Just talk to me." Elspeth lifted the covers away from her leg. "What's happening with the search?"

Heather paced the floor relating the previous day's events. She told Elspeth about all the villagers who'd turned out on the Brae, listing their names as she counted them off on her fingers. As she did so, Elspeth saw a dawning on her daughter's face.

Heather sat down on the edge of the chair, and, for a moment, Elspeth thought she looked almost peaceful. She stared at Elspeth and then shook her head.

"You know what's weird?"

Elspeth waited.

"I thought I was alone, I mean, that no one here was connected to me anymore, apart from you and Murdo."

Elspeth nodded.

"But all those people. Most of them hadn't seen me in over a decade, but they showed up when we needed them."

Elspeth felt her throat tighten as Heather continued to process her epiphany.

"Even Kirsty was there." She looked at her mother and held her hands out at her sides.

"I know. These people never forget, Heather. Even if it doesn't always show, this is a community that cares."

Heather leaned back in the chair and let her head drop backward.

"I just can't conceive of losing him, Mum. I won't survive it."

Elspeth turned as she caught sight of a shadow at the door.

Fraser stood in the doorway. He was staring intently at Heather, and he was smiling.

"Fraser, come in." Elspeth pushed herself up in the bed just as Heather jumped up from the chair, her face draining of its remaining color.

The big man walked into the room, and even before he could speak, the sight of his face was giving them the news they were waiting for.

"Heather, he's OK. We've found him."

Heather stood rooted to the spot. Her hands hung at her sides, and in profile Elspeth thought that she looked like a cutout doll, her thinness was so alarming.

After what seemed like minutes, she launched herself at Fraser and wrapped her arms around his neck. Elspeth wiped her eyes and watched as he folded her gently into his chest, like he was protecting a baby bird. He rocked her slowly as the sobs finally came.

"Oh, Brett. Oh, my God. I can't . . . I couldn't . . ." Her voice was muffled as she spoke into his chest, but both Elspeth and Fraser had heard what she'd said.

Elspeth held her breath as Fraser, catching her eye, shook his head. She felt herself relax as he mouthed, "It's OK."

Half an hour later Murdoch walked into the room with Max. Seeing his mother, the boy broke away from his uncle's hand and threw himself at Heather, who had sunk to her knees.

"Oh, Max. My darling boy. Where were you?" She sobbed into the head of messy curls. "I was so scared."

Max had linked his arms behind her neck, and his eyes were tightly closed as she rocked from side to side. Neither seemed willing to let go of the other.

"I'm sorry, Mom. I'm sorry." Max sniffed and then crammed his face into her neck. "I'll never run away again."

Heather gradually released her grip and leaned back, taking in her son's face.

"You're filthy." Tears streaked her face, but Heather let out a laugh. "What a ragamuffin."

Max smiled, shoving his mud-spattered sleeves up over his elbows.

"I'm not that bad." He looked down at himself and shrugged.

Behind mother and son, Murdoch and Fraser stood shoulder to shoulder, like two massive titans. Murdoch was smiling like a loon as he leaned down and helped Heather up from the floor. She leaned her head against his shoulder.

"Murdo."

"I know, Wee Blister. It's OK." He patted her back. "Everything's OK."

Behind them Fraser stood still. Elspeth's heart went out to him, as it was obvious he was feeling suddenly awkward in the room. As he shifted his feet and made to step back out the door, Heather, hearing him move, turned to him.

"Fraser, I'll never be able to thank you enough. What you did—what you . . ."

Fraser patted the air.

"Forget it." He smiled, and Elspeth caught a slight redness bloom across his broad cheeks.

Heather walked over to him and, on tiptoe, wrapped her arms around his neck.

"I'll never forget it, never." She raised her lips and kissed him on the cheek. "Never."

Having disentangled himself from her arms, Fraser waved his goodbyes and slipped out the door.

Murdoch had fetched them all a drink. He sat on the windowsill sipping from a paper cup as Heather, having been out to the bathroom to wash her face, settled back on the chair across from the bed.

Elspeth reached for a tissue and blew her nose as Max stepped cautiously toward her.

"I'm sorry, Granny. I didn't mean to push you." His voice was almost inaudible, and his startling eyes, so like his mother's, were glistening. Elspeth patted the blanket.

Max perched carefully on the edge of the mattress and placed his head on her shoulder. He whispered, "I thought you were dead."

"Shh, now. Shh. I'm fine, sweetheart." Elspeth patted her grandson's back. Her eyes sought Heather, whose relief was tangible in the room.

"So, this Davy helped you?" Elspeth looked over at Heather. "How did he find you?" Elspeth sipped at a glass of water and tried to focus on what Max was saying rather than on the ache that was creeping back into her leg.

"Well, the first night I slept in a barn. There was lots of hay and some empty sacks, so I made a bed. It was cold, but I was OK." He wiped his nose on his sleeve.

Murdoch grunted. "Seems like he was in one of old man Ferguson's barns." He looked at his mother.

"Archie Ferguson?" Elspeth flinched. "That far away?" She stared at Murdoch, who shrugged.

Max continued.

"Then the next day I stayed in the barn for ages, then I went for a walk. I passed lots of sheep and then crossed a little stream."

Elspeth noticed Heather's face blanch, behind his back.

"I was really hungry, but I found some berries and had a drink from the stream."

Heather grimaced but stayed silent, apparently not wanting to stem the flow of information.

"I followed a long fence and then went under a gate." He paused. "But the weird thing was that after walking for a really long time, I got back to the same barn again." He grinned.

Elspeth moved some hair from his eyes.

"So you'd walked in a big circle then?" She smiled at her grandson.

"I guess so. But by that time it was really dark, and I didn't want to be cold, so I was heading back into the barn when I saw a light in the trees."

Heather's face paled.

"I walked toward it, but then Davy was there. He was out with his dog. It was so dark, I think maybe the dog sniffed me out." Max frowned.

"Were you scared?" Heather spoke from behind him.

"Yes. No. Not really." He paused. "Uncle Murdy and Fraser were out looking for me. And the police, too." Max sounded proud of the havoc he had caused.

"Well, everyone is just very happy to have you home. No more running off, young man. No matter how bad things get, that's not the answer." Elspeth frowned and poked Max's shoulder.

"I know. I know. We talk about it, we face it, and we fix it, together. Mom's told me." He turned to his mother. "Can I go and get another drink?"

Heather jumped slightly.

"OK. But you come straight back. Deal?"

"Deal."

She reached into her bag and pulled out her wallet. With a pound coin in hand, Max headed toward the door but then paused and turned back to his grandmother.

"I'll never leave my stuff on the stairs again. I promise."

Heather shifted on the chair and tightened her grip on her mother's hand.

"God, Mum. It was the worst two nights of my life. I was convinced—"

Elspeth cut her off. "I know. I can only imagine. But stop now. He's home and he's fine." She reached over and cupped her daughter's cheek. "Enough now."

Heather nodded and shook her head, trying to banish the negative thoughts. Her mother looked frail in the bed, and her left leg was obviously causing her significant pain. Apparently there was nothing to be done for the pelvis except bed rest, and her other injuries would heal in time, too.

Heather was suddenly flooded with guilt.

"I'm sorry I wasn't here, Mum. I wanted to come, but the police . . ." Her voice faded.

"For heaven's sake, stop. I was fine—safe here and fast asleep half the time. You needed to be at home, for Max and Megan." Elspeth dismissed the apology. "So, who is this Davy person?" She focused on Heather's face.

"An old guy who lives in a caravan on the moor, over by Achachork." Elspeth eyes widened.

"I know." Heather swallowed.

"So what happened?"

Having been given a rundown of the events by Murdoch, before he left to pick up Megan and take her home, Heather explained about Davy Gunn. She told her mother about the caravan and how he had fed Max baked beans and then let him sleep. Elspeth listened intently, nodding and frowning.

"Not to be dramatic, but what do you know about this Davy?" Elspeth was leaning forward, and her gaze was piercing as Heather, understanding her mother's meaning, nodded.

"Turns out that he's the one who sold the croft to Murdoch when he lost his son a few years back. Apparently he's a good person." Heather smiled. "And Max seems none the worse for wear, so . . ."

"Oh, right. I remember him now. Well, it's a blessing that he found him." Satisfied, Elspeth sank back onto the bank of pillows behind her. "We'll need to thank him properly."

Heather nodded. Of course—she would make sure to seek out this Davy Gunn and let him know that he had saved her life.

"You must be exhausted." Heather stroked the thin hand underneath hers. "We should go and let you get some rest."

Elspeth smiled.

"I'm a wee bit sore now, to be honest." Her mother's voice sounded less grounded than usual.

"Right. You rest and we'll come back later. Do you want anything from home?"

Elspeth nodded.

"My nightie. This thing is awful itchy." She yanked at the hospital gown and grimaced.

"Anything else?" Heather pulled out her phone to make a list.

Elspeth chewed her lip.

"My toothbrush and perhaps the book that's by my bed, and my glasses." She smiled at her daughter, then her eyes widened. "Oh. I meant to ask you. How was the cottage you went to see the other day?"

For a moment, Heather had to think what her mother was talking about. The two-bedroom cottage that she had been walking around just forty-eight hours earlier had been erased from her mind with all the turmoil. Now, when she thought about it, she remembered that it had been exactly what she had hoped for. The pristine, whitewashed former croft house in Peiness was so picturesque it was almost clichéd. It had three perfectly spaced dormer windows above and two beautiful bays below, a dark wood front door, and matching chimneys on each end, like cheerful parentheses. A small garden and a circular driveway looked over the surrounding countryside. She had even caught a glimpse of Loch Skeabost from the upstairs bedrooms.

Elspeth lay and looked at her, waiting for a response. Heather took in her mother's sallow appearance and swallowed her enthusiasm. There was no way she could move out now, with Elspeth needing care, and who knew how long it would be until she would be able to get around the Forge and cope by herself. No, the cottage would have to wait.

"It was fine. A bit small and probably too far out, to be honest." She shrugged. "Not sure about it, really."

Elspeth nodded.

"Well, the right place will show up at the right time, love."

Heather turned the car into the long driveway of the Forge and saw Murdoch's Land Rover tucked in at the end. Max was already unclipping his seat belt.

"Take it easy. He's not going anywhere." Heather chuckled as she made her way into the house in her son's wake.

Both Chick and Charlie were jumping around, welcoming them, and Murdoch was at the Aga with Megan, who was wearing Elspeth's apron. A huge pile of pancakes teetered on a plate, and the kitchen table was set.

"Breakfast all around?" He stretched his arms wide.

Megan, grinning, trotted over and hugged Max.

"Where were you?" She assessed her brother. "We were scared that something bad had happened to you."

Max hugged her back and then gently pushed her away.

"Nothing bad happened, though, did it?" He smiled. "But I'm starving."

"Well, there's a mountain of pancakes." Murdoch laughed.

Heather had hung her coat up and padded into her father's old office to check the answering machine, as Elspeth had asked her to. Not that they were expecting many guests at this time of year, but it was still possible that someone had called looking for rooms.

As she passed the desk, the light was flashing on the machine. She pressed the button and listened to the message. A couple from Edinburgh wanted a room for three nights, from December 19 to 21. As she listened, Heather glanced up at the calendar on the wall. December 19 to 21 looked absolutely empty. Her immediate instinct was to call them back and cancel, until something held her back. Could she manage to take the reservation, install Elspeth back at home, and still be able to ferry the children around as needed?

She had always loved working in the bed-and-breakfast in the past. There was something so satisfying about the feel of clean sheets as she smoothed them on the beds. She enjoyed seeing the line of unfamiliar cars in the driveway, scanning the variety of faces at breakfast in the conservatory and breathing in the smell of local bacon browning under the grill each morning. She would come downstairs to see her dad at the stove, flipping fried eggs and dark rounds of black pudding in the huge skillet. He would tuck a tea towel into his belt and have the radio quietly playing Gaelic music. She had loved living at the Forge, with its tide of interesting, odd, and, admittedly, sometimes annoying guests. She wouldn't have changed that part of her childhood for the world.

Murdoch was serving up their breakfast as she came back into the kitchen.

"I asked Fraser to join us, but he's knackered. He's gone home to sleep." Murdoch slapped three big pancakes onto Heather's plate.

"That's too many." She grimaced.

"Just eat what you want, then. I've made enough to feed an army." He laughed.

"I can see that, you loon." She laughed up at her bear of a brother and then, seeing his good-natured face, she realized that she had not said the most important thing of all.

"Murdo. I couldn't have coped without you."

"Aye. Well, some things never change then, eh?" Murdoch winked, flopped down in a chair opposite her, and shoved the butter dish toward the twins at the other end of the table. "Slap it on, wee ones. It's good for your bones."

Heather pulled the heavy plate toward her.

"Davy Gunn lives near your place, right?" She reached for the jam and twisted the top off the jar.

"Aye." Murdoch spoke around a mouthful of pancake. "About half a mile or so." He eyed his sister. "Thinking of going up there? I can take you tomorrow if you want."

Heather nodded. "Yes. I want to thank him in person. Maybe take him something." She cut off a piece of pancake and popped it into her mouth. The batter was light, the jam sweet, and until she'd started eating, she hadn't realized just how hungry she was.

CHAPTER 33

The oddest part of Max's adventure had been that Davy Gunn, the old man who had sold Murdoch the croft, had found him. At the time of the sale, Murdoch had invited Davy to drop by anytime, but it had apparently been too difficult for Davy, so they had hardly seen each other since.

Murdoch had sensed how deeply attached Davy was to his land, his flock, and his life as a crofter. From talking to him, he knew that when Davy had lost his son, the event had drawn an ethereal but finite line under the life the old man lived on the land. Murdoch had felt bad for him, but his desire to own the croft had outweighed any guilt he felt at relieving Davy of his lifetime home.

With an image of his cozy croft house in mind, Murdoch now sat with Heather in the Land Rover outside the place where Davy lived today. Seeing it again made Murdoch's stomach flip. The mildew-covered mobile home crouched under the giant oak tree, and the same sallow light he'd seen the previous morning was glowing from the small frosted window.

Beside him, Heather ran a hand down her thigh and craned her neck to look out the window.

"This is where he lives?" She sounded dubious. "It's a bit run-down."

Murdoch nodded.

"Aye. It's not the greatest." He turned his head and took in the impressive prospect over the moor, the land undulating down toward Achachork's impending sunset. "Nice view, though."

Heather opened the door and slid out of the car. She lifted the casserole she carried up against her stomach and looked down, apparently searching for some solid ground.

"Careful there." Murdoch pulled his hat over his ears, stepped down into the mud, and slammed the driver's door. "C'mon then." He held a hand out to his sister, helping her navigate the sludge underfoot.

When they got to the door, Murdoch knocked on the upper door while Heather hovered behind him, nudging the heavy casserole up her middle.

"Who's there?"

"Eh, it's Murdoch MacDonald again, Mr. Gunn, and my sister's here."

Heather took another step back.

"Just a minute."

Davy opened the door. He wore a heavy coat and a woolen hat.

"What's this, then?" His questioning gaze slid between the two siblings.

Feeling awkward, Murdoch shoved his hand out and stepped forward.

"We're here t' thank you for taking care of wee Max."

At this, Heather also stepped forward into the dull light that emanated from the open door. She lifted the casserole away from her body and held it out toward Davy.

"I can't thank you enough, Mr. Gunn. My son, well, Max, he . . . he could've—" She stopped as Davy raised a ruddy hand.

"Enough now, lass. I just did what anyone would have. And it's Davy." Davy's leathery mask broke into a smile, and Murdoch could see the relief flood his sister's face.

"Davy." Heather exhaled the name, and once again lifted the casserole out toward him. "This is for you—a small thank-you."

Davy leaned down and took the dish from her.

"Jeepers, what have ye' got in here? Half a coo?" A surprising chuckle escaped the old man, and with it Murdoch felt himself relax.

"It's stew and dumplings. It's my mum's recipe."

Davy stood holding the dish for what seemed like an age, then he turned and walked back inside the caravan. Not sure what to do next, Murdoch looked over at Heather and shrugged. She held her hands out in front of herself and grimaced. After a few moments, they heard a grunt.

"Well, are you no' coming in?"

Murdoch grinned as Heather put a hand over her mouth, he guessed to stifle a giggle. As he watched her enjoying this moment of nervous relief, Murdoch couldn't remember the last time he had seen his sister laugh.

Davy had unfolded two chairs for them, and they sat side by side at the narrow kitchen table. As the temperature inside the little home began to rise, they had shed their coats, and when Davy pulled out the photograph album he'd been working on, Murdoch saw the dregs of Heather's reserve melt away.

They each held a teacup full of whisky, and Davy was perched on the low platform where Max had been sleeping. There was a packet of Ritz crackers on the table, and the photo album lay open.

A shoe box full of more pictures sat on the floor. Murdoch could see that the majority of them were of Davy's children at various ages.

Many were faded, and some had tears in them, but, as Davy explained, it was a project that he was determined to finish.

"I'm going to send it to my daughter, in Melbourne. Remind her that she had a family here. Call it a last-ditch attempt to reach her."

Obviously moved, Heather reached out and turned the album toward her.

"This one of them in Edinburgh is gorgeous." She looked over at Davy, who nodded.

"Aye, that was before they'd argue with every word we said." He smiled ruefully. "Good times indeed."

Heather flipped the page.

"Was this your wife?"

"Aye. She was a looker, was Morag."

As the night outside began to engulf the little window of the caravan, Heather glanced at her watch.

"Oh, we need to get back. Marj can only stay with the kids until four thirty." She looked at Murdoch expectantly.

"Right enough. We'd better shake a leg." Murdoch stood up, his huge frame dwarfing the inside of the caravan. His head all but scraped the ceiling, and with him standing, the kitchen area was full.

Davy slid out from behind the table and folded away the chairs.

"Well, thanks for the stew. You didn'y have to do that, you know." He looked over at the casserole that sat on the counter next to the doll-size sink.

Heather pulled on her coat. "Yes, I did. It's nothing. I can never thank you enough for what you did, Davy. You literally saved my son's life." Her voice cracked. "I am forever in your debt."

Davy blushed under his tan and flapped his big hands.

"Well, all's well that ends well, eh?"

Heather moved to pass him and then, to Murdoch's surprise, she leaned in and kissed his red cheek. "You're a hero."

Davy, obviously stunned by the spontaneous contact, stared at Murdoch, openmouthed. Feeling the man's pain, Murdoch sprang into action.

"C'mon now, woman. Let's leave Davy to enjoy his dinner." He slid a hand under his sister's arm and guided her down the narrow steps.

Night had cut off the view of the moor, and even the shape of the Land Rover was faint against the sky. When it got dark up here, it really got dark.

CHAPTER 34

Ten days later, Heather brought Elspeth home from the hospital and installed her in the downstairs office. Murdoch and Fraser had moved a single bed down from the top floor, and Heather spent an entire morning rearranging the furniture, switching out the rug and laundering the curtains to freshen up the atmosphere. She threw the windows open to air the room while she cleaned, then made the bed up with a soft lemon-colored duvet set. She then added several pillows against the headboard so that Elspeth could prop herself up to read.

Heather had also been into the village the day before and bought a tray table, a good reading lamp, a small crystal water jug and glass, and a tiny porcelain bell that Elspeth could ring if she wanted anything. She looked at her purchases, neatly arranged on the bedside table that she had harvested from her own room, and was pleased with the overall effect. The once underused, dusty little study now smelled fresh, and with the curtains pulled back, the morning sunlight streamed in through the window and pooled on the gleaming wood floor.

Heather had spent two full days cleaning and organizing the rest of the Forge in preparation for Elspeth's return. It wasn't that the place was unclean, more that with her fresh eyes she was seeing things that needed attention—things that, perhaps, during Elspeth's daily routine of tidying, washing, cooking, and running the business, had become invisible to her. As Heather emptied the tall linen cupboard on the upper hall, she pulled several of the guest duvet covers out and shook them open. To her amusement, three of them were the same covers that she had helped her mother tuck around the thick mattresses when she was a child.

Elspeth and Matthew always bought good-quality linens, as Matthew had insisted it was an investment. Here, almost twenty years later, holding a blue-and-lemon-striped cover her father had chosen, Heather was overcome with memories of him padding into the rooms, dawdling in the doorways, as she and her mother made up bed after bed in the busy season.

Elspeth would shake her head and scold him.

"Have you nothing better to do, Matthew MacDonald, than follow us around like a wee lapdog?" She would tut under her breath. "Get out from under my feet."

"Just checking on my investment, woman." Matthew would chuckle, pat her mother's behind, and leave her blushing as he whistled his way back down the stairs.

Heather methodically separated the linens that were badly faded then moved them into her own room. As she lifted the heavy pile onto the blanket box at the end of her bed, Heather knew that while this issue needed to be addressed, it must be handled with kid gloves. The last thing she wanted was to imply that Elspeth's standards were slipping.

Once she was finished with the linens, she went through each bedroom with a lined pad and pen and noted anything that she felt needed attention. There were some curtains that had seen better days, several throw cushions that needed to go, and three bedside rugs that should be replaced due to tiny holes or loose threads.

With her lists in hand, the offending carpets and faded bedcovers all piled in her room, Heather had set to work on preparing the guest bedroom for the couple arriving from Edinburgh. Before long, the four-poster bedroom on the first floor was made up with a crisp white bedcover, and clean towels were stacked in the bathroom at the end of the hall.

Downstairs, the fridge was stocked with everything she could think of that they might need for the breakfasts. The copper pans that hung on the laundry frame over the kitchen table gleamed, the table had been given a coat of beeswax, and the chair cushions had been washed and replaced.

Out in the conservatory, where the guests ate their breakfast, she had removed the faded checkered table covers and washed and replaced the glass on the rich red pine tabletops. Each small table had a new vase at the center and a matching miniature cut-crystal salt-and-pepper set. The tall Welsh dresser that housed the willow pattern dishes that Elspeth used for the guests shone from the polishing she had given it. All the windows sparkled from the vinegar and lemon juice she had used on the small panes. There was a citrus scent in the air, and a kaleidoscope of light fell on the brick floor, giving the room, which tended toward chilliness, a layer of additional warmth.

With all the preparations completed, she now stood in the kitchen, looking around at her accomplishments. Her lower back ached, her biceps twinged even as she raised the mug to her mouth, and her thigh muscles acknowledged every step she took. She was tired, but underneath her fatigue, she felt undeniably exhilarated.

Heather was excited to bring Elspeth home to see everything she had done, but at the same time there was a nugget of concern floating under her ribs. This had been her parents' territory, a finely etched life that they had established together. The Forge had been a sanctuary for them, and for her and Murdoch, a place where they had grown together as a family. With the changes she had made, she hoped she'd been respectful of that.

◆　◆　◆

The day before, the twins had helped Heather decorate a Christmas tree that now glimmered at the side of the living room fireplace. As they covered the lower branches with the selection of small tin airplanes and glittery pony baubles that Murdoch had bought for them, they'd talked about Brett.

"Remember last Christmas, in Virginia with Aunt Chrissy, Uncle Frank, and Phil?" Max stood on tiptoe, hanging a silver biplane. "Daddy was away flying." He dropped the plane into the depths of the tree branches. "Dammit."

"Max Forester. Language, if you please," Heather scolded him gently. Not wishing to stem this sharing of memories, she shimmied under the lower branches to retrieve the plane.

As they worked on the tree, they talked about the Christmases when Brett had been home. They laughed about his awful ho-ho-hos and the fake, ratty white beard he would don to greet them when they came downstairs on Christmas morning. Then, after a while, they retreated into silence, as if with each layer of baubles, tinsel, and lights, the realization that this was the first Christmas since he had left them for good settled over their little family unit.

Now, despite the sadness that their reminiscing had evoked, as she looked at the white lights flickering on the tree and inhaled the sharp piney scent, Heather felt a tiny stirring of excitement about buying gifts for the children, her mother, Murdoch, and, of course, Fraser.

The thought of her brother's friend brought a smile to her face. He really had been a tremendous support during Max's disappearance. As she remembered the way he had kissed her cheek and held her so gently, Heather felt her face warm. What was she thinking about that for? Fraser was almost family, and yet, there were undeniable qualities that intrigued her. Despite his height and presence, he could sometimes appear like a lumbering puppy that needed caring for. Embarrassed by her unexpected musings, she shook her head. The last thing she needed now, when the dust of the recent chaos seemed to be clearing, was to start thinking about Fraser Duncan.

Over the past few days, as she scrubbed and dusted, hoovered and arranged, she had worked through some of what Brett used to call brain sludge—garbage that clogged up the works. All the while she had been going through her childhood home assessing, correcting, preparing for the guests to arrive and for her mother to come home, she hadn't been focusing on her loneliness. Instead, she had been thinking outside the bounds of her own heart, about how she might enjoy focusing on the care of other people for a while.

For months now, her mother had been her rock, and Heather had needed and appreciated Elspeth in that role. She had boarded the plane in America with her children, three suitcases, and her broken heart and had arrived on Skye, quite happy to let Elspeth care for her until she found her feet. Now, as a result of an unexpected twist, she stood with her sleeves rolled up, her hair freshly washed, the Forge gleaming from her efforts, the larder stocked, and confirmed guests arriving soon. Looking around the spotless kitchen, Heather recognized a feeling of contentment that she had been missing for a long time.

The twins were watching TV in the living room, and she strained to hear what program was on as she stirred a pot of soup. Elspeth was napping in her new room, and, while Heather cooked with one eye on the clock, she waited for the sound of Murdoch's car in the driveway.

Knowing that the children would not want the vegetable soup, she had, as a special treat, given them the choice of what they would like to eat that evening. Megan had asked for roasted cheese with tomato slices, and Max had asked for beans on toast.

"Beans on toast?" She laughed when he said it. "Since when do you like that?"

"Mr. Davy gave me beans, and they were so good," Max quipped.

"Oh, well. If Mr. Davy eats them, they must be good."

Max had nodded earnestly and gone back to coloring.

Heather had made a conscious decision not to grill Max about his running away. She knew her son, and if she crowded him about his experience, he would clam up, jutting his little chin out at an angle and biting down on the information. The only details he had volunteered were that he had been very cold, that his foot had hurt where he had lost his shoe, and that the darkness had been scary until Davy had found him.

In the time that Elspeth had been in hospital, Heather had been back to see Davy Gunn three times. She wasn't sure exactly why, but there was something that drew her to the old man. She hoped it wasn't purely sympathy for his lack of family, or his slightly sad living situation, but each time she approached the caravan, she was aware of a lightening of her mood.

The first two times she had gone alone, taking a food offering with her. The third time had been the previous day when she had taken a dish of lasagna—and Max.

Max had drawn Davy a picture and wanted to give it to him to say thank you. It was of the caravan sitting under a huge leafy canopy. Next to it, in the long grass, was a small blue car and a dark blob, which Max informed her was Homer, Mr. Davy's dog. A huge yellow sun with a halo of tentacles hovered over the tree.

In the car on the way there, Max had been animated, chatting about school and a new boy whom he liked, called Gordon. She'd been thrilled to hear his voice filled with enthusiasm about anything, let alone school.

"You'll need to ask Gordon for tea, or a playdate." She looked at her son's face in the rearview mirror.

"When can he come?" Max's eyes were clear. He seemed to be making his way back from the shadowy place where she'd been unable to reach him since his father's death. Now, he was seeing her, hearing her, and the simple fact of having his attention again was enough.

Davy had obviously been touched by the picture and spent ages searching for drawing pins so that he could put it up on the small cork noticeboard that leaned against the wall in the kitchen. He had offered Max a caramel wafer that Max had devoured in three bites as Heather tutted and apologized for his behavior.

"Och, leave him. Kids need a good appetite." Davy smiled. "Max. Would you like another one?"

Heather laughed as Max nodded and took another biscuit. "Well, it looks like he's lost his appetite and found a horse's."

They all laughed at her father's old saying, and at that moment, Heather had stopped short. Davy, though a very different character, reminded her of her father. There was a slight irreverence to his humor, a wish to buck the norms, as was evident by his chosen lifestyle. He had a warmth behind his eyes that reflected a good soul crouching beneath the somewhat gruff exterior.

Now, as she stirred the soup and contemplated it further, she wondered whether Davy simply reminded her of how it felt to have a father around. As she pondered the thought she heard a car in the driveway.

"Kids. Uncle Murdy's here," she called over her shoulder and then winced, forgetting that Elspeth was asleep. Almost instantaneously, she heard the tinkle of the little bell, so she laid the wooden spoon down on the iron trivet and headed back to check on her mother.

CHAPTER 35

Elspeth shifted herself up in the bed. The duvet was heavy on her leg, so she pushed it off to the side and released her foot into the cool air of the room. The cast was cumbersome, and the tales that she had heard of the inevitable itchiness were proving true. She had developed a technique for gripping the cast at the top and gently rotating her somewhat withered leg inside it, just enough to alleviate the torturous sensation that crawled up and down her skin.

She had grown accustomed to sleeping in the little office downstairs, surrounded by Matthew's favorite things, and Heather had done a wonderful job of taking care of her during the two weeks that she'd been home. In that time, Elspeth had seen a subtle and yet marked change in her daughter. Not only had Heather been caring for her every need, but she had been baking, cooking, cleaning almost daily, shopping, managing all the twins' after-school activities and then playdates, since they had broken up for Christmas. To top all that general activity, she had made a wonderful Christmas dinner for them all the previous week.

Heather was gaining weight, her sharp features softening with a new layer of peace and her body filling out some of its harsh angles. Elspeth had even heard her humming as she worked in the kitchen and laughing with the children as they sat at the table doing their homework.

In between all the family and domestic tasks and keeping track of Murdoch and his general mess and mischief, Heather had also accommodated two sets of guests at the Forge, coping with each visit like a veteran hotelier. Elspeth had initially been surprised by the changes Heather had made to the conservatory, but found she liked them. It felt fresher in there now, and less chilly.

The second couple of guests had left that morning and, it being their third stay, they had stopped into her makeshift bedroom to say good-bye to Elspeth.

"Well, that was another wonderful weekend, Mrs. MacDonald. Heather is a chip off the old block." The lady had patted Elspeth's hand. "You must be very proud. It's so rare nowadays to see children taking on their parents' businesses. They're not usually interested in what we do, are they?" She'd sounded wistful.

The woman's words stuck with Elspeth, and as she lay and looked around at Matthew's books and the beloved maps of Skye that he had framed and hung on the walls behind his desk, a knot of concern gathered in her chest. While Heather seemed to be coping beautifully, would she feel trapped by Elspeth's accident? What if taking care of everything—the Forge, the twins, and even her mother—was too much too soon for her still-fragile daughter?

Elspeth wriggled her toes, sending a tiny needle of pain up through her calf. Damn that backpack on the stairs. This was not how it was supposed to be. She was meant to be helping Heather settle back into her home and find her feet again, not be lying here like a useless lump ringing a bell every time she needed to use the bathroom. Frustrated at her incapacity, she leaned over and jerked the duvet back over her now cold foot.

The TV was on in the living room, but she could make out Megan's voice above its low rumble. Max was laughing, and that sound alone was enough to make Elspeth release her irritation and smile.

He had been more engaged and communicative since the accident, and she suspected that it was primarily his relief at not being responsible for her demise. However, he had also been coming in to sit on her bed and talk, telling her about his new friend at school and showing her the games he played on his iPad. The speed at which he manipulated the characters was mesmerizing to Elspeth.

The twins talked to their aunt Chrissy each Sunday evening, and, as they'd picked up a slight Scottish lilt here and there, it was magical to hear them fall back into their American accents with ease as soon as those calls connected.

As Elspeth laid her head back on the pillow, Megan came into the room, carrying a plastic bag.

"Granny, do you want to play ponies?" Strawberry curls framed her granddaughter's cheeks.

"For a wee bit, love. Just until Mummy gets back from the shops." Elspeth shifted over in the bed to create a narrow strip of duvet where Megan could line up her toys.

"You can have any ones you want." Megan looked up at her grandmother expectantly.

"Well, I'll have the purple ones." Elspeth reached for the two ponies that she knew Megan was less attached to. "What shall we play?"

"We can play farms, or jumping." Megan shoved her hair out of her face, the gesture reminding Elspeth of Heather as a little girl.

The kitchen door flew open as Heather kicked it, her arms full of bags.

"Maximus, can you give me a hand, buddy?" she called into the empty room.

Max trotted into the kitchen.

"There's one more in the car." Heather nodded over her shoulder. Charlie jumped up at her, his tail wagging madly as she dumped the bags onto the counter. "Get down, you loony." She laughed at the dog as he circled the kitchen table, panting.

Max came back in with the last bag held up close to his chest.

"What's in here? Half a coo?" To hear Davy's words coming from her son took her aback. She had relayed the story of her first visit to the caravan to Elspeth, but Heather hadn't been aware that Max had been listening.

As his little voice lilted with humor, Heather allowed herself a second to soak up the lightness in his tone, and then she mocked annoyance.

"Max, you cheeky monkey."

He grinned at her as he lifted the bag onto the counter.

When it came to Davy, Max seemed to have a sense of possession, as if any information relating to the old man was his right to know and disseminate. He had asked question after question about Davy: why he lived in a caravan, why he lived alone, why he had no phone or TV, could he come for tea to the Forge, why did he tie string around his trousers rather than wear a belt, where were his family? Heather had eventually put a moratorium on further questions, telling Max that she didn't have the answers and that it wasn't polite to be nosy about people's private lives.

"But if we ask him and he tells us, then it wasn't private. Right?" Max's logic had rendered her speechless. Her son was becoming cleverer by the day, and Megan, tickled by the renewed, audacious version of her brother, giggled and egged him on.

The dynamic between the twins was getting back onto solid ground, and when they were out of sight for any time at all, Heather inevitably found them together in their room, using their iPads, reading books, or playing snap.

"Can you please get Megan so she can help unpack?" Heather pulled her boots off and left them at the back door.

As Megan slid into the kitchen in her socks, Heather patted her daughter's head.

"Can you help Max with the groceries, please?"

She padded through the living room to check on her mother and as she walked into Elspeth's room, she heard Max calling.

"Mom?"

"What, honey?" she called over her shoulder and rolled her eyes at Elspeth.

"Uncle Murdy called and said to tell you that Fraser is coming for dinner tonight." There was a pause. "I was supposed to write it down."

Heather frowned and shot Elspeth a questioning glance. Elspeth shrugged and held her hands up, as if protecting her chest.

"When did he call?" She turned and walked back out into the hall.

"Dunno. A while ago. I was supposed to write it down," he repeated, a slight pout tugging at his lower lip.

Heather couldn't bear to see the happy face of just moments ago slide away, so she casually retucked her shirt into her jeans.

"Hey, it's fine. Never mind. You remembered to tell me. That's the main thing."

Max smiled nervously.

"Good job, buddy."

Murdoch sat on the sofa with his socked feet crossed at the ankle. He wore jeans and an Arran sweater, and his face was still ruddy from the cold wind and the day spent outdoors. Megan was on his lap. Her silky head leaned against his collarbone as she trotted a pink pony up and down his forearm. Chick and Charlie had wound themselves into two tight curls and lay at his feet.

Fraser was sitting on the floor near the fire. His blond head bent over Max's iPad as they looked at a website about Scottish Blackface sheep. Max had been firing questions about the animals at Fraser all evening, and Fraser, appearing to be flattered by the boy's interest, had taken time to answer him, show him pictures of the breed, and explain how in the winter they sold the lambs to farmers on the mainland, so they'd have richer pastures to live on.

Max was fascinated.

"Can I come and see your sheep?" Max leaned back and stretched his feet out toward the fire.

"Aye, sure. Next time you come to see your uncle Murdo, he can bring you up to see my flock." Fraser nodded, looking over his shoulder at Murdoch.

Murdoch nodded.

"Aye. No problem. Fraser has a much bigger flock than me. Lots more lambs."

"Lambs?" Megan sat upright on Murdoch's lap. "Can I come, too?"

Fraser laughed and nodded. "Uh-huh."

"Oh, fine. You want to see Fraser's lambs more than mine, eh? Traitor." Murdoch wrapped an arm around her waist and tipped his niece back on his knee, her head dangling toward the floor as she giggled.

Heather tutted.

"Murdo, we don't need her to throw up her dinner, thank you!"

"Och, she's fine." Murdoch lifted Megan back up. "You're fine, aren't you, princess?"

"Uh-huh." Megan glanced at her mother. "Can Mommy come, too, Fraser?"

Fraser stood up, his height all but obscuring the fireplace.

"Of course. If she wants to."

"Sit doon, Fraser. You're blocking the heat." Murdoch chuckled at his friend and slid Megan off his lap.

Heather glanced at Fraser and felt sudden heat in her face. Megan was watching her, all eyes and innocence.

"Do you want to come, Mom?"

"We'll see." She widened her eyes at her daughter. "We'll see."

CHAPTER 36

Heather walked back into the kitchen, leaving Davy perched awkwardly on the edge of the sofa. The twins were sitting on the floor in front of him, and Elspeth, now able to leave her bed for short periods, with her foot propped up on a stool, presided over the group from the armchair at the fireside.

As Heather clanged the dirty pots against the sink, she realized that the noise she was making was competing with a Vivaldi piece that was playing on the CD player. It was Elspeth's favorite. Heather shifted the next pan more carefully as she tried to hear the conversation filtering through from the next room.

They had decided to invite Davy to Sunday lunch as a further thank-you for his good deed. He had seemed reluctant to accept, but Heather had insisted. Now, he sat wearing a pair of clean corduroy trousers and an Argyle sweater, which seemed to be making him itch. His boots were shiny from a recent lick of polish, and Heather noticed that he had even cleaned the dark line from underneath his fingernails since the last time she'd seen him at the caravan.

She had watched Davy earlier, over lunch, as the twins peppered him with questions. While his body language told a tale of his mild discomfort at his surroundings, his way of communicating with the children had impressed her. He had been patient, listening intently to them, then he had spoken to them openly and in a way that Heather knew had made them feel relevant, rather than simply humored.

Her father had been the same way with the twins, and it was something that she had appreciated about Matthew when she was growing up. He never made her feel like a child in an adult arena. He valued her opinions and encouraged her to voice them. Not that Matthew was above correcting her if she was wrong, or guiding her when she threatened to stray from a safe course, but he had given her her head to a large extent.

Of their parents, Elspeth had been the worrier—the one who said no first, then would soften her position after due consideration. She and Matthew had often crossed swords about issues concerning their children.

When Heather was twelve and her parents had clashed over whether to allow her to take the ferry to the mainland on her own, she had crept into Matthew's office and asked him if they were getting a divorce.

"No, pet. We're just airing our differences."

"But you were shouting, and Mum said that you never listen to her."

Matthew had laughed softly and patted his knee. "You're getting too big to be up here."

"Never." Heather had given the pat response that, even now, she would have given him, had he been here.

The thought of her father pulled her throat into a knot. How long would it be before she could think of him and not push down tears?

She knew that Murdoch felt the same gratitude for Matthew's parenting style, and a couple of years earlier when they'd been reminiscing, he had told Heather that he intended on giving his own children the same courtesy.

"You'd better get a move on then, brother. Time is a-wasting," she had teased him.

Brett had made a game of pretending to set Murdoch up with any suitable single woman he knew. He even offered to sign him up for an online matching service, but Murdoch had threatened him with a beating should he try. As Heather thought about the banter between Brett and her brother, she smiled.

"Mommy. Can we have dessert in here?" Megan called through to the kitchen. "It's cozier in here."

Heather remembered the many times that she had asked Elspeth the same thing.

"Sure. If Granny doesn't mind."

She scooped up the apple crumble from the counter and set it on the table as Megan trotted in.

"She doesn't mind." Her daughter smiled up at her and then turned to leave.

"Hey, missy. Come back and get the plates, please." Heather widened her eyes. "This diner doesn't offer waitress service, you know."

Megan swiveled back to face her mother.

"Saw-reeee." She held her hands coyly under her chin and grinned before sliding over in her socks to lift the plates from the table.

"You need to wear your slippers, Megs. I've told you that." Heather looked down at the small, pink-clad feet.

Before Megan could respond, Max shouted from the other room.

"Mom. What's for dessert?"

Heather picked up the crumble, five spoons, and the jug of cream and followed Megan into the living room.

"Just hold your horses. Your slave is going as fast as she can." Heather walked in behind her daughter to see Davy sitting on the arm of Elspeth's chair as she flipped through a photo album. Their heads were close together, and Davy wore a pair of wire-framed glasses that she had not seen before. At her voice, they both looked up, startled. Davy stood up from his perch and settled himself back on the sofa, this time at the end closest to Elspeth.

"I was just showing Davy the photos of you horse riding." Elspeth had a slight flush to her cheeks, and for a moment Heather wondered if she was getting overheated, sitting so close to the fire.

"Ah, the infamous gymkhana pictures. Right?" She rolled her eyes and then set the bowl, jug, and cutlery on the coffee table.

"You have a good seat on a horse, lass." Davy nodded approvingly as he tucked the arm of his glasses down the neck of his sweater. "A confident stance."

Heather smiled her appreciation at the compliment, her eyes flashing back to her mother, who was smoothing her hair over her ears and staring at Davy.

Before their guest had arrived, Elspeth had insisted on Heather helping her into a nice skirt and cardigan and having her fetch her coral-colored lipstick from the bathroom cabinet upstairs. While Elspeth had initially been somewhat wary of Davy, asking him questions about his time at the croft, his children, and how he filled his days now, in the three hours that he had been in their home, she appeared to have let go of any reservations that she held about this diffident loner.

"She was a great rider, Davy." Elspeth nodded, her tone almost conspiratorial. "You should take it up again, Heather. Take the children along and get them some lessons." She beamed at her daughter.

Heather dug a spoon into the golden crust on the dessert.

"Who's for crumble?"

Davy waved from the end of the driveway. Despite being told to park there, he had left his little Morris out on the Brae. As he left he had thanked them profusely for the wonderful meal.

The small bunch of daisies that he had brought sat on the broad wooden mantel in a tall glass vase, and the scent of citrus that had emanated from his freshly washed hair hung in the warm atmosphere of the room.

"Well, it seems we are no longer concerned about Mr. Davy Gunn's pedigree?" Heather looked over at her mother.

"What do you mean by that?" Elspeth sounded offended and Heather regretted her sarcastic tone.

"Oh, I didn't mean anything by it. Just that you seem to like him." She leaned over to pour more tea into Elspeth's cup.

"He's a gentleman, in the best sense. They don't come along often, anymore." Her mother sounded wistful as she lifted the cup to her lips. "A rare thing indeed."

Heather filled her own cup and sat back against the cushions.

"Kids, can you go upstairs and run the bath, please?"

The children were in Elspeth's temporary bedroom and, from the gradual rise in the level of giggling coming from the doorway, she suspected they were jumping on the bed. The laughter stopped abruptly and then throaty whispering floated out into the hall.

"Kids." Heather tried again. "Come in here, please."

The twins came into the room, Megan on tiptoes and Max walking toe to heel as they playfully shoved each other.

"I hope you haven't left Granny's bed in a mess."

Megan shook her head and trotted over to Elspeth's side.

"I fixed it." She smiled and settled herself on the arm of the chair.

Max slid onto Heather's lap, a tactic to avoid bedtime that he had employed more frequently since arriving in Skye. She felt his bony shoulder press into her ribs and involuntarily wrapped her arms around him.

"Megan wants to come to Davy's caravan with us next time." He spoke into her shoulder. "She wants to meet Homer."

Heather smelled his sweet breath as he burrowed in closer to her side.

"Well, we can't just invite ourselves, can we?" She winked at Megan.

Max sat up and pushed himself away, sitting cross-legged on the seat next to her.

"He said we could go, all of us. He said to bring Uncle Murdy and Chick, and that we can all go for a walk with the dogs." Max's eyes were bright.

"That was nice of him. We'll talk about it tomorrow, OK?" Heather reached out and squeezed his toes. "Time for bed, please."

Megan slid down the side of the armchair and rolled into a ball on the ground, next to Charlie on the fireside rug.

"No. It's so warm in here. I want to sleep here tonight, with Charlie."

Elspeth gently nudged Megan's back with her toe.

"Up, missy. Listen to your mummy."

Megan sighed and then pushed herself up from the floor.

"Max, come on." She pouted at her brother.

"I'm having my own bath tonight. I'm too big to share with you." He stuck his tongue out at Megan.

"I don't care, anyway." She stuck her tongue out in return.

"Right, that's enough. Go and get the bath started, and Max, you can use my bathroom tonight. I'll be up in five minutes to check on you both. Scoot." Heather gave Max's foot a gentle shove and then watched as the twins jostled to get through the door into the hall.

"It's so good to see his humor coming back." Elspeth leaned over and placed her cup on the table.

"Yes. He's coming back to us, all right." Heather smiled at her mother. "Do you think we should all go and see Davy?" Heather scanned Elspeth's face as the flush that she had observed earlier returned.

"You could. The children might enjoy it, and he's invited you . . ." Her voice trailed off.

"Perhaps we should wait until you're well enough to join us?" Heather crossed her ankles on the coffee table. She didn't want to tease her mother where Davy was concerned, but it seemed to be becoming a reflex.

"Don't be daft. That'll be weeks." Elspeth shook her head and edged toward the front of the chair. "Can you help me to bed, love? I'm sore sitting here."

Heather, accepting the deliberate change of subject and feeling suitably corrected, stood and helped her mother up.

"I'll get you to bed then finish cleaning up the kitchen."

Elspeth nodded as Heather walked her back into her bedroom.

"Mum. You know I'm just teasing you, right?"

Elspeth patted Heather's hand.

"I know, love. I don't really mind that. You know that your dad was the love of my life. But sometimes I do get tired of being alone."

CHAPTER 37

Murdoch whistled to Chick.

"Come on, boy."

The wind was cutting the flesh from his face, and with the day's work completed, he wanted to get inside the house and batten down the hatches.

The dog streaked across the field and circled Murdoch's legs before laying its belly on the ground.

"Good boy. Let's away in." He reached down and ruffled the silky head. "Perhaps you can stay inside th'night."

Murdoch strode toward the house with the dog close at his heel. At the front door, he pulled his boots off and set them on the step, the practice being a hangover from Elspeth's house rules at the Forge. As he leaned his shoulder against the heavy wooden door, a metallic flash pulled at his peripheral vision. He squinted into the fading light as a small blue car drew up at the side of his grain shed. He didn't recognize it, and yet something tugged at his memory.

Chick's ears went up as Murdoch leaned over and pulled his boots back on. As he watched, the car door opened and Davy Gunn got out. Murdoch's eyebrows shot up. He'd invited the old man to drop by numerous times, but he had never seen him here since the day Davy had handed him the keys.

The wind tugged at Davy's jacket as, with his head down, seeming not to have noticed Murdoch standing there, he strode across the path to the cottage.

"Davy. Hello." Murdoch shouted into the wind.

Davy raised his head.

"I was passing by. Thought I'd drop in." Davy smiled and extended a hand.

Murdoch shook it.

"Good to see you. Come on in. I was just about to stick the kettle on." He jerked a thumb over his shoulder. Dirty boots forgotten, he shoved the door open and beckoned to Davy.

"I don't want to bother you." Davy stepped inside and ran a hand over his windblown hair.

"No bother at all. Chick and I were done for the day." He gestured toward the dog, who had taken up his favorite spot on the rug.

Seeing Davy hovering by the door, Murdoch tried again.

"Take your coat off. Have a seat, man."

Davy's hunched shoulders visibly relaxed. He shrugged his coat off and draped it over the back of a chair as Murdoch knelt and put a match to the stack of firewood.

"I've been meaning to come over for a week or so." Davy perched on the sofa and looked awkwardly down at his boots.

"Oh, aye?" Murdoch fanned a small flame with a folded newspaper.

"I had a nice lunch with your family last weekend." Davy hesitated. "I thought you might be there?"

Murdoch pushed himself up from the floor and slid the battered fireguard into place.

"Aye. They told me you'd been over. I was up to my eyes wi' the vet. I thought I had a ewe wi' foot rot, but it turned out to be just an infected cut." He walked into the kitchen and began filling the kettle. Then, thinking better of it, he turned back into the lounge.

"Davy, do you want a cuppa, or would you prefer a dram, to keep out the cold? The sun's officially over the yardarm."

Davy laughed.

"A dram would be excellent, thanks, Murdo."

As he stood at the sideboard pouring whisky into two tumblers, Murdoch watched Davy. The older man was sitting with his back to him, but Murdoch could sense his unease, see the tension across Davy's back. As he pondered the somewhat awkward atmosphere, Murdoch had an epiphany.

This croft had been Davy's home for many years. This was where his parents had lived, where Davy had been born, where his own two children had been born and grown up, where he had lost his wife and then his son. How strange it must be to see someone else living here, to feel like a guest in the home that had been in your family for generations.

His heart felt suddenly heavy for the older man, as Murdoch couldn't imagine how it would feel to see strangers living in the Forge.

"This must be difficult for you." He reached over and passed Davy a glass. "I hope you think I'm keeping the place up OK?" He sat opposite his guest and started to lift his foot on to the coffee table when he noticed the muddy boot still on it. "Um. I usually take them off at the door." Murdoch blushed and leaned down to pull off the offending articles. With the muck-laden boots tucked at the side of the fire, he settled back in the chair.

"Morag was aye on my back about the same thing." Davy shook his head. "Never let up, that woman." A smile pulled at his mouth.

Murdoch heard the pain underlying Davy's words, but, as usual, he felt inept when it came to talking about emotional things. He opted for the practical.

"So, what brings you here? It's good t'see you, mind." Murdoch sipped his drink.

Davy had finally leaned back against the cushion and was beginning to look more relaxed. He glanced around the room and then nodded, almost imperceptibly, before sipping some whisky.

"It's good to see the old place. Brings back memories."

Murdoch swallowed.

"Aye, I can imagine." He waited for some revelation or poignant memory to come tumbling from Davy's mouth. Instead, Davy leaned forward and set his glass on the table.

"I was wondering, if you don't mind me asking, what's your mother's favorite flower?"

CHAPTER 38

Heather's midweek morning walks had petered out with the encroachment of the children's school routine. She missed the time alone, and despite several efforts to slip out, now, with Elspeth's injuries, she was even more tied to the house than before.

Murdoch, seeming to sense her need for silence, had stayed with the children a few times after Sunday breakfast, tossing her his car keys so that she could drive up into the hills.

This morning, she had left Elspeth ensconced in the chair in the living room. The twins were coloring at the coffee table, and Murdoch was due to arrive within half an hour. Elspeth had promised not to move from the chair and had told her to go.

"I'll be fine, love. I've got my book and the phone, and Murdo is on his way. Away you go and walk."

"I'll call you before I head up the hill, just to make sure he's here." Heather spoke over her shoulder as she pulled on her coat. "I won't be long."

Megan lifted her head from her task and looked over at her mother. "Can we come?"

Elspeth leaned over and cupped Megan's cheek.

"No, darling. Mummy needs to go on her own today."

Unperturbed, Megan shrugged, shoved her sleeve farther up her arm, and returned to her coloring.

Kneeling next to her, Max ripped the page he was working on out of the book and screwed it up into a ball, a tight frown creasing his forehead.

"Hey, why did you do that?" Heather's hand rested on the doorknob.

"I messed it up." Max met her gaze.

"You didn't have to tear it up." Heather walked back to the table.

"Yeah, I did." Max was sullen, his lower lip protruding. His shoulders slumped under the weight of his mood.

Heather slid behind the table and knelt down between him and Megan. She pulled him toward her.

"You don't mind me going out for a bit, do you? I won't be long."

Max leaned away from her and sniffed.

"Nope. I don't care."

Stung, Heather sighed and pushed herself up from the floor. "Well, if you don't care, that's fine then." She glanced over at her mother, who was frowning, and mouthed, "It's OK."

Max, seeing his grandmother's expression and seeming to sense that he had overstepped, reached up and grabbed Heather's hand.

"I didn't mean I don't care. I meant, it's OK." He swallowed. "We can all go out later. Maybe with Uncle Murdy and the dogs?"

Heather leaned down and smoothed his copper hair.

"Sure, buddy. We'll do that."

The Quiraing had always been her favorite spot. Matthew had often brought her and Murdoch up here, purportedly to give Elspeth some peace. Heather had soon realized that the point hadn't been their mother's peace, but that the hill served as a sanctuary for her father from the daily routine of the business. Not that he didn't enjoy what they did for a living, but being tethered to the village for much of the week made him antsy for the outdoors.

These hills were in his blood, after all, and his connection to them was his life force. When the winter grayness of Portree weighed heavy on Matthew, a walk up the Quiraing was like a shot in the arm that rejuvenated him. Heather remembered seeing the color flood back into his cheeks as he would stand with his hands deep in his pockets, filling his lungs with what he pronounced the cleanest air on the British Isles. She and Murdoch would run around while Matthew stared out to sea, a small but visible smile on his ruddy face.

After leaving the car at the Bealach Ollasgairte, she had hiked up the familiar hill. Her coat now felt heavy across her back, and her legs trembled from the unaccustomed workout. She stood, letting the wind dry the thin layer of sweat on her upper lip as she soaked in the view.

The land fell away at her feet, a patchwork of color from gold and green to brown and purple. Just below her, the familiar row of rock pillars jutted from the ground, and behind them, far in the distance, she saw a thin strip of white surf slapping the curve of Staffin Bay. The small smudge of the island out in the bay was clearly defined today, and as she had so many times as a child, she counted the tiny white homes that peppered the hill above the shoreline.

Brett had loved this view, too. They had brought a bottle of wine up one afternoon, a year before the twins were born, and sat on a tartan rug, looking over the bay. The wind had been vicious, and Brett had ended up wrapping them both up in the rug and tucking them in at the base of one of the stone fingers behind the Table, an elevated plateau that provided some shelter.

"This place gets under your skin." He'd spoken to her numb cheek as they huddled together, passing the wine bottle back and forth. "I could live here, you know."

As she pictured them sitting just below where she now stood, Heather realized that she couldn't hear his voice anymore. After he'd died, for months, when she imagined him or replayed memories such as this one, she'd been able to conjure his voice in her head. Now, rather than hearing him speak, she could only see his words, like a script, stark on a page. The meaning of the things he had said remained the same, and yet their essence had gone. Every day that passed, Brett's edges were fading, no matter how hard she tried to grip on to them.

She stuffed her hands into her pockets. Brett's Virginia Tech sweatshirt was bulky under her coat, but she lived in it these days.

They had been on Skye for three months now, and while she missed him every day and still sometimes felt like a knife in a drawer full of forks, life was beginning to take on a sense of normalcy. The twins were settling in and making friends, and despite causing Elspeth's accident and bolting into the night, Max was more himself again. She would occasionally still see the flash of a dark mood from him, as she had that morning, but on the whole, her bookends were close to being back in balance.

Murdoch was a great support. He stepped in with the children wherever he could, and most days she wondered what she would do without her big, brash brother.

Recently, he had been noticeably missing from a couple of Sunday lunches, and Heather had teased him about the fact that his absences seemed to coincide with Marjorie's daughter Jenny's visits from Inverness. Murdoch had batted her off, but she had seen him blush. Her brother, she was fairly certain, was falling in love.

As she thought about the prospect of Murdoch potentially marrying the petite architect, Heather was surprised by the clutch of jealousy that snatched at her chest. He had every right to be happy, to find that person who would balance him out. Heather had been the dusk to Brett's dawn, and together they had made a perfect twilight. Murdoch deserved that, too. She wanted it for him, but she wasn't sure that she was ready to share her brother yet.

Shocked at her blatant selfishness, Heather shook her head. Her feet were freezing, so she shuffled her boots and stamped back and forth, waiting to feel the blood rush back to her toes.

She had woken that morning on Brett's side of the bed, and as soon as she had orientated herself in the dim morning light, she had quickly shifted back to her own side. Chrissy had told her that when she could sleep in the middle of the bed, she would be letting go.

Heather closed her eyes. She was nowhere near ready for that yet. The idea of letting Brett go choked her, and until it didn't, she would breathe in and out, sleep on her own side of the bed, and take each day with whatever it brought.

A gust of wind slapped her cheek, and she brushed the hair out of her eyes.

She missed her practical sister-in-law. They talked on Skype every weekend, but Chrissy's presence was large and lively, and her absence had left a hole in Heather's daily life. The last time they had spoken, Chrissy had promised to visit them soon, and the twins were thrilled, telling her what they wanted her to bring them from the States.

As she'd listened to their conversation with their aunt, Heather was taken aback when Max had referred to it as "Virginia." Based on the time when she'd eavesdropped on Megan, she fully expected that the children would still consider America "home." Hearing Max say that had lifted a few pounds off the burden of guilt she still carried over the move.

Looking out at the horizon, Heather wondered . . . if asked, where would she say home was? For years, it had been wherever Brett and the twins were. She had believed that if they lived in a tent in the Amazon, if they were together, then that would be home. Staring out over Staffin Bay, a view that was etched on her heart, she marveled at her naïveté.

For years she had dreamed of leaving Skye. She'd struggled against its constraints. She had read books and fantasized about traveling to foreign climes and experiencing different cultures and ways of life. Underneath all that desire for change, had she been kidding herself? Had she simply been kicking furiously against a tide that would inevitably pull her back? Here she was, back on the island where she had been born, where her parents had lived and loved each other for almost forty years, where her brother and she had fought and played, ridden horses, fished, and raced. Amid all this, the life she had led in Virginia was becoming blurred.

Heather emptied her lungs, pushing her diaphragm up to force the air out, along with a twinge of disappointment in herself. Had she chickened out of her life in the States, or had she done a reasoned and understandable thing, coming home to her family? Could this really be her home again?

CHAPTER 39

Davy stood in the doorway. A bunch of pink alstroemeria was wrapped tightly in paper, which he held close to his chest. This was the third lunch invitation to the Forge that he had accepted, and Heather knew that both the twins and Elspeth were enjoying his visits.

Heather had told Max to let Davy in when he arrived, so Max had been waiting for him, his little head poking out the front door. Charlie was wedged between the boy's legs, and as Davy approached, the dog barked.

"Wheesht, Charlie. It's just Davy," Max chided the animal, stepping back to allow Davy inside.

"Well, hello there." Davy slid his wet coat off and hung it on the rack in the hall. "How's everybody th'day?" He carefully wiped his feet on the mat.

"Great. Mom made curry. It smells funny, but I tasted it, and it's pretty good." Max skipped ahead into the living room where Elspeth sat near the fire.

"Hello, Elspeth. How're you today?" Davy pushed the flowers toward her.

"Oh, Davy. Those are gorgeous. How did you know?" She took the paper cone from his hand.

"A little bird told me." He grinned as Heather walked in carrying a tray.

"Let me help you." Davy took the tray from her hands. "Where do you want it?"

"Thanks, Davy. Just put it there." She gestured toward the coffee table. "I thought we'd have a glass of wine before lunch."

"Lovely." Davy nodded and placed the tray down next to a pile of decorating magazines.

"Someone doing some painting?" He nodded at the pile and then sat at the end of the sofa, nearest Elspeth.

"Heather's thinking we need a bit of freshening up around the place." Elspeth inclined her head toward her daughter.

"Is that right? Well, it must be catching," Davy blurted. Heather noticed that he looked embarrassed.

"Sorry?" She frowned as she pushed the bottle opener toward him.

"Oh, it must be spring fever. I've been doing a wee bit o' work on the van, too." His face looked flushed.

"Oh, really?" Heather heard the sarcasm in her voice and flinched.

Elspeth was frowning at her but snapped a smile back on as she met Davy's questioning gaze.

"Well, that's lovely, Davy. It'll be spring cleaning fever that's got us all moving, right enough." She patted her skirt and then inspected the fire deliberately.

Davy pulled the cork out of the bottle, while Heather, feeling bad, turned the glasses the right way up.

"Will you pour, please?" She nudged the tray toward him.

Putting the cutlery together on his empty plate, Davy glanced over at Elspeth. Heather saw concern wash over his face, and when she took in the gray pallor of her mother's face, it was obvious that Elspeth was hiding considerable discomfort.

As if taking this as his cue, Davy folded his napkin and stood up.

"Thanks for a great meal. Another great meal." He smiled at Heather.

"You're welcome."

Elspeth heaved herself up from the chair and leaned heavily on the edge of the table. Just as Heather was about to help her to the armchair, Davy was quickly on his feet and standing next to Elspeth.

"Can I help you?"

He slid an arm under her mother's and walked her slowly toward the living room. "You still need to take it easy, m'dear."

Heather, feeling suddenly superfluous, watched in surprise as Elspeth blushed, reached across and patted his shoulder.

"You're a dear man, Davy Gunn."

For the first time since she'd met him, Heather was irritated by the old man's presence. Elspeth seemed to turn into a fluttery version of herself when Davy was around, and it bothered Heather. She wondered if this was how Elspeth had been with Matthew in the beginning.

No sooner had the thought struck her than Heather caught herself. What was she thinking? The beginning of what? Surely, there was no way that her elderly, terminally sensible, widowed mother had designs on, or actual long-term aspirations of, Davy Gunn?

Annoyed with herself, she gathered up the rest of the dishes and carried them into the kitchen. The twins had gone outside to play with Charlie, and so Heather began stacking the dishes in the machine while she waited for the kettle to boil.

Just as she was pouring the water into the teapot, she heard a peal of laughter coming from the other room. It was her mother, undoubtedly, but it didn't sound quite like her.

"Jesus," she hissed under her breath. "Get it together, Mum."

Davy balanced the teacup on his stomach. He had made to leave right after lunch, but Elspeth had insisted he have a coffee before he set off, so now he sat opposite her.

Heather had curled up in the armchair across the room. She knew that she had been distracted over lunch, snappy and less tolerant with the children than usual, and now, for some reason, she felt undeniably sad.

"The bairns did awf'y well wi' that curry." Davy spoke to Heather's side as she leaned down and prodded the fire with the poker.

She turned to look at him.

"Yes. We always encouraged them to try new flavors. Their dad loved Indian food." Her voice flat, she turned back toward the fire.

"It's grand, that. I wish our two had been open to new things."

Heather didn't respond and, seeming to sense that he should make a move, Davy tipped the last of the coffee into his mouth.

"Well, I'd best be off. Things to do and people to see." He placed his cup on the table and stood up.

"Don't let us keep you then." Heather was up instantly and heading for the hall.

Davy, looking slightly taken aback, flicked his eyes to Elspeth. Heather saw her meet his questioning gaze and then slowly stand up.

"Thanks for coming, Davy. The flowers are gorgeous."

As Heather waited at the door, Elspeth extended a hand to Davy. He took it, lifted it to his lips and kissed it.

Heather felt the kiss like a kick to her ribs.

"Beautiful flowers for a beautiful person."

"Oh, heavens." Elspeth laughed. "You don't have to say that." She flapped a hand over her chest.

"I don't have to, maybe, but the truth's the truth."

CHAPTER 40

Elspeth waited for the door to close before letting her anger bubble over.

"How could you?" she spat at Heather's back as she walked past her.

"Could I what?" Heather turned and met her mother with an eerily vacant gaze.

"Be so rude to Davy, just then." Elspeth leaned heavily on the walking stick and took several small steps toward the armchair. Heather, seeing her mother struggle, seemed to snap back into herself and trotted over.

"Come and sit down, Mum."

"I can manage, thank you." Elspeth lifted her arm away from Heather's hand and slowly lowered herself into the chair.

Heather sighed and turned to walk out of the room.

"Where are you going?" Elspeth's tone stopped her daughter in her tracks. "We need to talk." She pointed at the sofa.

"Not now, Mum. I have to clean up and get the kids in." Heather sounded petulant.

"I want to talk to you now. Sit down, please."

Heather's shoulders slumped as she flopped on the sofa.

"First of all, what did Davy do to annoy you?" Elspeth tapped the arm of the chair with her fingernails, as she was apt to do when angry.

"Nothing. Well, he was bit familiar. That's all." Heather linked her fingers in her lap. "He's taking liberties." Her eyes flashed at her mother.

"What on earth do you mean?"

"Bringing you flowers, like he's on a date, and helping you around like he belongs here or something."

Elspeth watched her daughter's face contort.

"It just feels forced. Like he's muscling in on the family."

Elspeth heard the crack in Heather's voice and felt a stab of regret at having lost her temper. Moderating her tone, she continued.

"Listen, Heather, he's a good man. He took care of Max that night, when God knows what could have happened, and he's asked nothing in return. You invited him here, and he's been nothing but polite." Elspeth swallowed. "He's kind and good with the children, and they enjoy his company."

Heather sank farther back into the cushion and looked at the ceiling.

"There is nothing for you to worry about. He is not muscling in anywhere that he's not wanted." Having said the words out loud, Elspeth felt that they sounded stark in their reality.

Heather's eyes snapped to life, and she sat forward on the couch.

"Mum. Are you telling me that you like him? I mean, really like him? In that way?"

Elspeth could hear the raw shock in her daughter's voice. She needed to tamp this situation down, and fast.

"I admire and appreciate him. That's all there is to say."

Heather let out a harsh laugh.

"God. Who would have thought it? My mother and Davy Gunn."

Elspeth felt the impact of the jibe in the center of her chest, and instantly her anger was back.

"Now you listen to me. I can take a lot from you, but blatant disrespect is not on the list." Elspeth's hands shook as she plucked at her skirt. "What's really the problem, Heather?"

To her shock, rather than defend herself, Heather folded at the waist and dropped her head onto her thighs. Her back began to shake, and for a moment Elspeth couldn't tell whether she was laughing or crying.

"Heather?"

Heather let out a groan and then sat upright as a sob escaped into the thick air between them. Elspeth felt her own heart tear a little when her daughter's face crumpled and she dissolved into tears. Elspeth tried to get up, but the walking stick was awkward, and her leg was aching terribly.

"Sweetheart, come here. Come here, please."

Heather rolled off the couch and crawled over to her mother. She was gasping for air as she reached Elspeth's side and then buried her head in her mother's lap.

A few moments passed while she patted Heather's back and let her cry. She could feel the heat emanating from her daughter's cheeks as she sucked in air and then howled against her legs. Whatever the reason for this outburst, it almost certainly had little to do with Davy Gunn.

Half an hour later, Heather sat on the sofa with a glass of brandy. The children were still outside, and Elspeth was thankful that they hadn't come in to find their mother crying. Heather's face was drawn, but she was breathing steadily now and her eyes, while red rimmed, were dry.

"Talk to me?" Elspeth waited.

Heather cupped the thin glass in her palms as she stared into the fire.

"I don't know what's wrong with me." Her eyes glistened. "One minute I feel almost together, and then the next I think I'm losing it."

Elspeth sat her mug on the table.

"I think I'm getting there, you know, making things work here, maybe even being open to new . . ." She paused. "And then I get so damn lonely. I'm actually jealous of Murdoch having Jenny, or even the promise of Jenny." She lifted the glass and sipped some brandy. "Then you and Davy, it's like everyone's lives are moving forward and mine is going backward. Everyone in my life is in love, and I am still sleeping on my side of the bed, wearing a man-size sweatshirt and wishing the days away." She sniffed and wiped her nose on her sleeve.

Elspeth's chest ached at this confession. She was painfully aware of Heather's loneliness but had not thought her own pleasure in Davy's company was contributing to that hurt. How could she have been so insensitive?

"Darling girl, you've been through hell, and you're coping with so much. You've lifted your family up and moved them across the Atlantic. You've helped the children settle into a new life, and you're working all the hours God sends taking care of them, running this place, and nursing me. Do you think maybe it's all just too much, too soon?"

Heather nodded.

"Probably. But the funny thing is, I don't mind the work part. I love it, actually. It's the downtime I can't stand." A single tear slid down her cheek. "At the end of the day, when you are all taken care of and the house is clean, the dishes are done, and the kids are asleep, it feels great. But then I lie up there and miss Brett so much, I can't breathe."

Elspeth nodded. "I know, darling."

"I want him back. I'm so angry at him for leaving me to cope with all this." She stared into the glass. "I want to slap his stupid face." She shook her head. "Then I think that if I could have just one more hour with him, I'd want to talk about the kids and tell him how proud I am of them and how well they're doing."

"He'd be proud, too."

"Yes. He would. He'd be proud of them, but perhaps not of me, right at the moment." She set her glass on the table and stood up. "I owe you an apology, Mum. And Davy, too."

Elspeth could feel the weight of Heather's exhaustion just from her stance. Her soul-deep sadness was tangible.

"There's time enough for apologies. Just focus on all the progress you're making instead of looking at what's not happening."

Heather walked over and perched on the arm of her mother's chair. She reached down and lifted Elspeth's hand in hers.

"You need to ignore me. If Davy makes you happy, you should grab that. You've had enough time on your own, Mum. He is a good person, and whatever you decide, I'll support you one hundred percent."

Elspeth squeezed her hand.

"Hold your horses there. We're not getting married or anything." She nudged her daughter's arm, and they both laughed.

Heather kissed the top of her head. "Not yet, anyway."

CHAPTER 41

Heather rapped on the caravan door. She could hear classical music coming from inside. It sounded like a cello, mellow and lilting, but not a piece that she recognized. After a few moments had passed and there was no reply, she tapped again and pressed her ear against the top section of the cold door. Perhaps he had seen the car and was purposely ignoring her? She knocked again and, beginning to lose hope, turned to take in the view.

The light was fading, and a vibrant sunset had begun to bleed across the sky. Though she had seen this view before, it still stopped her breath. It was entirely uninterrupted and starkly spectacular, rolling over the velvet moors toward Portree. She could totally understand why Davy had chosen this spot for his home.

Anxious about the time, she checked her watch. It was close to five, and having left the twins with Murdoch, she needed to head back there soon. Fraser had promised to take them up to see his flock, and rather than join them, she had taken the opportunity to slip away and visit Davy.

It had been almost two weeks since he'd been to the Forge for lunch, and her guilt had been percolating, heightened each time she saw her mother's stoic face as another day slipped by with no news from Mr. Gunn.

Heather sighed and then swung around to rap on the door one last time. She was startled to see the top section open and Davy standing inside the van, watching her. His hair was disheveled, a frown creased his brow, and he wore a thick Arran sweater that came high up under his chin. She noticed a layer of fuzz on his face indicating the absence of a razor, she guessed, for a number of days.

"Are you coming in?" His voice was low but not unfriendly as he turned and disappeared into the body of the caravan. Heather wiped her feet on the narrow mat at the top of the stairs and opened the lower door to let herself in.

The caravan smelled different, lemony and fresh. She hovered just inside the door and waited for an invitation to sit. She watched as Davy walked to the far end of the caravan to turn the volume down on the small CD player.

"Sit down. I'm makin' tea."

As she slipped past him and slid behind the small table to sit on the bench, Heather noticed the new cushions lined up along the back. The sleeping bag was gone, and now she sat on a clean bedspread that was tightly tucked around the mattress. As she moved her feet, the cloying stickiness was gone from the floor, and the window behind her was clean enough for her to see the trees surrounding the back of the van.

She unzipped her coat, pulled the hat from her head, and tucked it between her knees.

His back to her, Davy reached into the cabinet over the sink and pulled out two mugs. They were pale blue, different from the ones he had used before, and from what she could see, there was no evidence of the cracks, missing handles, or chipped rims that she had done her best to ignore on her previous visits. In the few moments that she had been inside, she could see the effort he had made to improve his little home.

It warmed her toward him and made her feel even more certain of the rightness of her mission.

He seemed to be taking an inordinate amount of time at the stove, and Heather was growing increasingly uncomfortable with the heavy silence that hung between them. Her regret at her treatment of him was threatening to choke her, and she couldn't wait any longer to speak.

"Davy. I need to apologize."

Davy turned to face her. He leaned against the counter and ran a hand over his silver-coated chin. As he eyed her, he appeared to be chewing something, his broad jaw ticking.

Seeing no sign of a potential response, Heather continued.

"I behaved badly when you were at the house, and I'm truly sorry." She felt her voice begin to crack. She really didn't want to cry. If she started, she had no idea when she might be able to stop.

Davy gave one nod, and then to her surprise, held a hand up as if stopping an oncoming vehicle. Heather clamped her mouth shut. He obviously didn't want to hear her belated apology, and she couldn't blame him.

"It's not necessary, lass. I think there was blame to be had on both sides." The big man held his hands out at his sides.

Heather frowned as she focused on Davy's clear blue eyes. Was he saying that she had not offended him? It seemed evident that she had. She shook her head and made to speak.

"Really, Heather. There's no need." Davy spun around and lifted the now steaming kettle from the stove. The boiling water splashed into the teapot as Heather tried to process what he was saying.

Davy sat down opposite her. As he poured the tea, Heather shifted on the seat.

"I really was rude, Davy. Please let me say how sorry I am."

He slid a full mug toward her and then nudged the milk jug closer to her hand.

"Naw. I was wrong." He nodded to himself. "I overstepped the mark, and I made you uncomfortable, lass."

Heather swallowed some tea and felt her eyes begin to prickle. She still found it hard to cope with overt kindness or understanding.

Seeming to sense her struggle, Davy continued.

"I came on too strong. I'm no' used to being at a family table. Getting to know the bairns and your mother and just feeling welcomed—it's been a long time." He blinked and blew on the surface of the hot drink.

He looked so vulnerable sitting opposite her, with his five o'clock shadow and messy hair. This man had been through so much. Like her, he had lost the love of his life. But then, to top it all, his daughter had emigrated and then his son had been taken from him, too. As she processed the thought, Heather felt a jolt of empathy. Imagine if she had lost Max that night. If Davy hadn't stepped in, she and he would now, in some twisted way, be even more intrinsically linked by their shared tragedies. As it was, he had brought her boy back to her, something that would never happen for Davy.

She reached across the table and touched his arm.

"You *were* welcome. We love having you. The kids so enjoy your company. I just have some of my own issues to work through, but I never should've taken it out on you." She smiled at his guileless face. "I was jealous. Plain and simple." Her voice caught as, feeling newly ashamed, she dropped her gaze to the table.

Davy placed his cup down.

"Jealous?"

Heather swallowed and met his gaze.

"Yes. Of you and Mum . . ." She hesitated. "Forming a friendship." She noticed his eyes widen.

"I know how much she enjoys your company, and I suppose I was afraid. Not ready to share her. Not yet, anyway."

Davy sat upright and let out a hearty laugh. Startled, Heather pulled her hand back.

"I cann'y imagine your mother would ever let the likes o' me get in the way of caring for you, or those children." Davy shook his head and then, as quickly as it came, the smile was gone, replaced with a look of genuine concern. "I wouldn't want that, either, lass."

Heather hadn't been aware of holding her breath but now felt herself exhale.

"There's no bones about it, I think your mother's a very special lady, but I would never do anything to get between the pair of you." He ran a hand over his hair. "Besides, I'd be flattering myself to think Elspeth would give me a second look."

In his questioning glance, Heather sensed a need for reassurance.

"Davy, there's no flattery involved here when I say that Mum is very fond of you." She smiled at him. "Very."

CHAPTER 42

Murdoch looked across the table at Fraser. They hadn't been out for a beer in a while. Early spring was a busy time for crofters, the demands of the sheep at their highest, and even being neighbors didn't ensure that they would see each other from one week to the next.

Murdoch was also aware that since Heather had been home, there had been an odd atmosphere between him and his friend, and it was bothering him. Consequently, he had been glad when Fraser had called and suggested they meet.

As he watched Fraser sip his drink, Murdoch felt a fresh pang of guilt at the harshness of his warning, a few months ago, not to crowd his sister. The way he had handled the situation had crept up on him and plucked at his conscience numerous times. He knew that he should have trusted his friend not to be insensitive to Heather's grief, because Fraser was the best of men.

As had been proven time and again, especially when Max had disappeared, whenever there was a crisis or he needed help, Fraser was the first person Murdoch turned to. In the entire time he had known him, Fraser had never let him down.

As he watched Fraser leaning over his food, he wondered whether he had perhaps interfered rather than intervened. Could Fraser, in fact, be good for Heather? Should he, even as a protective older brother, have stuck his nose into something that was, ultimately, not his business?

Heather was looking so much better than when she had arrived a few months ago, but at times he still sensed a deep-seated melancholy that filled the space around her, like an aura of sadness that emanated from her, preceded her into a room, and hovered around her, even as she smiled.

Feeling another lump of regret gather at his boorishness, Murdoch cleared his throat to shift it.

"So, the sheep are doing well?" Murdoch twisted his glass on top of a soggy beer mat.

"Aye. They're fat and happy." Fraser nodded. "Just right for market in a few weeks."

Murdoch stabbed a chip with his fork. Even after nine years of farming, he still had trouble with the selling of his flock. He knew it was sentimental nonsense for anyone who kept sheep, but nevertheless, he didn't enjoy this time of year.

Fraser swiped the last of the meat sauce up from his dish with a crust of bread and then pushed it away.

"That was great." He patted his stomach. "Almost as good as your mum's Bolognese."

Fraser twisted around and eyed the two men playing darts behind them.

"Looks like they've settled in for the night. We'll probably not get a game." He pulled the corners of his mouth down. "No chance to beat the arse off you, MacDonald." Stretching his long arms over his head, Fraser grinned.

"That'll be right. When was the last time you beat me, Duncan?" Murdoch laughed and shoved his empty plate to the edge of the table.

Fraser rolled his eyes and wiggled his empty glass.

"Another?"

"Aye, why not." Murdoch nodded and reached into his pocket for his wallet.

"Naw, these are on me." Fraser shook his head and walked toward the bar.

They talked sheep, lambs, market, grain feed, and pricing, and all the time Murdoch sensed that there was something else Fraser wanted to say. Having suggested the meeting, he was now hedging, it seemed.

"So, what did you want to talk about?"

"Heather. Of course." Fraser shrugged.

Murdoch leaned back in his chair.

"I thought as much." He nodded. "So?"

Fraser rested his elbows on the table.

"I don't want to overstep. You know how much I respect her— right?" Fraser's eyes were laser focused.

"Of course."

"I have stayed away—I mean, not asked her out or anything. I've mainly seen her at the Forge, when she came over to my place after she hit that car, and the first week when she was walking at the harbor."

Murdoch frowned. He hadn't heard anything of an encounter at the harbor.

"When was that, then?" He lifted his glass and sipped.

"The first week she was back. I was down at the harbor, very early one morning. I'd been up all night watching a sick ewe, so I went to get some fresh air. Heather was walking along the seawall, and we talked a bit." Fraser's face colored as Murdoch held his gaze.

"Oh, aye?"

"She was pretty tired. Not really ready to have company, so I left her be." Fraser sat back. "But it's been a while, and she's more like herself these days. So I wondered, if it was all right with you . . ."

Murdoch felt his friend's discomfort.

"You wondered if you could ask her out?"

"I did." Fraser nodded. "I won't if you think it's a bad idea. I'd never do anything to—"

"Fraser, it's fine." Murdoch cut him off. "I may have been a wee bit overprotective there." He eyed his friend. "She is looking better. Running the Forge, and my mother, seems to agree with her, right enough." He nodded, as if to reassure himself. "If you want to ask her, you do that." He watched as a smile crept across Fraser's face. "Just be warned—she might blow you out of the water, and if she does, don't say I didn'y warn you." He lifted his glass. "And if she says yes, and you mess her about, I'll break every bone in your body." Murdoch bit down on his lip to contain the laugh that was bubbling up.

Fraser looked startled.

"Oh, Christ, I'm kidding, man. Relax." Murdoch reached his glass across the table. "I can't think of a better man than you to see my Wee Blister. Cheers, my friend."

Fraser's shoulders visibly relaxed, and a nervous smile returned to his face as he met Murdoch's glass with his own.

"Cheers, you bugger. You had me going there." Fraser let out a laugh, and then the two men drained their glasses.

They walked toward their cars, the customary ease between them restored. The March night was clear, and a lacy sky revealed clusters of stars that shot through the blackness above.

Fraser pulled out his keys.

"So, I've been meaning to ask you. Speaking of going out with folk, what's happening with you and Jenny?" He pulled a hat over his ears and stared at Murdoch.

Murdoch was jolted by the question. He and Jenny had been seeing each other more frequently, and he had to admit, he looked forward to her visits more and more. He knew that Fraser was aware of his fondness for the talented architect—the only woman Murdoch had ever met, apart from his mother and sister, who took none of his nonsense. The qualities Jenny possessed were, if he was honest with himself, exactly those he would want in a wife. As he stood and stared back at Fraser, trying to formulate an answer, Murdoch asked himself why he was keeping the relationship tamped down, even keeping Jenny away from Heather, arranging to see her secretly and sometimes lying to his family about where he was.

Fraser stood still and waited, apparently not willing to let him off the hook.

Murdoch pulled on his gloves and fished the keys out of his pocket.

"I'm no' sure." He shrugged, knowing that the response would probably not pass muster.

"Are you joking?" Fraser eyed him, standing his ground.

"Look, it's complicated." Murdoch felt suddenly trapped, with his back up against the Land Rover and Fraser in front of him.

"I don't see why, mate." Fraser frowned. "It seems pretty simple to me."

CHAPTER 43

Heather watched Fraser walk up the driveway. She watched the space behind him, expecting to see her brother, but the closer he came to the house, the clearer it was that Fraser was alone.

Two hours earlier, Heather had taken the twins to Max's friend Gordon's house. Elspeth, enjoying her freedom from the walking stick, was sitting out in the conservatory reading a book and enjoying the March sunshine, which struck the glass and warmed the room in the early afternoon.

Flicking her eyes around the room, Heather felt suddenly exposed and vulnerable. As she watched, Fraser rounded the corner of the house and dropped out of sight. She threw the dishcloth that she was holding into the sink and swallowed over a flutter of nerves. Blowing the fringe from her eyes, she involuntarily grabbed Brett's ring, which still hung on the chain around her neck.

A few moments passed until she heard the knock at the door, and as she pictured opening it, her nerves suddenly turned to irritation. She didn't like the feeling of being cast open to anything that she wasn't prepared for. There was only one reason she could think of that Fraser would come alone, and she had no energy for firefighting of any kind, least of all the emotional variety.

In the time it took her to cross the room, and before the purpose of his visit had confirmed itself, she had constructed an awkward interaction in her mind that she knew, with an odd certainty, was coming. It would go like this: Fraser would be sweet, diffident, and polite. He would look maddeningly handsome and yet be, as ever, totally unaware of his physical impact on her. He would ask after the twins, her mother, and then, after a suitable period of time, would ask her out—perhaps for a drink or dinner. She would refuse but try to be kind. He would be visibly disappointed, and then she would feel bad for rejecting him. He would leave, and then she would question her decision, possibly feel guilty for a few moments, but then would come undeniable relief.

She opened the kitchen door.

"Hi, Fraser. What brings you here?" She sounded overly bright.

"I was in the village, so thought I'd pop in. Am I disturbing you?" He craned his neck, surveying the room behind her.

Although she saw him fairly regularly, Heather realized that she rarely noticed his height anymore. Fraser's head was dusting the top of the door frame. His hair was freshly cropped, and his startling eyes bored into her face. His shoulders went a long way to blocking out the daylight, which splintered behind him ethereally. He wore dark jeans and the usual heavy boots, and his long, lean arms extended from a black T-shirt.

"No, you're not disturbing me. I'm just pottering." She turned and walked back into the kitchen. "I've got to go pick up the twins in a while. They're at a party." She turned to see him still standing in the open door. His awkward stance was endearing. "Well, come in, you big eejit."

Fraser swiped his boots on the mat and closed the door behind him. "It's gorgeous out th'day." He nodded over his shoulder.

"It's pretty. Not sure it's quite T-shirt weather yet, though."

Fraser instantly colored at her jibe, looked at the floor, and shrugged.

A stab of conscience pricked her. She hadn't meant to make fun of him.

"Well, not for this wimp, at least." She jerked a thumb at her sternum and smiled.

Twenty minutes later, they were sitting at opposite sides of the kitchen table. They had drunk a pot of tea, and Fraser had eaten half a packet of chocolate biscuits while they talked about the weather, the children, Elspeth's recovery, and the upcoming bookings at the Forge. Heather told him about the reservations picking up and how much she was enjoying managing it all.

"So you don't think your mum wants to take back the reins yet?" He tipped some milk into her mug.

"She doesn't seem to. Which surprises me, actually. I thought she'd be dying to get me out of her hair and her business." She smiled at Fraser. "I found this great cottage, but—"

Fraser, seeming preoccupied, cut her off. "Perhaps she's glad of the help? Maybe she's just tired of it all?"

Heather, as ever, was mildly taken aback by the insightfulness of this diffident man. Was it possible that she was not seeing the signs? Perhaps her mother was, in fact, enjoying the release from the responsibilities of running the business more than just for the time of her recovery? How bizarre would it be if Fraser was right and she, Elspeth's own daughter, was missing something so obvious.

"You might be right, Fraser."

Having exhausted all the mundane niceties they could think of, a heavy silence drew them both in, and Heather felt her nerves gathering again. She stared into her cup, swirled the dregs of tea, and silently rehearsed the response she would give him when he ventured to where she knew he wanted to go. The suspense became unbearable, so she stood up abruptly and gathered the empty cups.

"I'll have to go, Fraser. The kids hate it if I'm late."

Fraser pushed himself up from the chair and followed her to the sink.

"Aye. I'd better be getting on." He hovered behind her as she placed the cups on the counter. She could smell the musk of his soap mixed with chocolate and the tart scent of her own nerves.

She turned back to face him and noticed that his face looked warm.

"I was wondering, if you're not too busy, if sometime we could go for a meal or something?"

Damn it all—he had done it. Her worst fear had been realized. She took a deep breath and dug deep, so as not to sound dismissive.

"Fraser. I'm . . . I'm just not there yet. There's so much I have to do here, and all the energy I have I need for the children and Mum and . . ." She saw his eyes empty as he raised a hand to stop her.

"It's OK, Heather. I sort of knew it. I just thought . . ."

She touched his forearm.

"Listen. If I was ready to go out with anyone, it'd be you." She watched as the corners of his eyes creased slightly, the minute movement wiping the defeated look from his face.

"I mean it."

Fraser squeezed her fingers.

"I understand. Just so you know—I'll wait, and then, in another wee while, I'll ask you again." He gave her a devilish smile and then, to her surprise, lifted her fingers to his mouth and kissed them. "See you later, m'lady."

Heather felt his dry lips graze her skin, and the unexpected intimacy of the gesture jolted her. It had been so long since anyone had touched her in a way other than familial that the sudden glaring absence of this kind of physical contact threatened to swallow her whole. She forced down a nut of loneliness and then gently withdrew her hand. Not trusting her voice, she met his gaze and managed a smile.

Fraser straightened up and playfully wagged a finger at her.

"You've been warned."

Heather watched his broad back disappear down the driveway. When he was safely out of sight, she clutched Brett's ring again and let the valve open on the pent-up loneliness that she kept at bay daily. Her chest collapsed and her stomach came up to meet it, rendering her breathless and nauseous at the same time. She closed her eyes tightly, leaned over the sink, and breathed into the pain that hovered under her ribs.

Suddenly, behind her, she heard a noise. Her eyes flew open, and when she swiveled around, she saw Elspeth standing in the kitchen door. Her mother's face was twisted in pain, and her cheeks were wet.

"Oh, Mum." Heather gasped and quickly made her way to Elspeth's side. "Don't you cry. I'm OK."

Heather felt her mother's capable arms clamp around her shoulders and smelled the sweet breath that had comforted her so often over the years.

"It's time to start letting him go, Heather. It's time." Elspeth spoke into her hair, all the time patting her back.

She clung to her mother and visualized the pats between her shoulder blades driving out the last of her sadness.

"I know. I'm going to try."

CHAPTER 44

Max lay on Murdoch's sofa. His legs were stretched out along the cushion, and he had folded his hands behind his head.

"This is comfy, Uncle Murdy. I could sleep here tonight."

Murdoch carried a jigsaw puzzle into the room and set the box on the table.

"You're not staying the night, pal. Get your feet down, please." He nodded at Max's shoes, and the little boy slid his feet over the edge of the sofa.

"Sorry." He grinned up at his uncle. "You're just like Granny."

Murdoch brought his hands up in front of his face and mocked a boxer's stance.

"Them's fightin' words, my friend." He jumped from foot to foot and then leaned over and patted Max's foot. "Gonna back them up?" He jabbed the air near Max's nose. "C'mon then—or are you chicken?"

Megan was curled up in the armchair and, at the sign of impending fun, tossed her book onto the ground and launched herself at Murdoch's leg, clasping on to his thigh like a limpet.

"Two against one." She squealed as Max leaped up from the sofa and attached himself to the other thigh.

Murdoch guffawed and began dragging around the living room with a twin attached to each leg.

"These trousers are so heavy. I—just—can't—seem—to move—my—legs." He jerked each leg forward and then shook it, trying to dislodge his passengers. The twins giggled hysterically and then finally, one after the other, let go, dropping onto the ground in matching heaps.

Murdoch ran a hand over his chin and laughed. These two had become such an important part of his daily life now that he couldn't imagine how he'd managed without them. He had offered to have them at the croft for a few hours to let Heather go to the mainland for some shopping. She'd been redecorating some more of the rooms at the Forge, changing paint colors, buying new bedding and curtains, and clearing out any chipped chinaware and glasses. Each time he went home, he noticed something else that she had changed, and despite his initial concern that Elspeth might feel put out, he had noticed how content his mother seemed to let Heather have her head.

Truth be told, for some time, he'd been worried about Elspeth continuing to cope with the business alone, so having Heather taking such an active interest was a positive thing. However, he knew that he would have to watch his sister and make sure she didn't bury herself in the demands of the Forge as a means of avoiding life in general.

"So, who wants to tackle the jigsaw?" He watched as Megan stood up and pushed the curls off her forehead.

"I will. Is it hard?"

Max stood up and pulled his T-shirt down where it had ridden up around his stomach.

"What's it of?" He craned his neck over the table to see the pieces that were already out of the box.

"It's the Quiraing—the hill we like to climb sometimes." Murdoch perched on the edge of the armchair. "It's quite a toughie, but if we finish it, I've got bananas and chocolate ice cream, and a film we can watch later."

"What film?" He had Max's attention.

Murdoch closed one eye. "Here's a clue. Yo-ho-ho and a bottle of rum, me hearties," he sang.

Megan flopped down on the sofa next to Max.

"Pirates?" She looked hopefully across at her uncle.

"You got it in one, young lady." Murdoch smiled at his niece and, leaning forward, started to shuffle the puzzle pieces around.

Max knelt close to the table and was searching for corners while Megan focused on finding bits of sky. Murdoch had set them these tasks, as his dad had for himself and Heather, saying, "Get the edges done and you're more than halfway there."

Murdoch smiled to himself at the inevitable map of life and the notion of history repeating itself. He carried so many of Matthew's characteristics, and despite the few rebellious teenage years when he thought his father was a strict old sod whom he'd never want to emulate, when he looked in the mirror nowadays—all he saw was his father looking back at him. Far from disappointing him, it made Murdoch proud.

He glanced from one twin to the other, the stark reality of their situation striking him once again. They wouldn't have the chance to emulate their own father, to admire and boast about him. Nor would they have the opportunity to grow recalcitrant and grumpy, contradict or annoy him, as they should. Life had stripped that possibility away for these children, and Murdoch resolved once again, as he watched them bending over the puzzle, to do all that he could to fill the gap.

The puzzle was almost three-quarters finished when there was a rap at the door.

"No, it's not time yet," Max whined and threw himself dramatically onto the sofa.

Megan ran around behind the armchair, giggling as she pulled the tartan rug off the back and draped it over herself. "I'm not here," she whispered.

Murdoch glanced at his watch and headed for the door. It was very early for Heather to be back. He pulled it open to see Fraser standing on the step.

"Well, hello there." He smiled at his friend. "It's OK, you two. You can relax. It's just Fraser," he called over his shoulder.

Fraser's eyebrows shot up as he stepped inside.

"What do you mean, just Fraser?" He laughed and pulled his coat off as the twins pelted across the room and flung themselves at him.

"Hey, take it easy." Murdoch rolled his eyes at Fraser. "Can I get you a drink?"

Fraser gently shook the children off, followed him into the kitchen, and opened the fridge. "Is the sun over the yardarm yet?"

Murdoch chuckled.

"Since when has that stopped you?" He nodded toward some bottles of beer on the top shelf. "Help yourself."

"Want one?" Fraser reached in and grabbed a bottle.

"No. Not while I'm watching the terrible twosome. I'll wait until Heather picks them up." He jerked a thumb over his shoulder. "We're going to watch *Pirates*, if you're interested?"

Fraser twisted the top off the bottle and threw the cap in the bin.

"Sure, but I wanted to talk to you first."

Murdoch frowned and leaned back against the cabinet.

"What's up?"

Fraser tipped his head back and took a long draft of beer.

"You were right. She said no." He shrugged.

Despite the gesture of resignation, Murdoch saw the disappointment in his friend's face.

"Oh, sorry, pal."

"It's OK. I wasn't really surprised." He nodded. "But I warned her that I'll no' give up."

Murdoch saw the return of a mischievous glint in the blue eyes.

"Oh, really?"

"Yeah. I told her I'd give her some more time and then ask again." Now Fraser was smiling.

"Well, you can't say fairer than that." Murdoch leaned over and punched Fraser's shoulder. "Never say die, eh?"

CHAPTER 45

Elspeth stood in the guest room on the second floor, at the foot of the four-poster. Heather had been gone since the early morning on a mission to Inverness to find new curtains for the room and to buy some replacement linens.

While she didn't like to admit that her standards might be slipping, it was true that Elspeth had stopped seeing the little things, like the faded bedcovers or the odd chipped cup or stained fork. It had been many years since she and Matthew had furnished the business, and overfamiliarity had softened her vision as she worked in and around these items on a daily basis.

Heather had sat Elspeth down a couple of weeks earlier and asked her if she minded if she made some more significant changes around the place. Elspeth had not hesitated to give her permission, as seeing Heather engaged in making improvements was heartening.

Elspeth had to admit that, despite her wish for Heather to move on with her life, she had an abiding desire to have her daughter close at hand, involved in her own life, too. She recognized it as selfish, but there it was. She was an old woman, and she felt that old women had a certain amount of license as regarded selfishness.

She leaned over, ran her hand over the soft new bedcover, and recalled the conversation that had taken her by surprise.

"Are you sure you don't mind, Mum? I won't change anything you're not OK with." Heather paced across the living room, holding a pile of interior design magazines. "There are some great ideas in here, and we can choose things together."

They had spent hours poring over the magazines, pointing out vases, rugs, and cushions as Heather made notes and e-mailed companies for fabric samples.

Although enjoying the exercise of out with the old and in with the new, Elspeth's main concern had been with the expense of all the activity. While she was managing financially, there were certainly no funds for renovations on any major scale. When she brought it up, Heather had reassured her.

"Look, don't worry about the money. I haven't mentioned it before, but I'm getting a sizable payment from the airline."

Elspeth had frowned, confused.

"Brett had a life insurance policy. Chrissy is helping me manage things on that end, but it'll be available to me within the next month or so." Heather scooted closer on the sofa and draped an arm around her mother's back. "You'll not have to worry about money, ever."

"But what about you buying a house of your own? You still need a car, and then the children, they'll need years of support, help with university and cars and rent and, well, everything." Elspeth was anxious, thinking through all the potential uses for this money that Heather was not yet considering.

"Mum, I'll have enough to take care of us all."

"And what about your own house?"

"I've been meaning to talk to you about that, too." Heather turned to face her mother and took both her hands. "How would you feel about me buying the Forge from you?"

Elspeth had been stunned by the question. While it was obvious that Heather was enjoying playing host at the bed-and-breakfast, buying the business outright was an entirely different situation with a very different set of responsibilities.

"I don't think you've thought this through, love." Elspeth held her daughter's hands tightly. "It's an enormous undertaking for you, so newly . . . I mean, so recently come back to Skye."

"I've given it a lot of thought, actually. I definitely want the kids to grow up here, like I did. And I want them to love Skye, to belong here. As far as the business goes, there aren't many things I'm qualified for or, to be honest, interested in, but this . . ." She swept her arm around the room. "This, I understand. This I can do. It's in my blood, Mum."

Elspeth stared into Heather's eyes and saw a light that had been missing for too long. This was really what she wanted, so there was only one answer to give.

"If you're sure—I can't think of anything that'd make me happier."

They had discussed all the logistics, the finances and the practicalities of them all living under one roof. Heather had suggested that while redecorating inside and making some minor repairs outside, they also renovate the large stone outbuilding at the end of the driveway. It was currently used for storage, but Heather had talked to Murdoch's girlfriend, Jenny, about it, and she was confident that they could make a roomy and well-appointed cottage for Elspeth for whenever she wanted privacy, or perhaps some peace from the twins.

Now, Elspeth spun around and scanned the bedroom. Another couple was arriving from Edinburgh the next morning, and Heather had the room already set up. New, soft sheers hung at each corner of the four-poster's frame, caught loosely into stylish knots that managed to look wholly accidental. A large cream rug with pale pink Chinese characters around the edge lay at the side of the bed, and a set of matching ginger jars flanked the mantelpiece above the fireplace. Three brass candlesticks sat on the low side table at the window, next to a beautifully illustrated book about Skye, and a wing-backed chair covered in a soft checked fabric faced enticingly out to the garden.

There was no doubt that Heather had a flair for this, and as Elspeth looked around her, not for the first time, the thought of relinquishing the reins of the business that had consumed her for thirty years brought with it a flood of not only relief, but of abject excitement. By handing things over to Heather, she would never have to face the possibility of the Forge leaving the family, at least as long as she lived. What more could she wish for?

There was a distant knocking, which snapped Elspeth out of her reverie. Davy was due to arrive, and while daydreaming up here, she had lost track of time. She glanced at her watch and then made her way along the hall. Despite her eagerness to get to the door, she continued slowly down the stairs. Her leg was so much stronger now, but the memory of her fall came back to her with chilling clarity each time she was on the staircase.

Reaching the bottom safely, she crossed the hall and headed for the kitchen.

"I'm coming. Just a minute." Catching a glimpse of her reflection in the mirror, she ran a hand over her hair.

She could see Davy's familiar silhouette through the small window panel in the door, and although his figure was distorted by the contours of the glass, she could still make out the strong nose, the flash of silver hair, and the dark-coated curve of his shoulder.

Davy always came to the kitchen door now, the one the family mostly used. Elspeth was glad that after the many weeks that he'd been visiting her, he was becoming visibly more comfortable in her home. *Her home.* As she reached out and opened the door, the idea that the Forge might soon belong to Heather struck her again. The more she played with the idea, the more strongly she felt that it was the right course of action and one that Matthew would have approved of, too.

"Hello, there." Davy smiled and placed a hand on each of her shoulders as he leaned in and kissed her cheek.

"Come in. Sorry it took me a while. I was upstairs." She felt her face tingle as the welcome weight of his hands seemed to hold her prisoner.

She and Davy had taken to walking together, usually along the edge of the harbor and into the village. Once she had assured him of her readiness to tackle it, they had walked up around Sron a' Mhill. She had been slightly nervous negotiating the stretch of narrow path where the hillside fell steeply away into the water, but with Davy close behind, she had felt safer. Elspeth particularly loved the elegant Scots pines that graced the hillsides along the circuit, and she would always stop to breathe in the view of Loch Portree.

Today they were heading to Waternish to have a late lunch at the Stein Inn, a favorite of Elspeth's and somewhere she hadn't been in years.

Davy's eyes crinkled as he looked at her, and then he reached into his pocket.

"This is for you. Rhubarb and ginger." He pressed a jar into her hand.

He had brought her some jam from a farm that he passed on his way into the village. He rarely arrived empty-handed, despite her protests that he needn't bring her something every time he popped in.

"Thanks. It'll go great with the scones I made this morning." She smiled.

"Are you ready to go?" Davy held a hat in his hand as he closed the door behind himself.

"Aye. Just need to get a jacket." She placed the jar on the kitchen table and walked over to lift a lightweight waterproof from the rack.

"You might need something a wee bit heavier. There's still a nip in the air."

Elspeth nodded and slung the anorak back onto the rack. Lifting a wool coat instead, she slid her handbag over her shoulder and flipped off the light.

"Let's go, Mr. Gunn."

The Stein Inn sat long and low, its white walls hugging the shore of Loch Bay. The watery afternoon sun was still making an effort as threads of shredded clouds streaked the sky. A soft, golden light splashed up the side of the inn, causing it to glow under the quivering shadows of the surrounding trees.

Elspeth and Davy sat on a bench at a wooden table on the grassy bank. The loch was glistening in front of them. She shivered as she cupped a glass of wine between her hands, and in response, Davy reached over and draped his own discarded jacket around her shoulders. She pulled the jacket closer around herself and leaned into the crook of his arm.

"So, Heather is certainly making her mark on the place."

"She is. She's got a wonderful eye, and great taste."

"Well, that's no surprise. Look at the stock she comes from." Davy squeezed his arm tighter around her, and Elspeth laughed.

"You're a funny man, Davy Gunn." She reached across and poked his ribs.

Davy pulled away slightly, so she raised her head.

"I wasn't joking." His eyes seemed paler than usual, the muted light draining them of their usual intensity.

Elspeth felt her face warm again. Davy had a way of making her feel like a teenager, all at once awkward, excited, and uncertain of herself.

As she stared out at the dark water of the loch, a tinge of guilt leaked into her contentment. Here she was, enjoying the attentions of this good man, while her daughter's broken heart was still healing. Was this wrong of her? Sometimes her happiness felt wrong on so many levels that Elspeth would cancel outings with Davy, concocting excuses that were flimsy at best. He never questioned her, gladly accepting whatever time she chose to give him and not complaining when she put the children or Heather first.

Heather's face floated into her mind. In less than a week it would be April 11, the first anniversary of Brett's death, and she knew that it was going to be a painful landmark for Heather and the twins. All Heather needed, as she was finally coming back to herself, was her aging mother waving a new romance in her face. Timing was going to be everything.

Elspeth sat up straight.

"She wants to buy the Forge. Take over the business formally and put me out to pasture, so to speak." Feeling warmer under the weight of both Davy's coat and his arm, she swept the hair off her forehead.

Davy drained his glass and plopped it onto the table.

"How do you feel about that?" He sounded curious but not, she noticed, particularly surprised.

"I feel wonderful about it." She nodded. "It's surprising, but I have no qualms at all." She turned to look at Davy. "I've said yes."

She wasn't sure what she expected from him with this revelation, and truth be told, it was really none of his business what she decided to do. Regardless, as she waited for him to speak, she was nervous.

"She and the twins will move in permanently."

Davy listened, his eyes steady. Then he smiled.

"Well, you'll be a lady of leisure then."

She felt the slight tension under her ribs release.

"It's a grand plan, Elspeth." He reached out and patted her hand. "If it makes you both happy, it must be right."

The simplicity of his acceptance, his trust in her reasoning, and his unquestioning support brought a lump to her throat. Until she had recently begun to feel these things again, she had forgotten how much she missed being part of a couple. Missing Matthew had been a given, but missing the reassuring balance of two people pulling together against the tide had been a heavy burden she had carried since his death.

As she thought about him, an image of Matthew's dear face appeared in the corner of her eye. He was smiling—as if giving her some kind of ethereal approval. But of what? Was it of her decision to sell their home to Heather, or of the concept of this man who now sat in his place? Matthew's shadowy visage floated behind Davy's shoulder and then, as she tried to focus on it, force some weight into its fading edges, the image dispersed with a flutter of breeze from the loch.

Turning to face Davy, she swallowed.

"It's going to work well." She laced her fingers through his. "And there's something else." She took a deep breath.

"Oh, aye?" Davy inched slightly closer.

"You know we're renovating the little stone building at the end of the driveway? Marj's daughter's working on some plans for turning it into a cottage for me." She halted. "So I can have some privacy."

Davy nodded.

"Sounds good to me." He winked at her and lifted her hand to his lips.

Elspeth felt her heart skip. It was time.

"I wanted to ask you if . . . not right away, of course, and not until Heather is settled and the twins are . . ." Her voice faded.

"What is it, Elspeth?" Davy now sounded concerned, the merry twinkle gone from his eyes.

"I wondered if you might live there, too—with me. Together. I mean . . . together." Her voice cracked, and as his eyebrows arched up, she pressed her eyes closed, waiting for the inevitable disappointment of being turned down, of being mortified by her forwardness and woeful misinterpretation of his intentions toward her.

It had been so many years since she had felt the flutter of new love that nothing about her situation appeared grounded anymore. Everything in her life was in flux, but this, the way she felt about Davy, she knew she could not risk letting slip away.

After what felt like an eternity, she felt Davy's hand under her chin.

"Open your eyes." His voice was little more than a whisper.

She raised her gaze to his.

"I know how difficult that was for you." His eyes were glittering. "I'm not exactly catch of the month." He ran a hand across his chin and chuckled. "But if you'll have me, then I'd be the luckiest old duffer on Skye."

Elspeth lifted her chin and kissed him.

"It might take some time to get everything organized, and I want to be sure Heather and the children are happy with everything. But I'll definitely have you, Davy Gunn."

CHAPTER 46

Heather packed the pile of sandwiches she had made into two plastic bags. A bottle of water and two tall thermos flasks sat on the kitchen counter next to a pile of kitchen paper folded into squares.

She loved a picnic, and today she, Murdoch, and Fraser were taking the twins to the secret waterfall. April 11 had been looming heavy on her mind, and knowing that Max and Megan were aware of it, too, a tiny gold star having been neatly colored on the calendar that hung in their room, she had decided to mark the day with something memorable and positive.

Murdoch and Fraser were due to arrive in ten minutes, and the twins were sitting on the floor at the back door, putting their shoes on.

"Why is it secret?" Megan called over her shoulder.

Heather laughed.

"Because it is."

Max turned to look at her over his shoulder.

"It's a daft name for it. It can't be secret, because people know about it." He rolled his eyes theatrically as Megan leaned over and shoved his shoulder.

"Shut up, stupid."

Heather heard the pout in her daughter's voice, so she padded over to intervene.

"Stop it, guys. This is going to be a good day. No grouching and no niggling. OK?" She knelt down and finished tying Megan's lace.

Max was hunched over his foot, and as she watched, he tied the lace and then tucked the loops back under the tongue of the shoe, as Brett had taught him.

"Like Dad?" She put a hand on Max's back.

"Yep." Max nodded and then jumped up from the floor. "When are Uncle Murdy and Fraser getting here?"

Heather stood up and pulled her T-shirt down over her hips. She checked her watch.

"Five minutes. Got everything?" She assessed the children from head to toe, taking in their jeans, the appropriate layers of T-shirts and sweatshirts, and their matching Virginia Tech baseball caps. She had packed rainproof jackets and extra socks for them in her backpack, just in case April was true to its reputation and they got caught out. Her own cotton sweater and jacket hung on the rack, and her trainers felt snug across her arches.

"Charlie!" Megan called over her shoulder. "Charlie, come, boy." The dog skittered into the kitchen, tail wagging. "Good boy." Megan jutted her chin out as Charlie began licking her cheek.

"Megs, please don't let him lick your face, honey. I've told you about that." Heather bent down and patted the dog's backside.

"Is Uncle Murdy bringing Chick?" Max's face brightened, and the slight shadow that had threatened to spoil his mood moments ago slid away.

"Yep. Chick's coming, too."

"Yes!" Max pulled his fist in and down to his hip, another Brett move.

"Is Granny coming?" Megan stood up, pulled her anorak from the rack, and tied the arms around her waist.

"No, love. Her leg isn't quite strong enough for this walk, so she's meeting Davy for lunch instead."

Max and Megan locked eyes, and Heather saw distinct smirks pass between them.

"Hey, you two. That's enough." She gently cuffed Max's hair.

Max jerked his head away from her hand but was now smiling.

"Is Granny dating Davy?" His eyes were clear as he scanned her face, and Heather, feeling cornered, shook her head.

"They're good friends who enjoy spending time together." She knew it was weak, but she wasn't prepared to discuss her mother's relationship with her soon-to-be eight-year-old children. Max held her gaze, a tiny glint in his eyes.

"Ooh, Granny has a boyfriend." Megan's lilting laugh was contagious, and soon the three of them were giggling.

"Now stop it. You hear me? It's not nice to tease Granny. So be polite and don't ask her a ton of questions, OK?" Heather patted Megan's head. "If Granny wants us to know stuff, she'll tell us herself."

Heather had discussed the decision to buy the Forge with the twins the previous week, and they had been delighted. She had explained that it would be their forever home and that she would run the bed-and-breakfast, just like Granny and Grandpa had.

Max had been excited.

"Cool. So we get to stay here? Can I have my own room?" He had then run along the top floor, going in and out of the rooms to see which one he wanted.

Megan had also seemed pleased by the news, but thoughtful.

"What's up, sweetie?" Heather had been surprised by the obvious concern in her daughter's face.

"But Granny had Grandpa to help her. Who do you have?" Megan's eyes had been cloudy.

"I can do it on my own, Megs, for a while, anyway."

Megan focused on her mother's face and then slowly nodded.

"I can help you. I make good biscuits now, and I'm good at stacking the dishwasher." The little face looking up at her was so earnest that Heather had reveled in a moment of joy at the good human being that she and Brett had created.

"You're a great help. And you make better biscuits than I do." She had pulled Megan into her arms and inhaled the lavender scent of the baby shampoo she still used on her hair.

"They're here." Max stood at the window. "Come on, Megs." He pulled the door open and ran out into the driveway.

Deciding to take one car, they had all piled into Murdoch's Land Rover. Heather had called shotgun and so had both dogs at her feet. Fraser's lanky frame was crammed in the back with the twins as the fourth rendition of "Ten Green Bottles" echoed around the car.

"God, can ye' no' sing something else?" Murdoch laughed as he guided the car around a pothole.

"Move over, fatty." Max leaned over Fraser and jabbed Megan with his elbow. "You're taking up all the room."

Heather spun around in her seat.

"Hey." She gave Max a mock glare and then smiled over at Fraser, who was holding his fists up in front of his face, boxer style.

"I'm fine. They don't scare me, much." He winked.

The road wound gently through the Greshornish Forest. Thick swaths of trees lined the route and disappeared into the horizon. Heather remembered that when she'd come here as a child, she'd been bored by the journey and the monotony of the trees. Now, the low, rock-covered banks, the dense green of the forest, and the rough track under the wheels were exhilarating. Her growing sense of belonging was undeniable, and as she soaked in the scenery, she felt as if she was in exactly the right place at the right time.

As Max started a raucous fifth rendition of "Ten Green Bottles," in the distance she spotted the blue strip that she'd been looking for as Loch Snizort came into view.

"Murdo, pull over. I want them to see this." She put a hand on Murdoch's arm, and he nodded, directing the car to the side of the road.

"Kids, look. That's the Trotternish Peninsula." She pointed through the windshield.

"Can we get out?" Megan was already unbuckling her belt.

"Of course." Heather slid from the front seat as both dogs leaped into the scrub next to the road. The animals bolted away from them, followed closely by Murdoch.

Max and Megan jumped out the same door as Fraser walked around from behind the Land Rover.

"Where's the loch?" Max squinted into the light and held his hand up as a visor.

"There. See the line of trees in the distance? Behind it is Loch Snizort. See the blue?" She stood next to him and guided his focus with her finger.

"Oh, yeah. I see it." Max nodded as Megan came up behind them.

"Show me, too." Megan stood on tiptoe as Heather leaned down and pointed across her shoulder at the horizon. "Did you come here with Daddy?" Megan spoke softly, focusing on the view.

"Yes, we came here before you were born." She placed a hand on each of the twins' shoulders. "We stopped right around here and then we had a picnic at the secret falls, which is where Daddy proposed."

Heather heard a shuffling behind her. Fraser was standing awkwardly, his hands shoved in his pockets as he scratched an arc on the ground with his booted heel. His outline was slightly blurred, and she blinked to clear her vision. His blond head was dipped toward his feet as he avoided her eyes.

Turning back to the view, she continued.

"It was the most amazing day. That's why I wanted you guys to see the falls today. I wanted to share it with you." She pulled the twins closer. To her pleasure, Max didn't resist, and the threesome stood still, deeply connected in the moment.

"Daddy was so much fun." Megan leaned her head into Heather's ribs.

"Yes, he was, honey." She bent over and kissed the strawberry curls.

Max stepped away and then suddenly took off into the grasses as Murdoch appeared with the two dogs at his heels. Heather gave Megan's arm a squeeze and then turned toward Fraser.

"Sorry about that." She shrugged.

"Hey. Don't apologize. It's important that they see this, and know your story." Fraser held a hand out and helped her step over a low rock that crouched between them.

"There's so much they don't know about Skye. I want them to learn it, and to love it like I do." She smiled up at him, and he let her hand go.

"Do you still? Love it, I mean?" His eyes were slightly hooded.

"I do." Heather shrugged. "Despite myself." A moment passed, and then the two of them laughed.

"I'm glad to hear it." Fraser jerked a thumb over his shoulder. "Shall we go?"

Back in the car, Heather held Charlie on her lap as Chick sat on her feet. Fraser was once again perched in the middle of the backseat as the children, having been tasked with spotting the sign to the falls, pressed their noses to the windows on opposite sides of him.

"First to spot it gets the Twix." Heather looked over her shoulder at Fraser, who had wrapped his arms across his chest in an effort not to crush either child.

Max squealed.

"There. There it is." He pointed over Heather's shoulder at the small green sign.

"Good job, buddy."

She watched as the sign grew bigger. The simple white lettering on the dark green background, so evocative and yet rudimentary, sparked a wave of memories. Brett had laughed loudly at the concept of a sign to a secret location.

"Only in Scotland," he'd jibed as she had feigned offense.

Murdoch indicated and turned the Land Rover onto a smaller track.

"You OK, Wee Blister?" He looked over at her.

"Yep. I'm fine."

As Heather watched the familiar surroundings unfold around her, she ran through a picture show of memories in her head. She remembered what she and Brett had been wearing that day, the day that he had asked her to marry him. She could see his broad back ahead of her and hear him puffing as he negotiated his way along the track. She had teased him about his need to get back to the gym, and he had thrown a handful of grass at her over his shoulder. He'd lost his footing and dropped the backpack at one point, and they had sat on the ground and scrambled through the contents, checking that the wine bottle wasn't broken.

She smiled to herself as Murdoch pulled the car to a halt in a small parking area next to a gate.

"Right, everybody out." He got out of the car and slammed the door, and they all made their way into the forest.

Twenty minutes later, a beautiful glen appeared on their left. It was deep and lush and in startling contrast to the fairly uninteresting path they'd been following.

"This way." Heather led the group with Murdoch and the dogs. Behind them were the children who flanked Fraser, talking across him in their twinlike manner. She pointed to her left and walked into the glen, where a sparkling burn splashed over glistening river rocks, all surrounded by thick grass and moss-covered mounds. Keeping the burn on their left, they walked carefully along an almost invisible path until they saw the falls ahead of them, white sheets of crystal water falling gracefully into the gorge below.

"Oh, wow," Megan shouted. "So pretty."

Max darted ahead of his sister and slid his hand into Heather's. She looked down at him, but he stared ahead.

"You OK, Maximus?"

Max nodded and squeezed her hand. She knew what he was saying, and it meant the world to her.

Murdoch slung an arm loosely around her shoulder.

"Gorgeous as ever, eh, Wee Blister?"

"Yes. It truly is." She looked over at her brother, and far from being overwhelmed by sadness at the sight of this precious spot, Heather felt a surge of happiness that took her by surprise.

CHAPTER 47

Elspeth watched as Davy lifted the large sheet off the kitchen table and looked at the outline of the plan. The conversion of the small stone building had begun, and Murdoch's girl, Jenny, had quite the eye for design. The one-level building would have a plethora of windows for maximum light, a full bathroom, a small kitchen, and a sitting room with a sliding door out to the back garden. The bedroom looked large—Elspeth had always struggled to envision spaces that were still undefined.

The plans showed a patio at the back with an arbor over it. All in all, it amazed her how much living space could be fitted into what appeared, from the outside, to be nothing more than a large stone shed.

Elspeth had made a point to involve Davy in the design process, and she knew that it had meant a great deal to him to be consulted. The thought of moving into the new cottage made her smile, and then a simultaneous tinge of concern bled into her contentment. They had still not told Heather of their plans to live together, and the delay was beginning to feel more dishonest than considerate. Davy said that he understood Elspeth's reluctance to tell her daughter, but that he suspected she was underestimating the young widow's ability to embrace her mother's happiness.

Elspeth, distracted by her thoughts, dropped a cup in the sink.

"Coffee?" She smiled at Davy, who was refolding the plans.

"Aye, coffee's great."

He padded over to the kitchen counter.

Elspeth spooned coffee grounds into the tall cafetière. He'd told her that he had never used one before meeting her, relying on the instant variety of coffee that he bought in a jumbo plastic container from the cash-and-carry.

"You make the best coffee on Skye, m'dear." He winked at her. "No denying it."

Elspeth tutted and swatted his arm with her palm.

"It's coming along nicely, isn't it?" She gestured toward the plans on the table. "I love the patio." She stirred the mahogany liquid with a long spoon as cream-colored froth gathered on the surface.

"Aye. It'll be a grand spot for the morning coffee." He leaned his forearms on the counter next to her. "All we'll need is a manservant, and we can call ourselves Lord and Lady Muck." He chuckled.

Elspeth shook her head and laughed softly.

"You're a case, Davy Gunn."

He reached out and took her free hand in his own.

"What time are the monsters due back?"

Elspeth looked at the wall clock.

"Not until three. Heather's taking them swimming after school." She poured milk into two cups, then filled them with steaming coffee. "I've got some gingersnaps somewhere."

"No, thanks. I'm fine." He lifted the mug she slid over to him and inhaled. "Ah, that's the stuff."

They carried their cups into the living room and settled on the sofa. Elspeth lifted the *Courier*, pulled the local news section out, and handed it to him. Accepting it, Davy kicked his shoes off and tucked them under the coffee table as he settled back to read. After a few moments, he folded the paper and tossed it onto the table.

"Nothing interesting?" Elspeth was startled at him discarding his favorite section so quickly.

"Nope. Not th'day." He shook his head.

"Oh, right." She hesitated before turning back to the travel section. "There's an article in here about Italy. The Amalfi Coast looks dreamy." She wafted the paper toward him and smiled.

Davy reached out and took the pages from her hand and laid them on the sofa.

"I want to ask you something." He pushed himself to the edge of the seat and cleared his throat.

"What?" Elspeth's eyes were wide.

"If you could go anywhere in the world for a holiday, where would it be?" He focused on her face as she chewed her cheek.

"Anywhere?"

"Aye."

"Sorrento." She nodded at the paper on the table. "In May." She laughed. "Not that I'm particular."

Davy edged off the sofa and dropped onto one knee.

"What're you doing?" Elspeth felt a jolt of alarm. "You'll hurt your knee." She slid her hand under his arm and attempted to help him up.

"No. It's fine. I need to be down here." His focus was intense.

Elspeth smoothed her trousers.

"What are you up to, Davy Gunn?" She squinted at him.

"How would you like to go to Sorrento with me?"

Elspeth gasped. "For a holiday?"

"Or for a honeymoon."

Her hand flew to her mouth, and then she thumped her cup onto the table, sloshing coffee over one of Heather's decorating magazines.

Davy dug into his pocket and pulled out a small box.

She said nothing, pressing her lips tightly together in case she exploded before he got the words out. But then, unable to wait, she grinned.

"I'd vote for the honeymoon." Elspeth leaned over and placed a hand on his shoulder. "Now, won't you get up off the floor?"

CHAPTER 48

Murdoch extended his leg across the bed, the chilled space indicating that Jenny had already left. It was still dark in the room, but the dawn light splintered underneath the curtain and, at his best guess, it was around five thirty a.m. He was usually up by this time, but they'd drunk a bottle of red wine with their dinner the night before. He often suffered a thick head after too much wine, but he hadn't wanted to spoil the evening by refusing it in favor of beer.

Jenny had gone to a lot of trouble, bringing all the ingredients to cook him a special meal. She had lit candles and put a cover on his rough-hewn kitchen table. When he came down from the shower, the normally utilitarian room had been transformed into a romantic setting, with flowers in a stone jug on the sideboard and his favorite Colbie Caillat CD playing. Jenny might be a diminutive, soft-spoken lady, but she had an undeniable presence and left a stylish and distinct impression in her wake, on both his heart and his home.

Murdoch bunched the pillow under his jaw and watched as the sliver of light from the window crept up the wall toward the ceiling. He could still smell her shampoo on the bedclothes, and with the scent came the sharp pang of longing that always settled on him when she left.

They had talked late into the night about their plans for the future. Jenny lived and worked in Inverness and had struggled to make her way within the prestigious architectural firm. After six years there paying her dues, she was finally feeling recognized for her skills. Murdoch knew how much her work meant to her and respected her for her tenacity and ambition.

In many ways they were much alike, he and Jenny. He had chosen a path that strayed from the expected, and now that he could truly call himself a crofter, every day that he was on his land, working his flock, he was living his passion. Murdoch believed that passion work did not drain the soul and therefore didn't feel like work at all. He knew that when Jenny sat in front of her wide drafting table or used the CAD program that she had described to him to create a structure or a beautiful space from nothing, she felt the same way. This similarity in their determination to dedicate themselves to something they loved was in fact what had brought them to an impasse in their relationship.

As he closed his eyes against the onset of the day, Murdoch recalled their conversation of the night before.

Jenny had been quiet, preoccupied. She sat at the opposite end of the sofa with her small feet draped over Murdoch's thigh.

"What're you thinking, Jen?" He had pinched her toe, making her snatch her foot away.

"Just that there's not much chance of me getting into one of the firms here on Skye." She hugged a glass of wine to her stomach and twirled a tendril of fair hair around her finger as she stared into the fire. "I've worked so hard to get to where I am."

"Aye, I know. But with the croft, and Mum, and now Heather and the kids being back, I can't see leaving." He scrubbed his hand over his chin. "It's a tough one."

Jenny nodded silently.

"You know I want to be with you, right?" He'd reached for her foot again.

"I know. I just can't see how we can make it work."

Murdoch had made them hot chocolate and, bringing it back into the living room, sat close to her on the sofa.

"We'll find a way, Jen." He wrapped an arm around her narrow shoulders. "Love always finds a way." He rocked her back and forth, hoping to lighten the mood.

"Don't joke, Murdo. This is serious." She frowned at him. "I don't intend to spend my life sitting around here, waiting for you to make your mind up about us."

Seeing his crestfallen expression, she'd softened.

"I mean, I want us to be together, too, but it always seems to be the woman who has to make the sacrifices, give up the dream." Her eyes had clouded over as if she was already envisioning their demise as a couple.

"That's not what I'm saying at all." Murdoch felt stung by her unfounded assumption of his expectation of her. "I'm not asking you to give up anything."

"Sorry. I'm just scared that this will all be too much, and we won't survive it." Her eyes had glittered in the firelight. "There's land and sheep in Inverness, too, you know?" She took in his profile as he stared ahead. "This could beat us, Murdo."

Pulling the duvet up over his head, Murdoch tried to banish the memory of the conversation and the angst that it had left him with. If it came down to it, would he let Jenny go rather than leave Skye? His instinct was to say no, but now that the problem was creeping into their conversations more frequently, casting a pall over their rare and precious time together, he knew that a decision would have to be made, and soon.

Reluctantly he threw off the covers and, shivering in the chilly room, headed for the shower.

◆ ◆ ◆

In the kitchen he spotted a note propped up against the jug of flowers. He lifted the folded paper.

M, I'm sorry about last night. You are so important to me. See you in two weeks. Call me tonight. J xxx

He smiled, refolded the note, and shoved it into his pocket. There was one person on the planet he could have talked to about this, but she was also the one person whom he was protecting from any more change or upset. Heather had been his sounding board for all his past romantic entanglements. Not that there had been many, but when they had arisen, she'd given him sage advice—not always what he wanted to hear, but inevitably correct. If only he could ask her what to do now. Fraser was a good friend, but when it came to relationships he wasn't the best resource, especially now, having been so recently rejected by Heather. No, Fraser wouldn't be much help with this conundrum.

Murdoch pulled on his boots and threw open the cottage door. The morning was bright and the sky clear of clouds. April was a good weather month on Skye, and he longed to be out on the croft, smelling the new grass and filling his lungs with crisp and uncomplicated air.

He shifted his feet in the sticky mud, and as he looked out over his land, an image of Heather and the children came to him. While he knew that she was an adult who had ultimately made her own decisions, he had been pressing her to come home. He'd been the one to keep telling her that Skye was the be-all and end-all of places to live, and the idea of being even partially responsible for her choice now made him nervous. How could he even consider leaving the island now that she'd taken this huge leap of faith?

He shoved his hands into his pockets and scanned the horizon, and as he searched for the white blobs of his flock, Murdoch was flooded with a cold certainty that if he wanted to be any kind of father figure, he could never go and leave those children behind. Not even for Jenny.

"Chick. Come on, boy." He whistled.

The dog emerged from the grain shed, skittered across the stone courtyard, circled Murdoch's legs, and lay down on the ground.

"Time to work, lad."

CHAPTER 49

Elspeth circled the kitchen, lifted a damp cloth from the sink, and wiped the clean surfaces again. The dishes and bowls she had recently used were all stacked away, and two loaves were baking in the oven. Being fully back to health, she was enjoying helping out again around the place but was being careful not to interfere. Her new role as back-of-house support occasionally felt odd, but overall, she was adjusting well to the new dynamic at the Forge.

Heather was coping beautifully with the coming and going of the guests. As she watched her daughter circulating in the busy conservatory, managing the turnover of the rooms, the bookkeeping and administration, and easily directing the two young students she had taken on as help for the summer—all while juggling the twins and the demands of motherhood—Elspeth was beyond proud. Her confident, capable daughter was back, and it lifted her heart to witness her reemergence.

As she scanned the tidy kitchen, Elspeth inhaled the warm scent coming from the oven. The smell of baking bread usually made her hungry, but today her nerves were working as an effective antidote.

Since he had proposed, she and Davy had talked at length about her need to tell Heather of their plans, and this was the day that she had chosen to break the news. Heather was dropping the children off at a birthday party, and there were no new guests arriving until that evening. An uninterrupted afternoon with a long walk in the fresh air, away from the familiarity of the home environment, seemed like a good setting for Elspeth's announcement, and as she rehearsed the words in her mind again, she tried to envisage Heather's response.

Heather had been good with Davy recently, and it appeared that she was genuinely becoming fond of him, but having him marry her mother was another thing entirely.

Elspeth looked out of the window at the hedge, which was sprouting new shoots, reaching eagerly skyward. It would soon be time to trim it again. As she imagined Murdoch up the ladder, wielding the chain saw with Davy standing at the foot, steadying him, she sighed. It was wonderful the way Davy seemed to have gotten to know her family so well. He had surprised her with his astute insights on more than one occasion, and his insistence that she might in fact be underestimating her own daughter had finally pushed Elspeth into deciding to come clean. She hated to have secrets from Heather, and her greatest hope was that once the news was out, they would all be able to share in her excitement, a sentiment that she had, at times, given up on feeling again.

She glanced back at the clock. Was there time for a cup of tea before Heather got back? Deciding that she was too nervous to drink it, she opened the cupboards and began rearranging all the canned goods, stacking them by size and then by label color. She lost herself in the mindless task until, within a few moments, she heard the door opening behind her.

"Hi, Mum. I'm gasping for a cuppa." Heather, bringing a waft of cool air in with her, kicked her shoes off, walked over to the table, and slung her handbag over the back of a chair. "Ah, four whole hours with no kids. Bliss." She moved over to her mother's side and put an arm around her shoulder.

Elspeth patted her hand. "It's such a beautiful day outside, I thought we could go for a walk."

"Sure, great idea. But can I have a cuppa first?" Heather hung her tongue out comically. Her hair was shiny as it fell in her eyes and, on a reflex, Elspeth reached out and brushed it aside.

Heather laughed.

"I do that to Megs all the time." She shook her head, and the fringe fell back onto her forehead. "Mother's prerogative, I suppose."

"Yes, I suppose." Elspeth smiled at her daughter. Heather's skin was glowing, and her eyes were clear. The sunlight from the window splintered across their green irises, like fireworks exploding. "You're looking so well, love."

"Well, thanks, Mum." She kissed Elspeth's cheek and then bobbed a curtsy. "All compliments gladly accepted."

Elspeth grabbed the kettle.

"A quick cuppa, then, and we'll go for a walk along the harbor. I don't want to miss the good weather." She wiggled the kettle and turned back to the sink.

Heather's arm was looped through Elspeth's as they walked along the Brae. The early-afternoon sun felt warm on their backs, and the light jackets they wore were more than enough to cope with the breeze that softly ruffled their heads from behind.

"Shall we pop in on Marj at the shop? I haven't had any good gossip for a few days." Heather nudged her mother's side.

Elspeth shook her head.

"No. Let's not. She just never knows when to stop chatting, God love her, and I want to make the most of the time with you." She reached over and squeezed Heather's fingers.

"Aw, you don't want to share me. How sweet." Heather momentarily leaned her head against Elspeth's shoulder before turning her gaze back to the water. It stretched out to their side like a dark blanket, moving slowly in gentle folds toward the steep harbor wall. A handful of colorful fishing boats bobbed on their moorings, and the breeze played a metallic tune as it meandered through the masts.

"I love it down here." Heather sighed. "I never get tired of this view." She lifted a hand and shielded her eyes.

Elspeth felt her nerves prickling her palms. It was now or never, but Heather seeming so happy was making it harder to broach the subject. She watched her daughter soaking in the familiar view and pushed her anxiety aside.

"Heather, I need to talk to you about something." She gently steered her toward the railing that ran along the top of the harbor wall. Unhooking her arm from her daughter's, Elspeth gripped the cold metal rail and looked down at the water.

"Sure, what's up?" Heather stood at her shoulder, and Elspeth could feel the Heather's focus on her cheek.

She took a deep breath.

"Davy has asked me to marry him."

Heather's face was smooth, remaining motionless except for her eyelids, which fluttered several times in quick succession. She stood completely still while Elspeth tried to read the distinctive green eyes that she knew so well. All she saw was their vivid color reflecting the warm afternoon light. Heather's mouth was slightly open, and as Elspeth stared at it, waiting for something, any sound to come out, she could see the tip of Heather's tongue darting to her top lip.

"God, darling. Say something. Are you very shocked?" Elspeth's voice cracked as Heather, repopulating herself, focused on her mother's face.

"No, I'm not shocked at all. I've been expecting it, to be honest."

Elspeth nodded, still unable to accurately gauge the reaction.

"And?" She dipped her chin, inviting more information.

"I'm so happy for you. Both of you." Heather's eyes glittered as she leaned over and wrapped her arms around Elspeth's neck.

Holding Heather close, Elspeth caught her breath. The relief coursing through her limbs was making her feel light-headed.

"Oh, are you sure? We want your blessing, or it just wouldn't . . ." Her voice left her.

Heather gently pushed herself back from her mother's grip.

"You don't need my blessing, Mum, but you have it, unconditionally."

CHAPTER 50

Heather clicked the reservation screen closed on her computer. The remainder of the spring and the summer seasons were filling up nicely. With the new advertising campaign that she had been running online, she had even begun wait-listing people for August and September. There was something painfully wonderful about saying, "I'm sorry, we're fully booked that week," and the thrill of seeing the room chart with virtually no availability until the autumn was intoxicating.

She checked her watch. Her sister-in-law was arriving for a visit in a few hours, and she needed to make sure she allowed enough time to get to Inverness Airport to meet the flight.

Heather had missed Chrissy immensely and felt a lilt of excitement at the prospect of having her friend see her here in her newly forged life. As she considered Chrissy's potential reaction to her situation, Heather felt a flicker of anxiety. She knew that Chrissy wanted her happiness above all else, but would it be difficult for her sister-in-law to see that happiness coming from a life that no longer included her brother? Heather shook the hair from her eyes. She would find out soon enough.

Satisfied that her reservation planning was done, she linked her fingers and stretched her arms above her head. Her knuckles cracked loudly, and she flinched, more from the sound than the popping sensation in the joints.

The twins were out in the garden with Charlie, and Elspeth and Davy had gone for a drive to Dunvegan Castle. Heather had noticed them whispering these past few days, thick as thieves, as her dad would have said. They seemed totally in tune, and as she watched them circulating around each other, it was obvious that they were comfortably functioning as one now. The idea of their togetherness had settled on her gradually, at first chilly to the skin, the sensation sending her senses into overdrive. More recently, when she heard them laughing together in the conservatory or their low voices melding as they talked in the living room, she found that she had acclimatized to their closeness, and it felt right.

When, a few days earlier, Elspeth had asked her to go for a walk along the harbor, Heather knew what was coming before her mother had even started to tell her that Davy had proposed. It had been surprisingly easy to wrap her arms around Elspeth and say, unreservedly, how happy she was for them both. Things were changing on all fronts, and as Matthew had always said, if we can't change, we die.

Heather stood up and leaned forward to stretch out her lower back. Elspeth had moved back upstairs to her own room until the decorating inside the new cottage was finished. The move had allowed Heather to turn the office back into a work space, with the addition of a small sofa and a television where the twins could play their video games and stay out of the living room when there were guests in residence.

As her spine settled, she scanned the maps on the wall and then spotted the family photograph on the windowsill. In it, they were on the beach in Oban, and she guessed that her parents were in their early thirties. Murdoch was wearing baggy shorts and was clinging to Matthew's leg, much as the twins did with Murdoch now, and she was peeking out coyly from behind her mother's skirt. Elspeth's hair was long and being tugged by the wind as she held a hand up to keep it out of her eyes. It was the color of Megan's hair, the soft copper that Heather's had also been until she hit her teens and it had started to darken. It was a classic picture. She suspected that almost every family in Skye had one similar, showing a time of life that seemed simpler, cleaner, and less angst ridden than that of today.

Heather walked over and lifted the frame from the sill. Their four faces were open, blank canvases ready to accept the colors of life's possibilities, not guarded or suspicious of what was to come. If only they had known then what they knew now. As she looked at the happy group, she wondered if that knowledge would have changed anything. Would she have been less keen to leave the island, knowing that she would meet the love of her life, only to lose him again? Would Murdoch have stuck it out at the bank or still have chosen the croft as his future, knowing that one day he might have to choose between Skye and Jenny? Would Elspeth have loved Matthew any less knowing that he would leave her prematurely and with little warning? Heather doubted it. She ran a finger over the top of the frame and carefully placed the photo back on the windowsill.

A crash from the kitchen made her jump. Snatching up the laptop, she darted out into the hall.

"What was that?"

"Dammit." Megan was standing at the fridge holding just the top of a milk bottle. The glass lay splintered across the floor, and a pool of milk quivered around her bare feet.

"Stand still, Megs," Heather barked as she lay the laptop on the table. "What've I told you about bare feet?" She scanned the floor around her daughter.

"Stupid bottle slipped." Megan scowled. "Sorry, Mom."

"Let me get the big pieces before you move, OK?" Megan nodded as Heather knelt down and picked up several large shards, then stood up and threw them in the bin.

"I can't see any more, so give me the lid." She reached out and took the top from Megan and tossed it in the bin. "I'm going to pick you up." She reached over the spreading puddle and scooped Megan up in her arms, lifting her over the mess and depositing her onto a dry patch of floor.

"Jeez, you're getting heavy, missy." She huffed.

Megan giggled. "It's all the caramel wafers."

Heather laughed.

"Funny girl." She moved Megan toward a chair. "Sit there until I get a towel."

With the mess cleaned up, and Megan's feet clean and safely in her slippers, Heather plopped herself down at the table opposite her daughter.

"Well, that was a right mess."

Megan studied her mother's face and smiled.

"What is it?" Feeling self-conscious, Heather ran a hand over her fringe, then her face. "Do I have something on my nose?"

Megan shook her head and tucked a curl behind her ear.

"No. You just look different now."

Heather felt a tiny jolt to her middle.

"Good different or bad different?"

"Good different. You don't look so sad anymore."

Heather reached across the table and took Megan's hand.

"I'm not as sad, sweetie. I'm getting better, more used to things . . ." She halted.

"Even though Daddy's gone?" Megan's clear eyes held hers.

"Yes, that's right." Heather swallowed.

"I think coming to Skye has fixed you."

As she looked down at their hands, Heather could see the last dots of the pearly pink varnish that Elspeth had painted on Megan's nails a few days before.

"You do?" She smiled at her daughter's serious face.

"Yes. You've stopped crying, and you don't yell much anymore. You laugh again, and you wash your hair all the time."

At that, Heather let out another laugh.

"Megan Forester, I always washed my hair." Even as she said it, she knew the statement wasn't strictly true. There had been a time when that small act of domesticity, of self-care, had seemed too mammoth to deal with and far too narcissistic to justify when the love of her life had been reduced to ash.

As she considered her daughter's observations, Heather realized that she had stopped keeping track of how she was feeling as she had done when they'd first arrived back on the island. Without consciously monitoring herself, she was, by default, no longer studying her sadness, either. The notion of moving forward had been terrifying, but now she knew that she was doing it. Day by day, hair wash by hair wash, she was doing it.

"I'm so proud of you and Max. You guys have been so brave." She squeezed Megan's fingers. "I couldn't have managed without you both."

Megan stood up and walked around the table.

"And Uncle Murdy and Granny, and Charlie and Fraser, and Davy . . ." Megan giggled as Heather rolled her eyes.

"OK, all of you."

"Love you, Mommy." Megan settled onto Heather's knee. "You smell like toast."

Heather laughed again.

"That's Skye for you. I always thought this place smelled like toast." She hugged Megan into her side.

"Do you mind that Granny's marrying Davy?"

Heather was caught short by the directness of the question and shifted Megan away from her so that she could see her face.

"Do *you* mind?"

"I think it'll be cool." Megan hesitated. "'Cause he'll be our grandpa."

Heather felt a tug under her ribs. The children had grown fond of Davy, and while he and Elspeth were already committed to each other, wedding or no, she didn't want Max and Megan to forget Matthew's existence.

"Well, he'll be like a grandpa, for sure." She nodded. "Just not Grandpa Matthew."

Megan frowned.

"Oh, yeah. I liked the way he used funny voices. He told jokes and gave us mints all the time." She dropped her head onto Heather's shoulder. "I miss him."

Heather raked a hand loosely through the mop of curls that was tickling her jaw.

"You're a honey bunch, Megan Forester. But you need a haircut."

Megan sat bolt upright.

"No, I'm growing it long. Like Merida." She tossed her head theatrically. "Like a Gaelic princess."

Heather rolled her eyes and pushed Megan gently off her knee.

"Well, please tell the Gaelic princess that she needs to get her shoes on if she is coming to Inverness to pick up Aunt Chrissy."

Megan squealed.

"When are we going?"

"We're leaving in half an hour, so please go tell Max to get ready. This is your thirty-minute warning."

Megan bolted from the room as Heather rose and pushed the chair back in close to the table. Chrissy was staying for two weeks, and the anticipation of her arrival had been driving the twins crazy. They had argued over who would sleep in beside her on the first night, and Heather had eventually mediated, suggesting that they let their aunt have her privacy the first night and then draw lots for the second night, and so on.

Heather was looking forward to some serious girl time, late nights with good wine, and talking until they were hoarse. With everything that she had rebuilt here on Skye, a good girlfriend was still missing from the equation. She met up with Kirsty occasionally and had even begun to get to know a few of the other parents at the school, who were growing more friendly, if still somewhat tentatively. Everything would come with time, but she was glad that she was at least trying harder to make connections.

The only other woman that she had spent any time with was Jenny, who had been ever present while the work on the cottage was going on. The more often she saw her, the more Heather had become convinced that Jenny could potentially be her sister-in-law someday, but now that the major work was completed on Elspeth's new "but and ben," Jenny was noticeably absent. She rarely joined them for lunches when she was over from Inverness, and Murdoch hardly mentioned her anymore. Curious about the glaring absence of the young woman, Heather had asked after her the week before, at the Sunday lunch table.

"It's all off with me and Jenny." Murdoch had spoken around a mouthful of roast beef.

"Oh, Murdo. I'm sorry." Elspeth, who was fond of Jenny, had looked shocked. "What happened?"

He had been vague, saying that it was mutual and not a big deal, but as they'd been doing the dishes, he'd confided in Heather.

"Neither one of us could compromise on our work or where we lived." He had shrugged. "So we agreed it was best to go our separate ways before things got even more difficult." His face hung as he spoke, and it had cut her up to see her brother hurting.

Since then, Murdoch had been uncharacteristically quiet, sometimes missing his usual breakfast visits, and Heather was worried about him. She'd asked him more than once if he was sure about the decision, but he'd had shut her down.

"Decision is made. Leave it alone, Wee Blister."

She'd seen the new shadows appear under his eyes and noticed that his usual voracious appetite had waned, but having been told in no uncertain terms to back off, she'd stopped probing. She was extremely sad for them both, but after a few weeks of moping around, Murdoch seemed to be coming to terms with the situation.

Heather knew that her brother had a great capacity for love. He often hid it behind his big-man frame and dry humor, but he was a tender heart. She also knew that he wanted to have a family of his own someday, so, trying hard not to sound callous, she had counseled him.

"If you both felt your careers were more important than the relationship, then the relationship wasn't right." She had been sitting on the floor in his croft house nursing a bottle of water while he cleaned his boots in the sink—a practice she was sure Jenny would not have approved of had she been there.

"Aye, you're right."

Murdoch had agreed with the sentiment, but regardless of his seeming acceptance of his lot, Heather had resolved to keep a close eye on him to make sure he didn't slip into a dark place.

Max darted into the kitchen and startled her from her daydream.

"Shoes on, coat on, ready to go sir." He saluted.

"Oh, my God, and ten minutes early, too. Who are you, and what have you done with my son?"

CHAPTER 51

Chrissy sat on the sofa with a twin under each arm. Her long, dark hair was wet and twisted up into a tight ponytail. The sweatshirt and casual tracksuit trousers she wore were oddly uncharacteristic, but even inside their sloppy outline, she was still lithe and elegant.

Heather smiled over at her sister-in-law and nodded at the empty glass on the coffee table.

"Splash more?"

"Yes, but I'll need a straw if these two don't give me an arm back." She laughed.

Megan tucked her legs underneath herself and pushed in tighter to Chrissy's side.

On her opposite side, Max grabbed her hand.

"You can't have this one." He giggled.

Heather leaned over and filled Chrissy's glass. "Come on, guys—let her move." She smiled at the matching faces flanking their aunt.

"A person could die of dehydration in this family." Chrissy slid her arm out from behind Megan and lifted her glass. "It's so good to see you all."

Heather folded her legs up into the armchair.

"I've missed you, Chrissy. We all have."

"So, give me all the gossip. Your mom's getting married?" She balanced the glass on her thigh.

"Yep. She and Davy are good together. They're doing it in the registry office next month. Honeymooning in Italy. Davy moved into the new cottage last week." She gestured toward the driveway.

Hearing the words out loud gave them more weight. Her mother was getting married. She had known Elspeth and Davy's plan for a while, but with business booming, the children being off school for Easter, and then Chrissy's impending visit, she hadn't allowed herself to stop and fully absorb it.

"He's a good guy? You like him?" Chrissy leaned back against the cushion as Max and Megan each released her and slid to opposite ends of the sofa.

Megan's eyes were heavy as Max bent over and lifted his iPad from the floor. Heather wagged a finger at him, and, acknowledging the sign, he closed the device and slid it down the side of the sofa cushion.

"Davy's a gem. Kind, clever, great with the kids." Heather nodded. "He's really good for Mum."

Chrissy smiled.

"Well, I think it's fantastic. Gives us all hope." A shadow passed across her eyes, and she blinked several times.

Heather noticed the odd change in her expression.

"OK, kids. Time for bed." She stood up. "It's adult time now."

To her surprise, the children didn't protest. Rather, they each wrapped their arms around Chrissy and kissed her cheeks.

"'Night, Aunt Chrissy," they both murmured against her shiny skin.

"Good night, monsters. See you tomorrow." She kissed them back. "What are we doing this weekend, again? What's special about it . . . I forget?" She winked at Heather.

Max piped up.

"It's our birthday, and we're going to Neist Point to see the lighthouse."

Chrissy nodded.

"Oh, right. Sounds great."

"Uncle Murdy and Fraser are coming, too." Megan stood up and yanked at her pajama top.

Chrissy's eyes widened, and she poked an elegant finger into Megan's pony-clad stomach.

"Is Fraser your boyfriend, kiddo?"

Megan let out a peal of laughter.

"No, silly. He's Mom's."

Heather felt her face flush. She shook her head abruptly as Chrissy's eyes flicked to hers.

"That's enough, madam. Bed, please." She pointed at the stairs. "Both of you. Don't forget to do your teeth."

Chrissy stretched her long legs out on the sofa and bunched a cushion up behind her head.

"OK, lady. Talk. Who's this Fraser?"

Heather scanned the beautiful face for any indications of judgment.

"He's a friend of Murdoch's. A nice guy. He's a friend." She stressed the final word.

Chrissy nodded slowly and folded her arm behind her head. Her face remained serene.

"You know, you can tell me if you're seeing him, Heather. It's no betrayal—it's just life, honey." Chrissy voice was low and her eyes steady.

"I'm not seeing him. He's asked, but I'm not there yet." Heather leaned forward and emptied the last of the wine into her glass. "Seems we need reinforcements." She waggled the empty bottle.

With a new bottle and the opener, she settled back into the chair. Chrissy's comment earlier about hope had sparked concern, and Heather wanted to delve deeper.

"So, speaking of life, how's yours? What's going on?" She slid the cork from the bottle and filled Chrissy's glass.

"Oh, you know. Work and more work. Blah, blah, blah, the usual stuff." Chrissy pushed herself upright on the seat. "I never hear from Phil, unless he needs money." She grimaced. "Had the roof replaced on the Virginia house, at great expense. Oh, and of course, Frank cheated on me." She dipped her head, stared into the glass, and then closed her eyes.

Heather felt the jolt of shock.

"God, Chrissy. No."

Chrissy lifted her chin and met Heather's gaze. She nodded.

"What . . . I mean, when?" Heather was up and moving toward her sister-in-law.

"Three months ago." Chrissy sniffed and tucked an imaginary hair behind her ear. "Seems the long-distance thing wasn't working for him, and an accommodating paralegal in the Atlanta office took care of the rest."

"But you were just about to move to Atlanta, too. I mean, you were, right?" Heather sat next to Chrissy and crossed her legs.

"Yep. It was all planned. Thank God I didn't sell the house or anything." Chrissy gulped. "I just didn't see it coming, and that's what makes me madder than hell. I am smarter than this." She swept her hands down in front of her body as her voice cracked. Heather shifted over and wrapped an arm around Chrissy's shoulders.

"I'm so sorry, Chris. I just can't take it in. It seems we've both been left in the lurch."

Chrissy's eyes fired to life again.

"At least Brett leaving you was not his choice." Her voice was brittle, and for the first time since the subject had come up, Heather heard bitterness. She pressed her lips tightly together and willed herself not to cry.

"Oh, Jesus, I'm sorry. That was shitty. But you know what I mean," Chrissy said, grabbing Heather's hand. "It's just so hard to know that Frank had a choice, but he still made a decision that ended us."

Heather let the painful truth hover between them for a moment, and then she stuck her hand in her pocket and pushed a tissue toward her sister-in-law.

"It's clean."

Chrissy took the tissue and blew her nose loudly.

"Not anymore." Chrissy offered the soggy mass back to her, and suddenly they both laughed, the sound cracking the film of tension surrounding them.

"What're you going to do, Chris?" Heather shifted back to the opposite end of the sofa and tucked her feet under a cushion.

"Well, I'm going to divorce him. It won't be pretty, two attorneys and all." Chrissy shrugged. "But he should've thought of that before he jumped Miss Paralegal-hormone-surging-boob-job-twenty-something's bones."

Heather laughed despite herself, and then her hand flew up to her mouth.

"Oh, sorry. It's just that that sounded more like the Chrissy I know and love."

"Yeah." Chrissy shrugged. "I hope he wasn't fond of his clothes, car, golf clubs, horse, fifteen acres of idyllic Virginia countryside, any of our friends, or the respect of his son." She lifted the glass and took a long swallow.

"Why didn't you tell me? We talk all the time, and you never let on." Heather shoved a foot out to make contact with Chrissy's thigh.

"What was I supposed to tell you while you were over here doing the whole widow thing, carving out a new life and barely surviving?" Chrissy eyed her. "'Oh, by the way, Heather, life sucks and no matter what you do, or how hard you try, it will still kick your butt'?" Chrissy bit her lip as tears trickled down her cheek. She swiped them away with the back of her hand.

Heather lay her head back against the arm of the sofa and counted the dark wooden beams that spanned the ceiling. She hurt for her sister-in-law, but she was also ashamed to know that she had been so wrapped up in her own struggles that she had failed to sense Chrissy's need for help. She was especially disappointed in herself for that failing, because Chrissy had been her support system for months after Brett died. She sat bolt upright.

"What can I do?" She looked directly at Chrissy, who was draining her glass.

"Fill 'er up, for starters." Chrissy pushed the empty glass toward her. "I say again, a person could die of dehydration in this family."

Ten days into Chrissy's visit, Chrissy and Heather had stopped for coffee on the way home from the supermarket. The café was busy, with a smattering of locals scattered among the tourists. The guidebooks, cameras, and binoculars would have given the visitors away had the smart walking gear and new boots not done that already. Most of the locals wore well-weathered boots to walk the hills, and they didn't use maps.

Heather looked around to see if any of her guests were among the crowded tables. Seeing no familiar faces, she turned her attention back to the newspaper. She had ordered two cappuccinos while Chrissy found the ladies' room, and as the waitress brought the cups over, Heather raised her head and smiled.

"Thanks, Kayla."

The young woman placed the cups down and nodded.

"Welcome. How's business? You full at the moment?" Her peroxide-blonde hair seemed incongruous, spiking around her sweet, round face. Her eyes were darkly lined with kohl, and a large metal stud nestled in the dip under her bottom lip, catching the light from the window.

"Yes, pretty busy. Only one vacancy, and some new people arriving tomorrow." Heather pulled the cup toward her, trying not to stare at the shiny stud that was an addition since last she'd seen Kayla. Kayla tucked her shirt back into the top of her jeans as Chrissy appeared behind her.

"Oh, sorry. Didn'y see ya there." She stepped back. "Your coffee's there." She pointed at the table and then walked back to the counter.

"Thanks." Chrissy slid into her seat and looked down at the coffee cup. "It's so small." She looked questioningly at Heather. "Is it a mini-cappu?" She rolled her eyes.

Heather laughed.

"No, it's just a normal size. Not super-Americanized megacappuccino."

Chrissy tutted and slid the cup toward herself. "Fine, I'll have to make do, then. Or just order another one."

Heather folded the newspaper, stirred the frothy liquid, and then looked up to see a young couple walk by the window of the café. They looked to be in their twenties. They were both fair-haired, and the woman's face was gently freckled. She spoke to the man, her voice muted by the glass, and then, in an excruciatingly intimate gesture, he leaned over and kissed her. Heather felt as if she was intruding, and yet she couldn't look away.

A young child was strapped into a stroller in front of the couple, and one small foot protruded from the side of the seat, clad in a tiny trainer. The chubby ankle bounced as the child kicked its leg against the edge of the frame.

Choked with emotion that she could not explain, Heather dipped her eyes back to her cup and took a swallow of coffee.

Chrissy was watching her, and even without looking up, Heather could feel the scrutiny.

"What's up, sis?" She touched Heather's foot under the table. "Feeling broody?"

Heather shook her head.

"No. Nostalgic, maybe." She met Chrissy's eyes.

"Man, I'm never nostalgic for those days. Phil was a nightmare of a baby. Colicky, a bad sleeper, a picky eater—you name it." Chrissy sipped some coffee. "Now he's nearly six foot—a grumpy eighteen-year-old who wants to be treated like a grown-up but insists on acting like a toddler."

Heather watched as Chrissy's face clouded over.

"How's he coping with the divorce?" Heather licked her teaspoon.

"He's angry with Frank. Well, furious, really." Chrissy shrugged. "I'm not in the right place to tell him not to be, though, so I guess I'm not helping."

"He has a right to be angry. Frank let him down, as well as you." Heather shrugged.

Chrissy nodded.

"I know. I just don't want him percolating all that fury for too long. It's not healthy."

"Shame he couldn't have come over with you."

"Yeah. I offered him a ticket, but freshman year is tough, and he's got exams coming up." Chrissy drained her cup and licked the line of foam from her top lip. "He won't even miss me, believe me."

The two women walked back toward the Forge, the shopping bags distributed between them. The afternoon light shone golden against the multicolored buildings of Quay Street, and the clutches of gulls that circled the high roofs called out to one another, their voices bouncing across the water. The twins were at home with Elspeth and Davy, and Chrissy had promised to make her famous mac and cheese for everyone that evening. Murdoch and Fraser were coming to eat with them, and then a game of charades had been promised to the children, who had already chosen the teams and filled a glass jar with dozens of folded squares of paper that bore clues for the willing victims.

Heather stepped off the curb to round a lamppost as Chrissy stopped to hoist a bag farther up her forearm. She looked over at Heather and smiled.

"You're doing such a great job here, sis. I mean it."

Heather stood still, waiting for a qualifier. Nothing came.

"I'm so damn proud of you." Chrissy's eyes glittered as she started forward again. "You really seem to have found yourself again."

The statement felt like a flash of sunshine on Heather's face. Her skin tingled with the truth of it, and while she knew it was *her* truth, hearing it coming from Chrissy somehow gave it more value.

"Thanks, Chris. That means the world." She swung a bag out toward her sister-in-law's leg. "You'll get through this, too, you know. There's no keeping us Foresters down."

Chrissy nodded.

"You're lucky to have your family so close. You guys are really there for one another. I'm quite jealous."

"You're family, too, Chris. You know that, right?"

"I know. It's just awesome seeing how they've rallied around you. Your mum is great—and Murdoch, he's fantastic with the twins." Chrissy focused ahead as they negotiated their way around an old man with a walking frame who was taking up all the pavement. He politely tipped his cap at them as he passed.

"Murdo's a good egg, and the kids adore him." Heather, now slightly ahead, spoke over her shoulder. "He's really stepped up since we've been home. I honestly don't know what I'd do without him."

Chrissy caught up to her in two long strides, and leaning her shoulder against Heather's, she spoke quietly.

"He's wonderful, all right."

CHAPTER 52

For the twins' birthday, Heather had planned an evening picnic at Neist Point Lighthouse on the most westerly part of Skye. It was another place that her father had often taken her and Murdoch on their Sunday walks.

She had baked a batch of chocolate cupcakes, filled a bag with sandwiches and drinks, and found two number-eight candles, which would work as long as the wind out on the point cooperated.

They were taking two cars, and Chrissy had brought her camera in order to capture the occasion for posterity. Fraser had told her there was a chance that they might see the aurora borealis that night, and Heather couldn't imagine a more spectacular way to celebrate the eighth year of her children's existence.

The mile-long path to the lighthouse, though steep, had level steps and handrails, so it was safe for Elspeth, who was happily tackling more challenging walks now. Heather was excited to show Chrissy An t-Aigeach, the Stallion's Head, a magnificent upright crag that loomed over the headland, which they'd have to round before reaching the Stevenson lighthouse. April nights on Skye were generally pale, but if everything went to plan, and they were extremely lucky, the sky would help to provide enough light for their little party.

As they set off from the cars, Murdoch took the lead with Chrissy and the twins. Elspeth and Davy were slightly ahead, and Heather followed behind with Fraser. The walk down to the lighthouse would take around forty minutes, and as the sun hung low in the sky, Heather began to worry that this might turn into a much later night than she had planned.

"I hope it won't be a problem, getting back." She stepped over a stone and hoisted the bag farther up her shoulder.

"It'll be fine." Fraser nodded. "The moon will help us out. It's so clear up there." He jabbed a thumb skyward. The strong line of his jaw, the piercing eyes, and the shock of fair hair took her by surprise again as she looked at him.

Heather glanced upward and saw that the sky was almost cloudless. The breeze was brisk but not buffeting, and she could see An t-Aigeach up ahead.

"But I've brought two heavy-duty torches, just in case." Fraser flashed a smile.

She had also insisted that the children bring the small lights that clipped to their baseball hats so that even if they did get caught out by unexpected cloud cover, they should find their way back without too much trouble.

The mood of the group was upbeat as they made their way down the path. She could hear the twins chattering, and then Chrissy's voice wafting back to her on the breeze. Her head and Murdoch's were close together, and as Heather watched them, she realized she'd never noticed how close to Murdoch's height Chrissy was. The twins were flanking the tall couple, and Heather had a momentary flash, or perhaps a premonition, of what Murdoch's own family might look like.

Fraser had caught her expression and tilted his head toward her.

"What?" His eyes were clear in the twilight as Heather filtered her thoughts.

"I was just thinking how good those two look together." She jutted her chin toward the group ahead.

"Aye, a handsome pair." He nudged her elbow. "Matchmaking now, are we?"

Heather laughed and shook her head.

"No, I know better than to interfere in my brother's love life."

Fraser shifted his backpack from one shoulder to the other.

"Aye, that'd be a minefield to avoid." He grinned, and then instantly a small frown split his forehead. "Do you think he's OK, about Jenny?"

Heather considered for a few moments and then nodded.

"Actually, I do."

The lighthouse stood tall against the early-evening sky, the startling white walls and towers iridescent in the cooling light. The tan detailing on the corners of the structure, along with the walls and chimney stacks, gave the group of buildings a castlelike appearance.

Next to her, Megan slid her hand into Heather's. As if reading Heather's mind, she said, "It's like a princess castle." She tugged at her mother's coat. "Can I go inside?"

Heather shook her head.

"No, honey. It's private property. We can't go beyond here." She drew a line in the air. "But this is a good spot, right?" She looked down at Megan, whose gaze was fixed on the light tower. Her hair was being gently separated by the breeze, showing the baby-pink scalp beneath.

"Yeah, it's so pretty here."

Heather spread two large rugs on the grass and, with Elspeth's help, unpacked the food.

Chrissy and Murdoch were wandering out to the cliff edge, and she watched their backs as Max took off after them.

"Maximus, stay with Uncle Murdy, OK?"

Max raised a hand over his shoulder and pelted toward his uncle and aunt.

Fraser had helped Elspeth into a lightweight camping chair that he had brought, and Davy began opening the flasks of tea.

"Quite a spread you've put on here, lass." He stood behind Elspeth's chair. "A birthday banquet, right enough."

Heather stacked the plastic plates at one corner of the rug and then tucked a pile of paper napkins under them.

"Not every day you turn eight." She smiled.

"Let me help you." Elspeth made to get up.

"Sit still and enjoy the view, Mum. There's nothing left to do." Heather laid the plastic box containing the cupcakes on the ground. "We're all set."

The weather had been kind, the breeze remaining steady and the sky staying clear as they gathered on the rugs and ate. Murdoch told the inevitable bad jokes, and then Elspeth and Davy started singing a song. It was supposed to be a round, but it quickly deteriorated into a melee of toneless shouting and mass hysteria, with the twins rolling around on the rug. Heather and Chrissy then cleared everything away so that they could arrange the cupcakes on the lid of the container.

"OK. Gather round." Heather beckoned everyone into the middle of the rugs. "I'll need some shelter to light the candles." She looked up at Murdoch, who was already pulling Davy, Chrissy, and Fraser into a rugby-scrum huddle.

Murdoch and Fraser stood shoulder to shoulder and opened their jackets to serve as a windbreak while Heather crouched down and lit the two number-eight candles. The flames took, flickering dangerously, but after a lightning round of "Happy Birthday," the twins blew them out and everyone applauded.

As the sun began to slide into the sea, and Elspeth and the children had added a layer of clothing, Murdoch produced a football from his backpack.

"Right, who's in for a quick game?" He dribbled the ball away from the group.

Fraser, the twins, and Davy were instantly up and running across the grass as Murdoch shouted instructions on who was playing against whom.

Elspeth called out to Davy.

"You be careful, you old codger. No broken bones, do you hear me?" She laughed as he turned and saluted her before heading into the fray.

Heather watched them all as they darted around, their crisp outlines gradually transforming into silhouettes against the warming colors of the night sky.

"God, it's beautiful here." Chrissy, having pulled a bottle of wine from one of the bags, plopped back onto the rug. Putting the bottle between her knees, she began opening it.

"I know. It's amazing, isn't it?" Heather looked over at her mother, who was staring out toward the lighthouse.

"You OK, Mum?" She reached out and placed a hand on Elspeth's knee.

"More than OK." Elspeth put her cold hand over Heather's. "This is perfect."

"You're getting cold. Where are your gloves?" Heather crawled over to the bags and began raking inside one of them. Finding a pair of her own gloves, she handed them to Elspeth.

"Thank you, darling girl."

Chrissy had filled three plastic glasses with wine and now handed one each to Elspeth and Heather.

"It's wonderful that you're here for their birthday, Chrissy." Elspeth bent over and touched her glass to the others'. "Can you not stay a few more days?"

Chrissy took a swallow of wine and then leaned back on her hand.

"Well, I might. There's definitely a lot to like about Skye." She winked at Heather. "The scenery is spectacular." Chrissy nodded toward the men, who were calling out to one another as the twins huddled around the football. Heather met her sister-in-law's gaze and saw a spark of mischief. She widened her eyes comically and raised her glass in the air.

"Stay as long as you like. The longer the better."

Turning back to watch the game, Heather felt the sense of calm that had been growing during the past few months take her over completely. As if on cue, Brett's face was suddenly there, a searingly clear vision in her mind. She so wanted to talk to him, to share this moment with him. *Were you here today? Did you see what we did?* A few feet away, their greatest achievements ran in circles around their uncle.

The three women sat in easy silence as the game began to wane. Davy dropped out first, to Elspeth's obvious relief, and then Max gave up, begging tiredness. He was followed quickly by Megan, who had broken a shoelace. Eventually Murdoch and Fraser returned to the group, panting and laughing, both red faced and grinning like giant boys.

It was approaching eight o'clock, and reluctantly, Heather began to pack the remaining picnic items into the bag. Murdoch and Davy were talking quietly as Chrissy and Megan shook out the rugs and folded them into squares. The light was dimming, but they could still see one another clearly as Max, who had walked away from the group and toward the lighthouse, suddenly called out.

"Mom, what's happening to the sky?"

Heather swung around to see a shot of green split itself away from the darkening horizon.

"Oh, my God, look. It's the aurora." She ran a few paces toward Max and pointed out to sea. "Look, everyone."

Shoulder to shoulder, the group stood in silence, afraid that if they spoke the moment would be shattered. The slice of green sky had burst into flames, bringing with it purple and crimson shards that linked to swaths of white and black. One color bled into the next, mixing oddly and perfectly, like a beautifully woven blanket. Behind the canvas that stretched as far as they could see, a crust of stars peppered the layers like fairy dust. As they watched, the whole spectacular painting flickered as if some celestial being were blowing on it from far above, moving the night sky simply for their entertainment.

As she stared out into the night, Heather instinctively reached up to grasp Brett's ring. Her fingertips diving inside her jacket, she pressed them against her empty breastbone. Her stomach flip-flopped as she remembered that she had taken her necklace off to shower and had left it on the bedside table.

Suddenly a large hand encapsulated her own. Fraser had moved in close to her side, and now she felt his formidable presence, not only through her fingertips and the bulk of her coat, but inside her head. She let him wind his fingers through hers, and without looking at him, she returned the pressure of his grip.

Finally, Max broke the silence.

"What's it called, Mom?" His voice was low, reverent.

Heather whispered.

"The aurora borealis—it's the northern lights."

Max nodded silently and leaned against her arm. "It's like a birthday party in the sky."

Heather leaned down and kissed the top of his head.

"That's exactly what it is, Maximus."

ACKNOWLEDGMENTS

Heartfelt thanks to everyone who supported me on this journey. Particular thanks to Miriam Juskowicz for her faith in this book, and to the wonderful team at Lake Union Publishing.

Special thanks also to Bev Katz Rosenbaum, Amanda Sumner, and Kelley Hoffman, and to Angela Allan, my friend and oracle on all things Skye.

To Lesley Shearer and Anna Marie Laforest, as always, my gratitude for the staunch support, advice, and encouragement.

And, as ever, to Bob, for his constancy and his unshakable faith in me.

ABOUT THE AUTHOR

Originally from Edinburgh, Alison Ragsdale now lives near Washington, DC, with her husband and two very spoiled dogs. Alison lived and worked in eight countries before settling in the United States. A former professional ballet dancer and marketing executive, she was educated in England and holds an MBA from the University of Leicester. She loves to read, spend time with family on both sides of the Atlantic, and throw parties involving bagpipers.

Alison's debut novel, *Tuesday's Socks*, and her second, *The Father-Daughter Club*, are both Amazon bestsellers. *Finding Heather* is her third novel.